Too Many Ass

By Kevin Ramsey

Too Many Assassins
© 2015 by Kevin Ramsey

The right of Kevin Ramsey to be identified as the author of this work has been asserted by him in accordance with the Copyright, Designs and patents Act 1988.

You may not copy, store, distribute, transmit, reproduce or otherwise make available this publication (or any part of it) in any form, or by any means (electronic, digital, optical, mechanical, photocopying, recording or otherwise), without the prior written permission of the publisher. Any person who does any unauthorized act in relation to this publication may be liable to criminal prosecution and civil claims for damages.

This book is the 2nd book in "The Andersen Plan" trilogy. The story continues from where Book 1, *Too Many Victims,* ended. If you haven't read Book 1, please go to my website **www.kevinramseyauthor.com** to find a special introductory offer for new readers.

The book is dedicated to all my friends and family who encouraged and helped me to attempt my first novel – and then demanded a sequel! Here it is.

In particular my wife, Eileen, has been a tower of strength, keeping me positive during the dark days when you think you are attempting the impossible.

Cover Design by James, GoOnWrite.com

TOO MANY ASSASSINS

PART 1 – The Gathering Storm

Chapter 1

The Englishman is a long way from home. In fact about as far away as you can be.

He is sitting in his hire car in a small car park in the Adelaide Hills, just a few kilometres outside Adelaide, the capital city of the state of South Australia.

He is one of the very few people who know that an incident will take place, today, at this quiet picturesque location, which will have enormous political ramifications not only in Australia but right back to the very heart of the political establishment in Britain.

He is waiting for the three men he had been observing for several weeks. Not all of them will walk away from this place alive. It is a chilling thought. He ponders on what he will witness and what he has to do.

He carefully observes the short stretch of road leading to the car park. It is early morning and there is very little traffic. A slight mist wraps the tall trees. He is surprised how chilly it is. Like many Englishmen he had imagined that Australia was always hot. Early morning in the Adelaide Hills at the onset of winter has cured him of that particular fantasy.

Eventually he sees what he is looking for; a white Toyota sedan is making its way down the slip road into the car park. He eases himself out of his car and creeps across to the spot he has picked out where, although he is concealed, he can follow what is happening. From this vantage point he can see the occupants.

He watches as the driver parks the Toyota and the passengers get out. There are the three men he has been expecting, but there is a fourth. He has been advised too late about the fourth man, who has ruined his carefully laid plan. Now he will have to improvise and make some unforeseen last minute changes.

He forces himself to be calm. Today is the culmination of a scheme which has its origins on a miserable winter's day in London more than six years earlier, in the political upheavals following the 2015 General Election.

Chapter 2

See amendment sheet to reflect 2015 election results

It was a dull November day in London. A slight mist came off the river adding its own finishing touches to the already grey atmosphere and sky. Sir Robert Smythe did not notice the air of gloom; he had other things on his mind as he sat in the back of the taxi while it made its slow journey from his pleasant town house in Kensington to Westminster.

Sir Robert was a large man in his late fifties. Still craggily handsome with a full head of hair, whose grey specks only served to give him a more patrician look, he was the acknowledged if informal head of a group of worried influential Tories.

Like many of them he was a wealthy man. He had inherited a family retail clothing business which over the years he had expertly managed until it was one of the country's biggest. His knighthood was for "services to the British clothing industry". He provided generous donations to the Conservative Party.

The group he was meeting consisted of a collection of wealthy and influential Tory MPs and backers, who were somewhat to the right of the prevailing philosophy of the Conservative Party leadership.

He had seen which way the political winds were blowing in the results of the recent general election of 2015, which had produced a result that many commentators had predicted.

Although the economy was still in a delicate state it seemed to be improving and the population were almost equally divided between those who believed 'if it ain't broke don't fix it' and those who wanted a change to the Labour party. Neither of the major parties had a convincing majority. The result was yet again a coalition government. There was no doubt the Tories still depended on other more left leaning parties to form a government, a fact which rankled with many Tories, particularly those on the right.

Sir Robert and his informal group, who had labelled themselves "The True Believers" believed strongly that the party was moving further to the left with the inevitable result that the right of the party was eroding, with the discontents moving to UKIP, The United Kingdom Independence Party.

UKIP had experienced the result that many had predicted. It had won strong popular support throughout the country, but not enough to give them many seats in their own right. In fact they had managed only a handful of seats which, as they were proud to point out, was the result of the first past the post voting system. Had there been a more proportional form of voting UKIP would have achieved many more seats.

Their main effect on the on the voting patterns had been to swing several marginal seats, some from Tory to Labour, others from Labour to Tory with the result that the Tories yet again had to accommodate a coalition partner to form a government.

Unlike many of their party, who were relieved just to be back in Government for another five years The True Believers recognised that UKIP was a force to be reckoned with and a strategy to deal with them had to be found before it was too late. Today's meeting was the latest in a series of sessions to try to work out such a plan.

The True Believers met at the office of MP Geoffrey Blaines, whose constituency was one of those which could be vulnerable to a further upsurge in UKIP support. He, Sir

Robert and eight others were gathered in his office. Sir Robert stood up.

"Gentlemen welcome, especially on this rather chilly day. Summer seems a long time ago already does it not?"

He beamed at his audience but received little response. He continued.

"Ahem, there is one item on the agenda today which I think is important enough to be considered on its own without being complicated by other business. Our colleague Geoffrey Blaines here has authored a plan which I believe could very significantly move forward our objectives."

He paused and noticed that his audience now seemed more interested.

"I will leave it to Geoffrey to explain the details. I would be grateful if you would give him your attention and support. Over to you Geoffrey."

Geoffrey Blaines stood up. He was short and stout with thinning hair and looked more like a friendly bank manager than a power broker, but behind his comforting and trustworthy appearance was a sharp calculating brain and an occasional ruthless streak when required. He flashed his avuncular smile at his audience and began.

"Thank you Sir Robert. Gentlemen, we all share the same concerns. In the eighteen months since the 2015 General Election UKIP is becoming stronger by the day. To date their popularity has resulted in a steadily rising share of the vote, but mercifully, thanks to our first past the post voting system, they have not translated this effect into seats in parliament. That will not last. At their current rate of growth they are likely to start winning many more seats at the next election. Most of those seats will be taken from us, that is from the right of our Party. This will result in a Tory party which will never again be able to rule on its own, but will have to continue to move further to the left in order to accommodate the demands of our various coalition partners."

As he paused to draw breath he was interrupted by Tristram Mainwaring, a wealthy land owner and an old school Tory member who represented a rural constituency in the East Midlands.

"Spare us the rhetoric Geoffrey. We all know what the problems are. The question is what are we going to do about them before we all lose our seats. Our verbal campaigns against UKIP have achieved very little and their popularity continues to grow. I say again, what do you think we can do?"

Blaines put on his best bank manager's patient smile and turned to face Mainwaring.

"My honourable friend is of course correct. I was merely reminding you all of how serious the situation is and that we have to somehow change the course of events. To do that we have to be bold, and it may involve some financial investment on our part. How do we all feel about that? What about you Tristram?"

Mainwaring twisted in his seat and tapped his fingers impatiently on the table top.

"Geoffrey, you know where I stand. Resources can be committed if we have any kind of plan of action. To date we have not been able to produce one. I think I speak for all of us on this. We will finance any form of sensible scheme that appears to have a chance of success. Do you have such a plan? If so let us hear it."

There were murmurs of agreement all round the table. It was Blaines' moment to announce his bold strategy.

"Gentlemen, it seems to me that attacking UKIP from outside is having little effect on them. It may even be making them stronger as we come to be perceived as negative. What we need is for UKIP to destroy themselves from within. At the moment they appear to be a very united party who speak with a common voice. They also have the benefit of a charismatic leader in the form of Nigel Farage who appears to have no serious opposition. These are the issues we must address."

Tristram Mainwaring again tapped his fingers on the table top. "And how do we bring about this miracle Geoffrey?"

Blaines smiled again and slowly looked at each member of the group.

"Simple really. We infiltrate them. If you like, we plant a mole."

There was a shocked silence around the table. Blaines continued.

"We will recruit our own mole. He will join UKIP and work himself into a position of trust and confidence. From that position he can do several things. Firstly he can feed back to us any snippets of gossip he hears, skeletons in closets, and all that sort of thing. We can use this information to discredit individual members and promote a general air of distrust about the party.

Secondly he can sniff out the seeds of disagreement and frustration and help to promote factions within the party. Once there are factions there will be power struggles and internal disagreements. We can use this information to create an aura of a party that is out of control.

Thirdly, and I accept that this is a longer term goal that is dependent on the first two steps, he will seek out and groom a challenger for the party leadership, with the ultimate objective of replacing Mr Farage with a less effective and liked leader."

"That's a very ambitious plan Geoffrey". The interruption came from the end of the table, Henry Truscott, a young and capable MP who also was holding a marginal seat. He was well liked and influential among The True Believers. If Blaines could get his support his plan would almost certainly be accepted. Blaines smiled at him as if he were a student who had managed to ask the right question.

"Quite so Henry. Fortunately time is on our side. The next election is still more than three years away. If we act now we have plenty of time for our plan to take effect. We could have them in disarray so that their effectiveness at the next election would be substantially reduced."

Truscott nodded in apparent agreement.

"How would we go about this? And how do we find the right person for a mole?"

"As it happens I have a good friend in MI5. They also are concerned about UKIP and the effect that any shift to a nationalistic far right position would bring. They say they have suitable people available that we could employ."

Tristram Mainwaring looked up and raised his forefinger.

"Geoffrey, if MI5 are so concerned why don't they simply plant a mole themselves? Surely they have the power and resources to do that?"

"It's not quite that simple Tristram. Although various members of the service, including my colleague, are concerned they also agree that at present UKIP present very little of a direct threat to the country, and the department does not wish to be criticised for interfering in the affairs of a legitimate political party. Privately of course they would give us all the help and support they can."

"And that support includes helping us find the right man for the job?"

"Yes it does, and also to set him up with a credible false identity that would stand up to scrutiny."

Mainwaring seemed to be warming to the idea, much to Blaines' relief. He turned around to face Henry Truscott.

"Henry, I'm beginning to think that this idea could be viable. I would value your opinion."

Truscott looked around the table and rose to his feet.

"Tristram, gentlemen, first I would like to thank Sir Robert and Geoffrey for their initiative in presenting this plan to us. It seems to me to be an opportunity we should take advantage of. We have already considered various options but none have appeared to be very effective. This plan however has possibilities. It would give us useful feedback from inside the party itself which could alert us to various courses of action we could take. And if we could destabilise the party to such an extent that a coup would take place which could result in a less attractive leader, well I think it would have been of great service to our wonderful country.

I think we should agree to this scheme in principle and request Geoffrey to proceed to the next stage."

There were murmurs of assent from around the table.

"Geoffrey, perhaps you would be kind enough to outline what our next steps should be?"

Blaines was delighted. He had passed the first hurdle.

"Thank you for your support gentlemen. I propose that I now go back to my MI5 colleague and begin the search for a suitable mole. Then I can come back to you with a more detailed, fully costed plan.

There is however one thing we need to consider. I believe that for the plan to succeed it is vital that the mole's identity is known to as few people as possible. His identity will be known to myself, my colleague in MI5 and to my assistant Michael Robinson. Michael will handle all day to day contact with the mole. He will not meet any one of you other than Michael and myself.

Apart from that small group I would value the services of one more person from this room to help me to select the right agent and to have an ongoing role in planning the strategy. Do I have a volunteer?"

The men around the table glanced at each other. Tristram Mainwaring again took the initiative.

"Gentlemen, I believe this is a role for a younger, dynamic sort of fellow. I think we have the perfect man for the job in Henry Truscott. What do you say Henry?"

Truscott smiled.

"Thank you Tristram. It seems that I've been volunteered. I would be delighted to accept and to contribute in whatever way I can."

"Henry, I am really pleased to have you on board" said Baines warmly. I will set up some meetings and get back to you. Gentlemen, I think that concludes our business for today. Would anyone care to join me in a celebratory sherry?"

Chapter 3

On a beautiful sunny afternoon in August St James Park was at its best. Tourists and Londoners alike were enjoying the warm summer days.

A thick set man of average height walked slowly around the lake. He found the water and trees soothing, a green oasis in a very busy London.

It was several months since he had been recruited to his present occupation, in many respects one of the easiest jobs he had ever had.

For over twenty years he had practiced a lonely and dangerous career. He left school with reasonable grades but without distinguishing himself particularly in any one area. He had grown up in a small village near Aldershot in Hampshire and when he looked at the prospects for a career he realised that in that particular part of the country most opportunities were centred on the large army presence in the area.

Inevitably he joined up, more because it seemed the sensible thing to do rather than with any burning ambition to be a soldier.

Following a period of basic training his life was changed dramatically when he was sent to Northern Ireland where The Troubles were still seething despite the best efforts of politicians and peace protesters. He had to grow up quickly and soon developed a definite talent for under cover and infiltration tasks.

Although he considered that what he was doing was worthwhile he was only too aware of the high risk nature of the life he lead, with the result that when his contract period was complete he chose to leave the army while he was still healthy and in one piece.

After considering several possibilities for a new career he joined the police force in London, more commonly known as "The Met". There he progressed rapidly and discovered that the same talents he displayed in the army were useful for a career as a detective. Again he became involved with undercover and infiltration operations. Out of the frying pan and into the fire he sometimes mused.

His unique talents resulted in him occasionally working on secondment to MI5, the security organisation responsible for anti terrorism in the UK.

Although approached several times to move to MI5 permanently he had refused. By this time he was past his fortieth birthday and was again starting to dream about a more normal and less dangerous job.

His opportunity came soon after New Year in 2017 when he was approached yet again by his MI5 contact. Initially he was wary but he agreed to meet with him in one of The Met's less obvious offices.

He was shown in but to his surprise his normal contact was not present. Instead a tall, elegant, well built man rose from his chair to meet him.

"Please come in" he said. "I'm very pleased to meet you. I'm Michael Robinson. Obviously I know who you are. Do sit down and I'll tell you what this is all about."

He sat and listened, unaware that he was being observed on a TV screen in an adjacent room by two members of the True Believers.

Robinson explained his plan to plant a mole in one of the political parties, seek out damaging information and foment dissent among its members. He was at pains not to reveal which party until they were sure they had the right man.

Finally Robinson sat back and declared "that's about it really. You would be given leave without pay from The

Met and you would be funded in this role by our contacts, and quite generously too. We would give you a new, plausible identity as a minor public servant and the rest, as they say, is up to you."

The policeman was wary. "It doesn't sound very demanding. Why me?"

Robinson smiled.

"Well of course we are impressed by your track record in much more dangerous roles than this one and in recent times you have made no secret of the fact that you are looking for, shall we say, a less stressful life. This should be perfect for you."

"You've done your research" the policeman declared. "I have to admit it's very tempting. Who would I report to?"

"Good question. That would be me. For obvious reasons this operation must be highly secret. Your identity will be known only to me, my boss and your contact in MI5."

"And just who is your boss?"

"That must remain a secret I'm afraid."

"I see" said the policeman. "Just which party are we talking about?"

"That will be revealed when we are closer to an agreement. Look, here's my card. Sleep on it and give me a call tomorrow."

*****

Robinson showed him out and back to Blaines and Truscott, who had observed the interview.

"What do you think?" he asked them.

Blaines smiled and said "I think we've found our man. His file was more convincing than the others and in person he is very impressive. What about you Henry?"

"I think you're right" said Truscott. "I think he's the best of the ones we've seen."

***

Following a further session with Robinson where the target was named as UKIP the policeman accepted the assignment and was very quickly transformed into Phillip Gardner, a minor civil servant in the Department of the Environment. He quickly joined UKIP and worked tirelessly to make himself indispensible.

As Gardner pursued his walk around St James Lake he thought about how his life had changed. As an eager volunteer with apparently lots of free time on his hands he had been well received in UKIP and was taking on more and more roles with them.

He had mixed feelings about the party he was becoming more involved with. He came to meet many of the senior members of the party, including the leader, and was really quite impressed with much of what he was hearing. Other members however he thought were substandard or even out on the lunatic fringe.

It was early days yet but he was beginning to come to some ideas about who might be worthy of further investigation and where the whiffs of scandal seemed to be.

He was enjoying the warm summer sun but he was shortly due to hold his regular meeting with Michael Robinson. He reluctantly abandoned his walk and strolled over towards Westminster.

Chapter 4

The summer that Gardner was enjoying faded into autumn. On another grey November day in London the True Believers met again in the offices of MP Geoffrey Blaines. It had been a year since the plan to plant a mole in UKIP had been agreed.

The members of the group, although aware that a mole had been recruited, were anxious to hear what progress, if any, had been made.

Sir Robert Smythe, as leader of the group, made the introductions.

"Welcome gentlemen. It is now one year since we elected to take the regrettable but necessary step of planting a mole inside UKIP. Extreme secrecy has had to have been maintained and I know little more than you do. The mole's identity and any other facts about him are known only to two of you in this group, Geoffrey Blaines, who is planning the strategy of this campaign, and Michael Robinson, who, as you know, is Geoffrey's trusted personal assistant in charge of the day to day tactics."

Tristram Mainwaring, an MP with a constituency in the East Midlands, interrupted.

"You make it sound like a military operation Robert. If you don't know anything relevant yourself, could we possibly hear from someone who does?"

Sir Robert coughed.

"Certainly Tristram. This is a very delicate operation and I must remind you that any leaks could be very embarrassing. However I don't wish to waste your valuable time so I will ask Geoffrey to bring you all up to date."

Blaines rose to his feet and smiled at his audience.

"Gentlemen, in the year since we conceived this plan much has been achieved. Michael and I, with help from my colleague in MI5, have recruited a suitable mole. He is a man very experienced in undercover operations and infiltration techniques, both in the army and the police force. We have great faith in what he will achieve."

"It's all very well to have faith Geoffrey" drawled Mainwaring, "but has he actually achieved anything? UKIP is rising steadily in the polls and we appear to be still powerless to stop them."

"I understand your concerns Tristram, but I did warn you that this is a long term operation and is unlikely to show many concrete results initially. However, behind the scenes we have been slowly making progress. The mole joined a branch of UKIP – I won't say which one but it is one of the London branches, to be closer to the centre of power, and has made himself very useful. He has become a trusted party member and is active on several organising committees. He has already identified signs of dissent in the leadership and is working to exploit them."

Mainwaring raised his forefinger, a habit he had when he was about to object.

"These of course are laudable long term goals. Are there any more immediate benefits?"

"As a matter of fact, yes. He has identified a few anomalies in the personal lives of some of UKIP's MEPs in the European Parliament, skeletons in closets if you like. When he has gathered more evidence we will be able to leak it, which will cause a certain level of embarrassment. I am personally delighted with his progress and look forward to some significant results in the medium to longer term."

Mainwaring seemed to be satisfied with this response but added "Don't forget Geoffrey, the 2020 election is now only about two and a half years away. We will need some significant results before then."

"And I'm sure we will get them. I shall report back to you as soon as there is something of interest to comment on." Blaines sat down.

Sir Robert rose to his feet.

"Gentlemen, on behalf of all of us I would like to thank Geoffrey for his efforts to date. We always knew this was going to be a long term project. Do not forget that from small acorns do mighty oaks grow. I feel we are still on the right track as nothing else appears to be working. Do we still have your support?"

There was a murmur of agreement around the table.

"Thank you gentlemen. That concludes this meeting. I will leave it to Geoffrey to decide when we need to have another."

Chapter 5

During the preceding year Phillip Gardner had enjoyed considerable success in his role as the mole. He had made friends with many of the key players in UKIP and had socialised with most of them. He kept his eyes and ears open for any titbit of gossip that might further his goal of exposing members of the party.

Some of the scandal he had unearthed had been leaked to the press resulting in great embarrassment for the individuals concerned as well as to the party as a whole.

Gardner viewed these scandals as little more than a means of gently upsetting the party. Mostly they died away when interest waned and had little long term effect on the party itself. Occasionally affected candidates were advised to resign but they were quickly replaced. In his view the more interesting and worthwhile task for him was that of promoting division and dissent within the party, which he executed with considerable skill.

While Nigel Farage was a capable and charismatic leader there were those who were growing impatient with his attempts to take the party into the safer middle ground of British politics and believed that an appeal to the far right would yield superior results. After all, with all major parties trying to win over the middle ground, UKIP was just "me too" and seemed to have less to recommend it as an alternative to the more established parties.

Gardner sensed that this was fertile ground for dissent and sought out the rising stars in the party's right wing to see if any of them might be capable of wrestling the great prize of leader ship from Nigel Farage.

After several false starts he settled upon Francis Ventrice. Ventrice was a tall good-looking man in his early fifties. He exuded charisma and spoke in a resonant deep voice.

He had had a golden start in life. His father had founded a small engineering business which, although not large or super profitable, made enough money for Francis to go to a good private school and then on to University where he gained an engineering degree with honours.

On graduating he joined his father's business and quickly proved his worth by helping to grow the enterprise and modernise it. Eventually his father retired and handed the reins over to his son.

Ventrice seemed to have only two major interests in life; running the business and indulging his love of right wing politics. He was a natural for UKIP as he despised what he called "professional politicians who have never had a real job" and had been member for several years.

He was well liked among some of the members, among whom he was widely regarded as destined for high office in the party, perhaps even leader one day.

What intrigued Gardner about him was that he was widely admired despite certain oddities. Most of the time he spoke in measured tones but when roused he was capable of turning from reason to rant, from a capable speaker to a shouting right wing demagogue.

Gardner liked this evidence of a split personality. He could be capable of turning off great sections of the voting public if he showed any tendencies to extreme ranting. Ventrice also had a rather bizarre personal life which interested him. He was unmarried and appeared to have no serious relationships. Some of the party members wondered if he were gay and on one social occasion over drinks Ventrice was asked the question by a member who had had one or two too many. While those in the vicinity turned quiet and looked embarrassed Ventrice merely laughed.

"Of course I'm not. I'm just too busy with my business and you lot to worry about a woman. If I were I would admit it and be proud."

Gardner had witnessed the exchange and decided to probe a little deeper into his private life and made it his business to socialise further with Ventrice.

He had already noticed that Ventrice rarely drove his own car, preferring instead to be chauffeured. His driver was a strikingly pretty young Asian lady, possibly Thai, Gardner guessed.

One evening over a few drinks in the pub he managed to guide the subject of conversation to driving.

"I don't drive a lot" explained Ventrice. "I like my wine too much. It's safer to have a driver."

"Yes I guess I would too if I could afford it but I'm stuck with public transport. I must congratulate you on your choice of driver though. I noticed her the other night when we left."

"Oh Alice, yes she's a little doll. Without them I don't know where I'd be."

"Them?"

Ventrice grinned. "Yes them. There are two of them, Alice and Grace. They're twins."

Gardner put on his best surprised expression. "You need two drivers?"

"No Phillip, they are a lot more than drivers, more like PAs really. They organise me and my house and generally make my life run more smoothly. I don't know how I'd cope without them."

Gardner smiled and deflected the conversation back to party matters so as not to appear too curious. However he believed he had just struck gold. A middle aged single man living with two young beautiful Asian women. He could just imagine the possibilities this might bring in any future schemes.

Chapter 6

The 12th of September 2018 was one of those beautiful days you sometimes get in London's early autumn, bright sunshine with a touch of warmth and clear blue skies.

Westminster was thronged with tourists enjoying the unexpected late burst of summer. However there were many people for whom the lovely weather was merely a distraction; far more interesting events were taking place on the political scene. The news, when it came, caused politicians, journalists, the media and various apparatchiks to go into overdrive.

For some months there had been rumours circulating that UKIP were in trouble and were heading for a massive bust up. Just where these rumours had started nobody really knew but they certainly caused lots of interest and many column inches.

The rumours, combined with revelations of graft and corruption among some of UKIP's MEPs had had an effect on the party. Their poll ratings had peaked and were beginning to drop, much to the delight of all the other political parties.

For them however, today's news was indeed the icing on the cake. There had been a leadership challenge and, against all expectations, Nigel Farage had been deposed and by a party member who had not to date enjoyed a high profile in the media. His name was Francis Ventrice, who some had taken as a figure of fun due to his occasional rants. Now it was time to take him seriously.

Newspapers and TV stations were vying with each other to get some copy on this relatively unknown politician who would now be one of the most watched leaders in the country.

Around Westminster journalists, politicians and public servants all scurried around trying to assess the impact of this event.

Among the thronging hoards a number of Conservative MPs were making their way to the parliamentary offices of MP Geoffrey Blaines. They had been summoned urgently by no less than Sir Robert Smythe. This could only mean one thing, an unscheduled meeting of the True Believers.

As they trickled in they noticed that Geoffrey Blaines, Sir Robert and Henry Truscott were already present. Something was brewing.

Sir Robert waited for a few minutes to allow others to arrive and then stood up.

"Gentlemen, I think most of us are here. I am aware of at least two members who cannot make it today, so I intend to begin. You are all no doubt aware of the dramatic events of today. I believe it is not an exaggeration to say that today's events are substantially the result of the operation we have been master minding for the past two years. I'll say no more for now; instead I will hand you over to Geoffrey, who can give you the background and answer any questions."

He sat down and Geoffrey Blaines rose to his feet looking like the cat that had the cream.

"Gentlemen, welcome to this special meeting of our group. We and our mole have been working for this moment for many months and we are delighted, and surprised, that it has happened so quickly.

Many of the rumours and scandals of the last few months have been a direct result of efforts by our mole, who is to be congratulated on the splendid job he is doing. These efforts have resulted in a general loss of confidence in the party leadership and declining poll ratings. Our intention was always to undermine the leadership of Nigel Farage but we are delighted that it has happened so quickly."

He paused. As usual Tristram Mainwaring was the first to comment.

"Geoffrey, let me offer you my congratulations on the splendid results you and your, ahem team, have achieved. Can I ask one question however? Were you specifically grooming Francis Ventrice for the role of usurper, and if so why did you pick him?"

"An excellent question as usual Tristram. We looked at various candidates for the role and initially Ventrice was not our first choice. He seemed to be too right wing, out on the lunatic fringe even. However, he appeared to be gathering quite a following as the party inexorably moved to the right, so we took advantage of the situation."

"Mm, how do you think he will go down with the electorate, as opposed to the party faithful?"

"That's the beauty of him. The party seem to have lost their common sense. While Farage is a capable and charismatic leader who appealed to many disaffected voters and stuck mostly to populist issues in the middle spectrum, Ventrice is a right wing fanatic. I believe the Great British Public will see him for the buffoon he is."

Mainwaring smiled and lifted his eyebrows. "Let's hope so. There have been many examples in history where right wing fanatics have achieved an unexpected level of power and control."

"You worry too much Tristram. We British have always been a middle of the road people; we do not like the extremes of the right or the left. I think we can safely say we have UKIP on the run. With less than two years to the next general election I think Mr Ventrice has a hard and thankless task ahead of him."

"I hope so. Do you intend to keep the mole operational, or has he now achieved the objectives we wanted? What do you say Henry?"

Henry Truscott looked at the members round the table. "Gentlemen, as Geoffrey has explained, the plan has succeeded beyond our expectations. However we are all aware that things can go wrong. I would suggest that the mole continue his excellent work for the foreseeable future, to make sure that the momentum is maintained. We wouldn't want to get too complacent would we?"

Mainwaring nodded.

"I'm with you there Henry. We would not wish our hard earned gains to be reversed. Let me offer my personal congratulations to Henry and Geoffrey for their excellent strategy to date. May it long continue."

Blaines was clearly delighted by the response.

"We'll keep the mole in place then to continue his useful work. Now, on a momentous day like this we should celebrate. I have some bottles of cold champagne here and I would be delighted if you would all join me."

Chapter 7

The efforts to discredit the UKIP leaders continued, but only with occasional success. Blaines received periodic reports from the mole via Michael Robinson but he was beginning to wonder if he would find anything that would achieve the results he wanted in the required time frame. He had hoped for a while that the mole would be able to find out more gossip about Ventrice and his young PAs but nothing further emerged.
"What do you think about this business of Ventrice' twins?" he asked Robinson at one of their regular meetings.
Robinson shook his head. "I don't know what to make of it. On the surface you would have to believe there's some hanky-panky going on but we can't find any hard evidence that would seriously embarrass him. He doesn't seem to put a foot wrong."
"Mmm I wonder if it's worth stirring the pot a bit."
"What had you in mind?"
"Well, suppose we were to leak a story to the tabloids. They would have a field day with it."
"But they don't have any more evidence than we have."
"They don't need evidence. With the right photos and some innuendo they can make a story about anything."
"But wouldn't Ventrice simply deny any improprieties?"
"Of course he would. But if you sling enough mud some of it sticks. And it's just the kind of story that would titillate the public. It could be enough to knock some of the confidence out of him and maybe damage him in the polls. Worth a try don't you think?"
"Well I guess it can't hurt; at least not us."
"Well said Michael; I think it's time you arranged a leak."

The tabloids had a field day. No-one knew where the story originated from but every paper picked up on it. The headlines ranged from mild to salacious, 'Ventrice and the Asian Connection', 'UKIP Love Nest?', 'UKIP Leader and the Asian Delights'.

The articles were accompanied by photographs of Ventrice and the twins. The fact that the twins were stunning and Asian added to the frisson.

The official response from UKIP was surprisingly muted. The party issued a solemn press release condemning the 'unwanted intrusion into our leader's private life'.

Ventrice himself, when cornered by a Daily Mirror journalist for a comment, merely said "I have always been a strong believer in a free press even when they are peddling this type of nonsense."

Eventually Ventrice was invited to appear on the BBC's Daily Politics show to put his side of the scandal. He was interviewed by George Denby, one of the rising stars in the beeb, an interviewer who combined incisive questions with humour.

Ventrice turned up looking immaculate in a dark suit, white shirt and old school tie, every bit a leader of the establishment.

Denby opened the proceedings with a handshake and a welcome.

"Mr Ventrice, thank you for coming onto the show."

Ventrice beamed. "It's my pleasure George; and please call me Francis."

"Right Francis, it seems you've caused a furore in the media."

Ventrice, relaxed and smiling, said "on the contrary. I've done absolutely nothing. The press appear to be working themselves into a frenzy without my assistance or anyone else's. "

"But you must admit they have some grounds."
"Which particular grounds are you referring to?"
"Isn't it true that wherever you go you are driven by a young beautiful Asian lady, who apparently has a twin sister, also in your employ?"
Ventrice laughed. "What of it? Would you prefer it if I were driven by a bald, boring, white, middle aged male?"
"I wouldn't. But you know how people will talk."
"Let them. I suspect many people would approve my choice of drivers."
"Don't you think it looks a bit James Bond-ish?"
"George you flatter me. I had never thought of myself as James Bond. Mind you the country has many enemies we need to attend to."
"You mean the issues that UKIP bang on about, immigration, Muslims, The EU?"
"Those and others are the valid concerns of many of our citizens who are being ignored by the traditional parties."
"But do you think it's appropriate for a party leader to have two young girls living in his house?"
"Look, I have a large house which has several self contained apartments. I need to have my support staff continuously available. I am a very busy man with my own business – a very successful one I might add – and my work for the party. The twins function as my PAs, driving me being just a minor part of that important work."
Ventrice paused and looked serious for a moment. "Do you think I'm corrupting these young ladies?"
Denby looked embarrassed briefly but recovered quickly. "Of course not, but can't you see that an unattached male with two beautiful women in his house is bound to attract comment?"
Ventrice seemed to be enjoying himself.

"Come now George, you seem to believe, as Jane Austen suggested, that an unattached male must be in need of a wife. Let me assure you I have no need of a wife. My passion is to work on behalf of our country. I have no time for anything else."

"There are those who claim that you don't like women at all."

"Ah the old rumours. A single man in middle age must be a misogynist or gay. I can assure you I am neither of those things, merely a busy man with a different set of priorities."

"And what would those priorities be?"

"George, as you well know, we at UKIP believe that as a country we have lost our way in the world, and the traditional politicians aren't listening. They are too busy furthering their own interests. It is our belief that UKIP, and UKIP alone, is willing and able to restore this country to its rightful place in the world. That is my goal in life."

"Francis, it's been a pleasure having you here. I'm afraid our time is up."

"Thank you George. Now perhaps the press will calm down a little."

*****

Following his TV appearance Ventrice seemed to have won the day. The tabloids had little new to write about. There were one or two last minute attempts to keep the story going and even the odd attempt at humour, 'Ventrice denies he is gay',' The James Bond of UKIP'.

The next round of political polling was good news for Ventrice but bad news for his opponents. His ratings in the polls had risen sharply from their already high levels.

Blaines was furious. His plan had come to nothing; in fact less than nothing as Ventrice was now even stronger. He sat in his office sipping a sherry wondering just what he had to do to get the better of this rising star.

*****

Ventrice was as happy as Blaines was furious. His gamble had paid off. By treating the newspaper stories with indifference and humour his profile with the public had improved by more than he had hoped. The latest poll results were the icing on the cake.

He watched the results of the polls on the TV morning news as he dressed, which put him in a good humour. He made his way to the large office where his personal assistants were already sorting the incoming mail.

"Good morning girls" he declared with a broad smile, "Have you seen the TV news?"

Alice smiled back at him and replied "yes it's in the newspapers as well. Here have a look."

She handed him a selection of the morning's papers. According to them there was no doubt that Ventrice and his party were on the way up.

"It looks as if it will be a long but enjoyable day in the party rooms" he remarked. "I'd better get down there."

*****

Ventrice returned from his day at the party headquarters with the words of congratulations still ringing in his ears. Even those who had opposed him in his leadership challenge had to acknowledge that he was bringing a whole new level of success to the party. He took pains to point out that his policy of keeping to the right of the other parties obviously appealed to the general public and he would be emphasising that difference in his coming speeches.

A tired but jubilant Ventrice was collected by Alice in the Range Rover and driven back home to Kensington. As they approached the house Alice pressed a button in the car and the large door to the underground car park slid silently open.

As the door closed itself behind them Ventrice remarked "thanks Alice, now I can forget the world for a while and look after myself."

"You must be tired" Alice agreed. "The hot tub is ready and waiting. Get in and I'll bring you a drink."

The hot tub was in a large room in the cellars which had been superbly renovated to resemble a miniature Roman baths, complete with columns and statues. The heated pool, for such was the "hot tub" gave off a turquoise glow from its concealed lighting.

Ventrice undressed in the adjacent changing room and manoeuvred himself into the hot water. Bliss! He began to unwind from the excitement of the day as the warm water soothed his body and the soft piped music calmed his brain.

He was almost asleep when he heard the door open and the soft sound of approaching footsteps. It must be his drink arriving.

It was rather more than a drink. He looked up to see the twins approaching, both totally naked and each carrying a silver tray. On Alice's tray was a bottle of French champagne, already open, in an ice bucket; on Grace's a platter of olives, biscuits, pate and salami.

They deposited the trays on the pool edge alongside Ventrice and walked gently down the steps into the pool.

He watched as the two girls approached him and grinned. "If those rumour mongers could only see me now!"

Chapter 8

The True Believers were gathering again at the office of Geoffrey Blaines. This time the mood was sombre.

The general election of 2020 had produced a result which no one had seriously predicted. UKIP had won a significant percentage of seats, stealing them from all three major parties, but particularly the Tories who were badly affected.

Three of the eleven members of the True Believers had lost their seats and some of the rest had managed only small majorities. Everyone was nervous.

Contrary to all expectations Francis Ventrice had proven to be a capable and electable leader. Now he and his fellow MPs were a force to be reckoned with. So great was the Tory rout that it was left to Labour and the Liberal Democrats to get together to form a coalition government with a slim majority.

Sir Robert Smythe was once more the chairman of the meeting. He waited until all members were present and stood up to close the door.

"Gentlemen", he began, "it is no exaggeration to say that we are facing a crisis. Our plan to undermine UKIP by supporting Francis Ventrice over Nigel Farage seems to have backfired, as we are now in a worse position than ever. My number crunchers have been doing their work and what they have told me is truly terrifying."

Tristram Mainwaring interrupted. He still held his seat, but by a very slim majority. He was not accustomed to having to fight very hard for what had always been a safe Tory seat. He was very alarmed.

"Robert, is it possible to imagine anything worse than the situation we find ourselves in? This UKIP rabble are making inroads right across the country. No one is safe now."

Sir Robert held up his hand.

"Tristram, things are indeed difficult at the moment but as I mentioned just now it could get much worse. I am told that if UKIP support continues to grow at its present rate they could hold more seats than any other party at the next election in 2025. This would make them the dominant partner in a coalition and, god forbid; they might even be able to form a government in their own right. I know, Tristram, what a struggle it was for you this time to hang on. Next time you may not be so fortunate."

Mainwaring blanched. "It's not just about my seat is it, although that's bad enough? What sort of a country will we have? Their extreme right wing policies are not conducive to our British way of life. How did we come to this? Henry, could you enlighten us?"

Henry Truscott was one of the younger MPs and was very popular and influential in the group. He was a capable politician and, along with Geoffrey Blaines, had master minded the mole operation which appeared to have gone badly awry.

Truscott rose to his feet. He seemed to have aged in the last few weeks. He addressed the group hesitantly.

"Tristram, gentlemen, I am the first to admit that what we thought was an excellent plan has fallen victim to the law of unintended consequences. Francis Ventrice was supposed to have destroyed UKIP's prospects but he has in fact enhanced them greatly. He has proven to be a far more compelling speaker than any of us may have predicted. We appear to have badly underestimated him."

Mainwaring impatiently raised his fore finger.

"But it's not just the way he speaks. Their policies are appalling. You would think that people would see through this nonsense."

"I have been analysing his speeches and what I have concluded is very disturbing indeed. It seems to me that he has studied the speeches of Adolf Hitler and brought them up to date."

"But that was more than eighty years ago. Surely they can't be relevant today?"

"On the contrary. He has a number of target groups that he blames for the present weakened state of our country; immigrants, Muslims, the French and the Germans. Not least he also blames what he calls 'The Ruling Elite'. He means the likes of you and me Tristram. He hasn't started attacking us yet but he will.

Look at the policies already revealed, forced repatriation of illegal immigrants, 'encouragement', whatever that means, of legal migrants to return home, the banning of the burqa in public, closures of mosques and a withdrawal from, as they see it, the French and German controlled EU.

The problem is that these policies, reprehensible though they are, are beguilingly attractive and have great appeal to the unsophisticated minds of much of the population.

I am very worried. I believe Francis Ventrice represents a significant threat both to our party, and to our country itself."

The members looked anxiously at each other around the table. Lynton Hardcastle rose to speak. He was one of those who had lost his seat to UKIP in the 2020 election.

"But Henry isn't our population more intelligent than that? They will see through this nonsense. Surely this is a temporary aberration caused by our flat economy right now? It will swing back as growth returns. Most people I know are openly laughing at the antics of UKIP."

"Think back Lynton. All through the 1930s many people laughed at Hitler and were openly contemptuous of the Nazis. Remember what happened?"

"I take your point but what can we do?"

"I'm not sure. Our mole reports that Ventrice' popularity with the party is currently very high, understandably so in the circumstances. He feels that attempts to undermine him at the moment would not be successful.

We do have time on our side however. Don't forget that the next election is not due for more than four years. We should be able to find a solution in that time. I suggest we leave our mole in place in order to exploit whatever may happen. You would agree with that wouldn't you Geoffrey?"

Geoffrey Blaines stood up and regarded the assembled members with his benign bank manager's smile.

"Gentlemen Henry is right. Time is on our side. I know that it is small comfort for those of you who lost your seats at the last election but rest assured we will ensure that next time you will be returned to your rightful place."

"I hope so Geoffrey" said Mainwaring, but it does seem that we cannot do much in the short term. However, before the next election we must do whatever it takes to rid our country of this menace."

He paused and looked directly at Blaines. "Whatever it takes."

As there was no other business to discuss the members one by one left the office. Blaines waited until there was only himself and Sir Robert remaining and said "Robert do you think I could have a word with you on another matter?"

"Certainly Geoffrey, what can I do for you?"

"Now it's just the two of us I'd like to review the Ventrice problem."
"But I thought we had already discussed that?"
"That was for general consumption. Between you and me I think the problem is much more serious than I reported. We have to do something about Ventrice."
"But you just said there is nothing we can do."
Blaines dropped his smile.
"I think Robert that in this serious situation, extreme measures may be needed. Ventrice must be stopped one way or another. As Tristram so eloquently put it; 'whatever it takes'. My colleague in MI5 is equally concerned and they are drawing up plans for various scenarios."
Sir Robert frowned. He looked around and lowered his voice.
"Do I understand you correctly? Are you seriously proposing that we find a way to eliminate Ventrice?"
"If he were to somehow meet with a fatal accident, would that be so terrible? It would solve our problems for us."
"But that's despicable. We couldn't be a party to something like that."
"Robert, look at it this way. Suppose we uncovered a network of terrorists who planned to wipe out most of the government and take over the country. If there were no other way would we not be justified in eliminating them?"
"Yes of course. But surely that's not a valid comparison?"
"Can you imagine a country led by Ventrice? It is no exaggeration to imagine that the events of Hitler's Germany could be repeated."
"Do you really think it's that bad?"
"The parallels are extraordinary, particularly if you study his speeches, which are eerily similar to Hitler's. And he

has already proven himself to be a capable and charismatic speaker even if we consider him a rabble rouser." If he gets into government there is no predicting what could happen, but I believe this country will be changed significantly – for the worse."

Sir Robert looked around nervously and lowered his voice still further.

"But what we are talking about is murder."

"I don't see it that way. What we have here is a war and he is an enemy that must be eliminated. We are protecting our state and our whole way of life."

"Well Geoffrey If you put it that way I see what you mean. Do you have any particular plan in mind?"

"Sadly no, but we need to find one. Whatever is to be done must be done in the not too distant future. The nearer we get to the election the more difficult it is going to be. Even if the end of Ventrice looked like an accident there would be no end of conspiracy theories about how it had been orchestrated by the so-called security forces. Remember the death of Princess Diana and how that stirred up all manner of nutty theories. There would undoubtedly be a reaction and it would need time to settle down. The longer we leave it the more difficult it's going to get."

"So what are you proposing?"

"As you are aware, my personal secretary Michael Robinson has been effectively running our mole for several years. I think we need to bring Michael into our plans. I trust him totally. He needs to work with the mole to tease out any opportunities to be rid of Mr Ventrice. Once we have identified opportunities we can make plans. Because of our mole we are perfectly placed to identify situations that would not be known to others."

"All right Geoffrey. Reluctantly I have to agree with you. But I rather feel like the senators in Rome must have felt when they were plotting to remove Julius Caesar. We rather resemble a bunch of assassins."

"Calm yourself Robert. Think of us as a group of patriots in wartime."

"I suppose so. But please keep me up to date on developments immediately. We may get lucky; this UKIP phenomenon may yet run out of steam of its own volition."

"You'll be the first to know. We will push on immediately."

"Have you discussed this with anyone else in our group?"

"No, no-one yet. I think we will restrict it to you, me and Robinson."

Sir Robert nodded, picked up his briefcase and left.

Blaines sat down and mopped his brow with his handkerchief muttering to himself, "Just as well I didn't tell him we have started already."

Chapter 9

The August weather remained warm and sunny and St James Park continued to be frequented by crowds of tourists and Londoners alike.

At one part of the lake two men, smartly dressed but without jackets, appeared to be enjoying looking at the ducks, but on closer inspection neither man seemed happy and relaxed.

Michael Robinson had organised one of the regular meetings with his mole, Phillip Gardner. St James Park was much more preferable in this weather to a dark, hot office in Westminster.

Robinson had just finished explaining to Gardner the idea that Blaines had had, namely that Ventrice had to be eliminated.

Gardner heard the news in silence as he continued to watch the ducks. Robinson waited nervously for a response. When it became obvious he wasn't going to get one he forced the issue.

"Well Phillip, you haven't said much. What do you think?"

Gardner took a deep breath.

"Michael, you have never told me who your boss is but up to now his decisions and ideas have been pretty good. I know things haven't always gone his way but that's life. On the whole he was on the right track. This idea is crazy."

"Why is it crazy?" asked Robinson anxiously. As far as he could remember this was the first time he and Gardner had disagreed.

"Let me see. It's illegal, dangerous, immoral, difficult and unnecessary. Apart from that it's fine."

"Phew" said Robinson, "you haven't minced your words. My boss believes it is necessary to protect the country from those who would destroy it. I'm sure you've dealt with a few such people in your army days."

"I did what I had to do, but that never involved a cold bloodied scheme like this."

"Well Geoff – er – the boss thinks this is something he has to do for the country. We may have to disagree on the morality of it, but why did you say it was difficult and unnecessary?"

"I don't think your boss realises how difficult this kind of scheme is" he replied, carefully committing to memory the name Geoff which Robinson had inadvertently revealed. It might be useful knowledge one day.

"First you have to find the right man. There are very few people who could pull off a stunt like this and it would require massive planning and lots of money. The boss needs to realise that. And if anything goes wrong – heads will roll."

"I'm sure he appreciates the difficulties and the risks. He's not a small thinker. But you also said it was unnecessary. Why?"

"I think you are just panicking at UKIP's short term success. If you take the longer view our current strategy will deliver results with fewer risks."

"I'm not sure I follow you."

"Look, Ventrice is an odd character with strange views that will catch up with him eventually if we keep chipping away. We know he has a strange personal life. If we can break into that we can destroy his career and his party without having to be heavy handed."

"Mm, the boss is really worried. He thinks they have a chance of being part of the government after the next election, maybe even *be* the government."

"I agree that's possible but unlikely. Even if it turned out that way they would make such a hash of things they would be out on their ear quick smart."

"But he's determined. He wants results."

"What does he expect me to do? I'm not an assassin. "

"No of course not Phillip. Just continue the excellent job you are already doing by keeping us up to date with Ventrice' movements and plans."

"OK but I still think it's a crazy idea."

"You may be spot on but right now he's very focussed on it. Maybe he'll lose interest when he realizes how difficult it's going to be. Anyway I'll keep you posted. Look, I must be off. I have another meeting shortly."

"Right, see you Michael. I think I'll stay here for a little while. It's peaceful and the water calms me and helps me get things into perspective.

**

The mole watched Robinson leave. He turned to watch the ducks on the lake as he tried to assimilate this latest news. Surely the boss, Geoff as he had now discovered, must know it would be insane to go ahead with such a scheme.

His military training had taught him to plan carefully and evaluate all the risks and opportunities before committing to a course of action. He wasn't at all sure that a politician with a short term focus, reinforced by the election cycle, would be as careful as he should be.

Not that he cared whether "Geoff" came to grief or not, as long as he was able to prove he knew nothing about it. He determined that there should be no evidence that he knew of this plot, just in case the silly fool did decide to give it a go.

Besides, he was enjoying this comfortable and well paid job and he was building up a level of respect for Ventrice.

He had some weird ideas but he seemed to be trying to do the right thing. He certainly didn't deserve this kind of treatment.

It occurred to him that he needed to take out a little more insurance for himself. He had long suspected the "the boss" was either a senior Tory politician or some grandee in the party. Now that he had a name to go on he should be able to get closer. After all, how many of them would be called Geoff?"

A first step was to maintain a level of surveillance on Michael Robinson. If he watched his comings and goings he would get an indication of who Robinson sees, which could shed more light on who Geoff might be.

He felt better now he had an action plan. Robinson would be an easy target to tail. He needed to keep close to this latest scheme and its authors, and to do what he could to prevent such a preposterous idea from becoming reality.

He didn't agree with all of Ventrice' ideas but he knew the man didn't warrant such extreme measures.

Chapter 10

After many months of trying to develop a sensible plan to be rid of Francis Ventrice, Geoffrey Blaines at last had an idea. He was aware that the lack of success of their previous efforts was having an effect on The True Believers with some of them openly questioning whether it was worth the continuing expense of running the mole.

His staff had long been instructed to refer to him any news items concerning Ventrice. He devoured them all, for what use they were. There were no suggestions of criminal behaviour on Ventrice' part and no personal scandals on which he might be attacked. He appeared to be Mr Squeaky Clean.

Reports from the mole, via his personal secretary Michael Robinson, had not identified any means by which Ventrice could be discredited, nor had they been able to suggest any ways in which his personal security could easily be breached.

Wherever he went he had his bodyguards with him; "personal assistants" as he preferred to call them.

A recent news item had given Blaines his idea. It was reported that Ventrice was intending to undertake a speaking tour in Australia in April 2022, just ten months away. He was aware that a far right party had appeared in Australia in recent years, which had titled itself "Our Nation". The name itself had echoes of another party which had been briefly successful in the late 1990s and early 2000s, Pauline Hanson's One Nation.

The policies of the new party were strikingly similar to the older one, a case of history repeating itself. As the Australian economy, which had brilliantly survived the 2008 crisis that had engulfed the rest of the western world, began to crumble, populist and protectionist sentiments resurfaced.

Our Nation emerged as a focus for these sentiments and grew rapidly, taking most of its support from voters disillusioned with the Australian conservatives, bizarrely named "Liberals".

Their collection of policies included severe curbs on immigration, a rebalancing away from multi-culturalism and strong support for Australian businesses, which were being "ripped off" by globalisation.

Their targets were immigrants, Muslims and global businesses and they held a general belief that an unidentified "ruling elite" were running the country for their own benefit and not for the good of the people.

Blaines reflected that Our Nation's policies were strikingly similar to those of UKIP as ruled by Francis Ventrice, so he was not surprised to hear that Ventrice had been invited to speak to various gatherings of Our Nation supporters.

The tour was to take place in a series of venues, starting in Brisbane and ending in Perth. In an interview Ventrice had declared that he felt privileged to be asked as Australia was a country he had long admired. He also admitted he was looking forward to a short break from his hectic political life in Britain and would be sure to take a well earned vacation while there to see some of Australia's famous sights.

This last point was the one which gave Blaines his big idea. While Ventrice was tripping around sightseeing in Australia he would be in an unfamiliar environment. Australia was known to be a dangerous place for the unwary and an Englishman off his guard could easily meet with a nasty accident. If such an accident were to happen in far away Australia it would be dismissed as unfortunate and the British politicians could publicly be shocked at this unfortunate occurrence. No-one in his right mind could credibly claim it was all a plot from political rivals in Britain.

There was of course the issue of Ventrice' bodyguards. Somehow it would have to be engineered that he spent some down time away from his minders so that a suitable accident could happen. That was a challenge but not impossible. He had learned from Michael Robinson that the mole he was running was now a part of the organising committee for the tour, which meant that there had to be possibilities.

At last he had the beginnings of a plan. He would study the details of the tour, supplied by the mole, and from that work out the method by which Ventrice could be separated from his entourage and led into a situation where he would meet with an unfortunate fatal accident.

Blaines left his office feeling more cheerful and positive than he had for some time.

Chapter 11

Sir Marcus Tomelly alighted from his first class carriage at Esher railway station. He was tall and patrician looking, a senior man in his field but still with a good head of steel grey hair. With his quiet demeanour and conservative clothes most people would have taken him for a senior public servant returning from a day at his office in London.

Had he been asked what he did he would have confirmed that impression with a vague "yes I have a very boring job at Whitehall". The truth however was that he was a senior figure in MI5, involved with Her Majesty's Government's continuing efforts to combat terrorism in the UK. No one really knew exactly what his position was and even to his small band of close and trusted friends he would only admit to "I help out a bit in the DDG's office".

The DDG in question was the Deputy Director General who reported directly to the Director-General.

The DDG was responsible for five important departments: International Counter Terrorism; Cyber, Counter Espionage, Counter Proliferation; Technical Operations, Analysis and Surveillance; Northern Ireland Counter Terrorism; Ethics and Review. To which of these departments Sir Marcus was attached was never revealed and in fact the identity of the DDG himself was known only to a small number of colleagues.

Tomelly enjoyed his twenty five minute train journey from Waterloo to Esher. It helped him to empty his mind of the day's affairs. He sometimes listened to music on his MP3 player, sometimes read a book or often just gazed out of the window watching the dull suburbs of South West London slip by until at last he reached the green and pleasant area of Surrey in which he lived.

His wife Penny would be there to meet him in the big, black Range Rover she was very fond of and in just a few minutes would whisk him in comfort to his spacious residence in a very nice corner of Claygate.

Sir Marcus was looking forward to this evening. He had been invited round to dinner at the house of his old friend Geoffrey Blaines and his wife. He and Blaines went back a long way. They met as two junior boys at Eton and were friends all through school. They made an odd pair; Tomelly tall, thin and serious, Blaines short, round and cheerful. Tomelly went on to read Classics at Cambridge while Blaines, who knew from an early age that he wanted to go into politics, went to Oxford to study PPE.

Throughout their careers they kept in touch and enjoyed each other's company and now, some forty years later, lived in the same elite part of Surrey, Blaines an MP and senior figure in the Conservative Party and Tomelly an influential public servant with his mysterious role in MI5.

As Tomelly changed from the formal business suit he habitually wore into more comfortable clothes for dinner he pondered about the evening to come. Although he and Blaines socialised on a regular basis this particular invitation followed closely upon a recent dinner at Tomelly's house. Normally they got together every two or three months but the dinner at the Tomellys had been only three weeks ago. Blaines had seemed very keen on a follow up. Sir Marcus wondered why. He wants something, he thought. I wonder what it is.

His thoughts were interrupted by a call from his wife Penny. "Darling, are you going to be much longer? We should be off soon."

"Just coming" he yelled as he descended the wide curving timber staircase. Penny was a stickler for being in time for social engagements. He didn't mind. She was not much of a drinker; typically she would consume only one or two glasses of wine in an evening so she drove the car, allowing Sir Marcus to indulge his love of whiskey and good red wine.

As they both lived in the same part of Surrey the drive was quite short. Cocooned in the Range Rover he looked at the Surrey countryside as he wondered again what Blaines was up to.

Blaines met them at the door with his wife Patricia, seemingly in his usual good humour. They exchanged handshakes and kisses. Patricia led them into the large lounge and waved her hand toward the drinks cabinet. "You men help yourselves to a pre-dinner drink. Dinner will be about twenty minutes. I need to finish it off. Come on Penny; tell me what you've been up to."

With that the two wives departed to the kitchen and Blaines moved over to the drinks cabinet. "Your usual Marcus?"

"Yes thanks Geoffrey." The usual was a stiff shot of Glenmorangie, a particular favourite of Tomelly.

Blaines poured the two drinks and they moved over to the fireplace with its wood fire giving out a cheerful warm glow. As they stood with their backs to the fireplace Blaines coughed slightly and said "Marcus, there's something I'd like to sound you out about."

Here it comes, thought Tomelly, and he's in a hurry to tell me.

"What's on your mind?"

"It's about Francis Ventrice."

"Oh, he's on everyone's mind. What's he done now that you find so interesting?"

"It's not so much what he's done but what he's going to do."

"And what is that?"

"In a few months time he's going on a lecture tour in Australia, as a guest of the Our Nation party."

"Yes I'd heard about that. But what has it got to do with us?"

"It's just that it presents us with an interesting opportunity" said Blaines a little nervously.

"I'm afraid I don't follow you Geoffrey. You're going to have to spell it out for me."

"Look at it this way. Ventrice is a clear danger to the UK political system. The Australian security services know what he has achieved here and that Our Nation are trying to repeat the same success there."

"But isn't that Australia's problem? I can't see what it has to do with us."

"Come on Marcus; I know that you are in regular contact with your colleagues in the Australian security service. ASIO isn't it?"

"Geoffrey you know I can't tell you about confidential chats with other agencies."

"Surely you must have discussed the Ventrice phenomenon with them?"

"Of course we have but what of it?"

"Don't you think they would like to see the back of Ventrice?"

"Undoubtedly. Probably as much as we would. They don't want the already bad situation in Australia to escalate into Ventrice-style extreme politics. But it looks as if we are stuck with him for a while yet. He doesn't put a foot wrong."

"I might just have a solution."

"Might you? That's interesting. And just how would you pull off this little miracle?"

Blaines took a deep breath. This is the moment, he thought.

"Let's just say that while he is in Australia he will be in unfamiliar territory and off his guard. If he were to meet with an accident there it would be tragic but there would be no blame attached to anyone in this country."

Tomelly gave Blaines a hard look.

"Geoffrey, what makes you think he would meet with an accident?"

"Well I thought one could be arranged. I'm sure it's not beyond the wit of ASIO to come up with something."

"This is pretty serious stuff Geoffrey."

"I know but desperate situations require desperate measures, wouldn't you say? We have responsibilities to our citizens which sometimes require unpleasant solutions."

Tomelly pondered for a moment. "It would certainly be fortuitous for such an - er – accident to happen away from these shores, although I'm not sure how ASIO would react."

"It would solve their problem as well as ours. Surely they could put it down to some lone nutter?"

"Perhaps, but you know it would be very difficult to find the right – er – agent to handle a job like this. And it's not just about doing the job. He would have to have an escape plan that is foolproof. After all we wouldn't want any aspect of the affair to be traceable back to us."

"But couldn't MI5 and ASIO be of some help?"

"I don't know. They wouldn't put obstacles in our path but I'm not sure just how much positive help we would get. They would be very concerned that they are seen to have nothing to do with it"

He paused and appeared to ponder for a moment before resuming.

"I'll tell you what I'll do. I'll have a quiet word in the right ears and get back to you. We have plenty of time. It's a despicable idea Geoffrey, but it might just work. Certainly food for thought. Speaking of food, I expect dinner will be just about ready. Shall we go and see?"

The two men, both deep in thought, slowly made their way to the kitchen.

PART 2 – Preparation

Chapter 12

By March 2022 Geoffrey Blaines had to admit that recruiting an assassin was not quite the easy task he had expected. Ventrice' tour of Australia was due to start in the near future and Blaines was still occupied with the search for his candidate.

Otherwise his plan was in good shape. Funding had been secured from Sir Thomas and also from Tristram Mainwaring, who had proven to be, as Blaines had gambled, enthusiastic to do something to prevent UKIP from usurping what he considered the Tories' rightful place.

Meanwhile, far away in Australia, a search for a different kind of assassin was under way. Brian Chambers, a Detective Inspector with the South Australian Police, who was stationed at the normally sleepy tourist town of Mannum on the River Murray, had for some time been observing the activities of a local minor hard man, Tony Andersen, who he suspected could be responsible for one murder and another murder or kidnapping in his area. Although he had no proof that would stand up in court he had collected a mass of circumstantial evidence that in some way Andersen was connected with the unfortunate events that had befallen the two British tourists.

The further he investigated the more he became convinced that Andersen was part of a scam run by his brother Greg in England, whereby naïve young British men, out of work and with a declining future in Britain, were lured to Australia by Greg Andersen with the promise of highly paid jobs in the Australian mining sector.

By this time it was almost impossible to gain a work visa in Australia unless you were a qualified and experienced mining engineer. Greg Andersen's pitch to the gullible young men was that he had contacts in the Australian Immigration Department and with sympathetic small miners who were desperate for men with a willingness to work in the harsh outback conditions for wages which were astronomical by British Standards.

All this came at a price of course, and the life savings of the young men and their families were handed over to the Andersens in the hope of a better, more rewarding future. Once in Australia the hopeful immigrants were met by Tony Andersen and taken to some remote location and then quickly abandoned. The unlucky ones died in very suspicious circumstances; the lucky ones discovered they had been duped and swindled out of a lot of money, in many cases the life savings of themselves and their families.

Technically they were only tourists on a tourist visa and had to make their way back to England sadder and poorer. When they tried to track down the perpetrators they found the web site had been closed, the mobile phone dead, and the contact person had vanished without trace.

Greg Andersen was continually creating new websites and new identities for himself, so any enquiries from the aggrieved party would lead to nowhere.

Chambers had been helped in his investigation by an English reporter, John Foster, who had unearthed useful evidence in Britain about the activities of the Andersens and had travelled to Australia to follow the trail of vanished British tourist Alan Warner.

Foster, more by luck than judgement had been able to alert Chambers to the fact that Tony Andersen was fleeing the area in the company of Alan Warner who he had kidnapped.

The final confrontation had happened when the police had caught up with Andersen at Forster Lookout on the Murray River, where Warner had been freed. In the confusion Foster's guide and lover, Debbie Simmons, had been wounded in the leg and Andersen had fallen from the cliff top into the river a hundred feet below.

Chambers did not know if Andersen had died in the fall or had somehow survived it, but by this time it was too dark for a thorough search of the area, so it was called off till daybreak.

Chapter 13

Tony Andersen felt very relaxed. He seemed to be just floating along. The air was warm and fragrant and the only sounds were the lapping of water and songs of birds. The light was beginning to fade, turning the sky into a vivid mix of orange and purple. He wondered where he was and why.

He looked around. He seemed to be floating past towering cliffs on one side. On the other side were green trees and grasses with the water gently lapping at them. He realised his left side hurt but otherwise he was so beautifully relaxed, just floating along. I must be dead, he thought, and this is heaven. It's really kinda nice, very peaceful.

He drifted along, willing his memory to give him some inkling of what had happened. He decided to sit up for a better view. He tried to sit up and realised with a shock that he *was* in water. And he really was floating. What the hell was going on? Think, Tony, think.

The more he thought the more pain he could feel. It wasn't just his left side any more. His right ankle was very painful and boy did he have a headache.

Now that he was more conscious he had to move about to stay afloat. How long had he been floating? And why? He manoeuvred himself closer to the bank. The tall cliffs came sheer out of the water but surely there must be a ledge or something. He was starting to panic when his wish was granted. For a moment the sheer cliffs were fringed at the bottom by a rocky outcrop.

He kicked his legs, wincing at the pain, but was able to beach himself on the outcrop. He pulled himself out of the water and sat on the rocks panting. He looked around, relieved to be on solid ground once more. The pain in both legs seemed stronger now that he was out of the water. He gazed around and willed his memory to return, but to no avail. He fell asleep exhausted.

*****

He woke with a start. It was dark and the air was chilly. In the moonlight he could see he was on one bank of a river with towering cliffs, but the other side was flat with small trees. Hang on, he thought, I'm not in heaven. This looks like the River Murray. What am I doing here? And why have I got all these aches and pains?

Slowly his memories returned, but the experience did not make him any more relaxed; quite the contrary. He remembered waving his gun at the police. The policeman had stepped forward to take the gun. He had involuntarily taken a step back. Christ, I must have fallen off the bloody cliff; no wonder I hurt so much. He was amazed that he had actually survived the fall and appeared to be more or less intact.

So where were the police? Were they searching for him or did they think he was dead? He needed to get away from here before daylight. He'd be a sitting duck when the sun came up. What time was it? He looked at his watch but it had stopped. Whether it was the water or the shock he didn't know. With a sigh he took it off and threw it in the river.

His phone! His phone was a waterproof model he had bought for his frequent fishing trips. This would be a test for it. Would it have survived the water and the shock? Or would the battery be flat?

He prayed as he fished it out of his inside jacket pocket. Please work! He pressed the power button. Miracle – it works! Now, is there any signal? Yes and not a bad one considering where he was. And how much battery was left. Mm, not a lot but enough for the one phone call he wanted to make.

He opened his contact list and made a selection. It seemed a long time until a tired sounding voice said simply "yeah?"

"Terry, it's Tony."

"Tony, what do you want at this time?"

"Why, what time is it?"

"Tony, have you had too much piss? It's nearly midnight."

"Oh, sorry mate, I hadn't realised. Look, I need your help. I need you to come and rescue me."

"Rescue you? You haven't been rootin another bloke's wife again have you?"

"Very funny Terry. You know I'm not like that. No I've had a bit of a fall and I need a lift."

"Where are you?"

"I'm not sure exactly."

"Whatdya mean you're not sure. How the bloody hell am I supposed to find you if *you* don't know where you are?"

"It's not that bad. I'm somewhere near Walker Flat. Could you meet me there?"

"Well I guess. It'll take me a while to get dressed and get there. You know this is going to cost you a few rounds in the pub?"

"Thanks Terry, you're a good mate. Look, you know the car park by the ferry? Be there and I'll meet you there, say in about an hour."

"OK I'll get going."

"And Terry! Don't tell anyone about this, and if anyone asks you haven't seen or heard from me. OK?"

"Jesus Tony, you're getting paranoid. What's all this about?"

"I'll explain later mate. See you soon."

Tony hung up and considered his position. He knew he was probably only a few hundred yards downstream from Walker Flat but he was on the wrong side of the river. Walker Flat was on the other bank. He could try floating downstream a bit further until he had cleared the steep cliffs then walk back to the ferry along the cliff top. The ferry would take him right to the car park. But he wasn't sure how long the steep cliffs lasted, and then there was the problem of the ferry. At this time of night the ferry didn't run to a schedule. You had to pick up the phone by the ferry stop and call the ferryman. In itself that wasn't too much of a problem but then the ferryman was sure to remember him, being the only passenger at that time of night, and on foot in this remote location. Very suspicious he would look. He wondered if his vehicle was still at the Forster lookout car park but dismissed the idea. Surely the cops would have taken it away.

So that option didn't look so good. He wondered if he could steal a boat to get to the other side, and looked up and down. But there were no boats on this side because of the high steep cliffs. Plenty on the other bank. A fat lot of use that was!

He was cold and wet and his head ached. There was only one way left and he didn't much fancy it. He had to swim across. He was a strong swimmer but this was a bit daunting, especially at night and with sore legs. But he didn't have any choice. Thank god this wasn't one of the widest parts of the river. The current would probably carry him a bit further downstream but that didn't really matter. It was a short walk back to the car park. The area was sparsely populated and it was unlikely he would meet anyone at this time of night.

What about the snakes? He knew there were snakes in the river. He wasn't paranoid about them but he wasn't anxious to tangle with one either. They could be quite poisonous. He had to do it. He closed up his phone, put it in one of his zip pockets and gently eased himself back into the water. Christ it seemed even colder. He headed out towards the other bank, which now looked quite a distance away.

He paddled along at a leisurely breast stroke, figuring that he could keep going for longer like that without getting tired. He felt something slimy slide along his leg. Snake!

No it wasn't. It was just some long vegetation floating in the water. Get a grip Tony, he thought.

Christ his left leg hurt but he paddled slowly forward. After a while he realised he had travelled quite a distance and the opposite bank didn't look so far away any more. That cheered him up and gave him the strength and confidence to carry on.

His left leg was feeling very stiff and sore. He worried that he wouldn't make the other bank but he ploughed slowly on. Gradually he realised he wasn't all that far from the bank. He scanned it for a good landing position that wasn't too steep and spotted a small stretch of beach downstream. Perfect! If he just kept paddling along he could let the current take him there.

Easy now. He could see the occasional house and some moored boats on the approaching bank. Not long now. He felt more slimy stuff slide along his body and hoped that it was vegetation not snakes. His left leg really hurt and he wanted to stop just to ease the pain, but he couldn't. Must keep going.

Finally, within striking distance just slightly downstream was the small beach. It gave him renewed strength. Part floating and part kicking he soon found himself at the beach and gratefully hauled himself out of the water. He was stiff, sore and exhausted but he'd done it. The swim of his life.

How long had it taken him? He couldn't remember what time he set off but he figured it was less than half an hour, which gave him plenty of time to get to the car park.

He allowed himself a few minutes rest to get his breath back and to massage his sore legs. I'm getting too old for this, he thought. He elected to follow the river bank back to the car park and set off slowly. He figured it was only ten to twenty minutes walk so he could afford to take his time.

He needed to be vigilant and wondered if the cops had left someone at Walker Flat just in case. He would keep his eyes open and he had the advantage of darkness.

He crept slowly along, past the occasional beach house and several moored boats. In the distance, on the other bank, he could see where the steep cliffs ended. Good! That was where the ferry to Walker Flat was, so he was quite close. At this time there were no lights in the houses and absolutely no one about. Passing close to one house he froze as he heard a dog barking. Then he heard a tired voice yell "Shaddup" and the dog quietened down. He hurried away and saw or heard nothing else until he could see the small village. From a vantage point behind a tree he surveyed the car park. Not a single car to be seen and absolutely no sign of life.

He sat down and massaged his legs while he waited and watched. After a few minutes he heard the sound of an approaching vehicle. He stayed behind the tree; you never knew who it might be. Then an old Holden Ute pulled into the car park and stopped. It was Terry. He knew that vehicle well. He had switched off the engine and sat there silently. Tony waited and observed. No one had appeared and all was quiet. This was it. He walked as quickly as he could over to the ute and pulled open the passenger door. Terry looked round, startled.

"Christ mate you gave me a shock. Look at you. What a sight. Where have you been?"

"Never mind that. I'll tell you on the way. Let's get out of here – quick."

Terry swung the car around and headed back to Mannum, a journey of some twenty five minutes on this road.

"OK Tony, what's this all about? What are you doing here, all wet at this time of night?"

"Mate the cops are after me. I've had a hell of a time keeping away from them."

"What have you been doing for the cops to be so interested in you?"

Tony nodded sagely.

"It's a case of mistaken identity" he stated with as much dignity as he could muster.

"What do they think you've done?"

"They think I kidnapped this guy, but I was just giving him a lift. I'm lucky to get away. They were about to shoot me."

He's lost it now, thought Terry. I'd better humour him till he sobers up.

"Well you're safe now mate. I'll soon have you home."

"No I can't go home. I'm a wanted man. They are trying to pin all sorts of things on me. Can I stay over at your place tonight?

He's flipped, thought Terry.

"Yeah OK, but you'll have to sleep on the sofa."

"Thanks mate, you're a real pal."

With that Tony fell asleep exhausted while a mystified Terry drove back to his house on the outskirts of Mannum.

*****

Tony woke up with a start as Terry pulled into the driveway of his house and turned off the engine.
"Where are we?"
"We're at my place mate. That's what you wanted isn't it?"
"Yeah, but we've got something to do first."
Terry groaned. Tony really didn't seem to have a grip on things tonight.
"What do you have to do at this time of night?"
"I've got to get something from my house."
"But you said the cops were after you. That's why you're coming to my house, isn't it?"
"Oh yeah, I didn't think about that, but I've got to get something. Take me round there won't you. It'll only be a minute or two."
"OK mate, then can we go home and get to bed?"
"I told you we'll only be a minute. Now let's get round there and keep your eyes peeled for the cops."
Terry drove slowly round to Tony's house just a few streets away wondering if Tony had had a bang on the head which was affecting him. Mostly Tony made some kind of sense, despite his violent temper, but this was a Tony he hadn't seen before. As they approached Tony's house Tony crouched down out of sight and said "Terry, just drive past and see if you see anything unusual."
Terry did as he was asked and pulled over just around the corner.
"Well?" said Tony, "what did you see?"
"It's pretty quiet mate but there's a car parked just down from your house and I thought there was someone in it."
"What, a police car?"

"Who knows? It's just a plain Nissan hatch."

"It could be them watching out for me."

Terry decided to go along with Tony's ramblings in the hope that he could soon get to bed.

"What do you want me to do then?"

"Just stay here for a minute, while I go in the back way. Give me ten minutes then drive back out and pick me up back at the corner."

"Whatever you say."

Tony carefully made his way round the back of the property and approached his back door cautiously. There didn't seem to be anyone about. He extracted his keys from a zippered pocket and quietly eased his way into the house. He stopped and listened. Silence. Good. He very carefully made his way to the kitchen and opened a corner cupboard. Right at the back, in the corner, behind a stack of bottles was a bag. Tony grabbed it, carefully replaced the bottles and closed the door.

Next, emboldened by how easy it had been so far, he moved slowly towards the bedroom, grabbed some clothes and placed them in the bag. Job done. He quietly made his way to the back door and locked it behind him. He looked around. There was no one about so he walked down the lane that ran along the back of his property, made his way to the connecting street and stood behind a tree to wait for Terry.

After only a few minutes he heard the sound of an approaching vehicle. It was Terry. He stepped out from behind the tree and waved. Terry pulled over.

Tony opened the door and got in.

"All done. Let's go home."

"What's going on Tony? I got stopped."

"What do you mean you got stopped?"

"That Nissan hatch really was a cop car. When I came back round he put his blue light on and pulled me over. He searched the car and then asked me what I was doing there."

"What did you tell him?"

"I told him I was just dropping off a mate who'd had too much to drink. He seemed to buy that but he still checked my licence. What have you got me into?"

"You worry too much. Let's just go home and I'll tell you all about it in the morning."

Chapter 14

Saturday morning dawned clear and hot, as was typical for this time of year. Tony Andersen had slept in late despite the lack of comfort in Tony's lumpy sofa. He sat up, looked around and listened. He could hear movement from the kitchen. Terry must be up already.

He heaved himself up and walked awkwardly to the kitchen, conscious that most of his body ached, particularly his left leg. He shuffled in and Terry turned around.

"G'day, you're up at last. You don't look much better than you did last night. Do you want some coffee?"

"Yeah thanks."

"OK, I'll make the coffee and you tell me what's going on. Right?"

"I told you last night. It's a case of mistaken identity. I'd got a job to take this guy across to Sydney overnight. We stopped for a break and before I knew it the cops had arrived and accused me of kidnapping him. They started getting all heavy and I tried to escape. That's when I fell off the cliff."

"What cliff?"

"The one at Forster Lookout."

"Jesus mate, you're lucky to be still alive. Those cliffs are huge."

"Tell me about it. I've got the aches and pains to prove it."

"What were you doing at Forster Lookout?"

"He wanted to see the view before he went home."

"What do you mean, went home?"

Tony thought hard. In his estimation he was telling a good story so far.

"Do you remember the pommie guy who disappeared?"

"Yeah, the one the two sheilas were looking for?"

"That's him. I was providing some security for him but it turns out he was here illegally. I hid him at my dad's shack for a few days and then I was driving him to Sydney so he could fly home from there."

"What happened?"

"His bloody girlfriend turned up with the cops and they all started accusing me of kidnapping him."

Terry seemed to be satisfied with this explanation.

"So why don't you just go to the cops and clear up what really happened?"

"They'll never believe me. I need to get away for a while till the fuss dies down. That's where you come in."

Terry worried at the thought of getting involved.

"Why do you want me to get mixed up in all this?"

"You're my mate aren't you? No, this is easy. I need a vehicle and I need it quick. I want you to go and see some of your car dealer mates and get me a cheap car."

"Is that all? And what do I use for money?"

Tony opened the bag he had taken from his house earlier. He took a few clothes off the top and to Terry's amazement the bag was full of money. He peeled off a wad and handed it to Terry.

"There, that's five grand. Go out and buy me a vehicle – today."

"Where did you get all that cash from? You been robbing banks?"

"Don't be silly. You know that most of the work I do is for cash. I don't want the tax man to see it and I don't trust banks."

"Neither do I. Ok, but you won't get much for five grand."

"Just as long as it'll get me up to North Queensland, then I'll dump it."

"Wow, you are serious about this."

"Course I'm serious. I know you've got a few mates who deal in dodgy motors. Go and get me one. Can you do it now? I want to get away tonight before they come after me."

"But look at the state of you. Shouldn't you be seeing a doctor?"

"Nah, a shower and some tucker and some pain killers and I'll be as good as new. Now, are you gonna go and get me that car?"

"OK, keep your cool. I'll go now. I've got a mate in Murray Bridge who deals a bit and knows to keep his mouth shut. Just give me an hour or two."

"Thanks Terry, see you in a while. I'll have something to eat then I might go back to bed for a while."

Terry headed off on his mission while Tony raided the fridge. He found some bread, cheese and cold meat. That would do; and a nice cold beer to wash it down. He sat in his chair and very soon was fast asleep.

He woke, hearing the sound of engines outside. How long had he been asleep? He looked at the wall clock; almost three hours. He pulled back the front curtain slightly and glanced outside. Terry had reappeared in his Holden. Two other vehicles were behind him. A large middle aged man with a bald head, wearing a tight black t-shirt sat in a bright red Ford Mustang. That's nice, thought Tony.

The other vehicle was an older model Holden Commodore. The young man driving it got out and went over to the Mustang. He got in and the Mustang roared away.

Terry locked his car and came into the house.

"Well I did it. Isn't she a beauty? It's a bit long in the tooth and done a few miles but it'll be ok to get you to Queensland."

"Thanks Terry, it looks fine. How much did you pay for that?"

"Well he wanted six grand but I kept saying I only had five and had the cash with me now. So he gave in. Delivered as well. It doesn't get any better than that does it?"

"No you've done well. Has it got any fuel in it?"

"Yep, I made sure he filled it up for you."

"And you didn't tell him about me?"

"No, I didn't mention you. I just said I wanted it for my girl friend."

"Great, as soon as it starts to get dark I'm away."

Tony spent the rest of the day preparing for his trip, getting some food and water together and packing his few possessions. He frequently peered anxiously out of the window to make sure the cops hadn't decided to call here. He wasn't to know that those same cops were doing a thorough search of the area round Walker Flat.

He had a long journey ahead of him, some three thousand kilometres or so, but it didn't bother him. He'd made this same journey many times before as part of his business deal with his brother Greg.

Greg! He'd better tell him what had happened. He rummaged in his bag and pulled out a mobile phone he had managed to retrieve from his house. It was an anonymous pay as you go phone which only he and Greg used. He switched it on. The battery was dead. No matter, he would charge up the battery and ring him later. He had to tell him the whole story and warn him to lie low for a while. That wouldn't be a pleasant conversation.

He dozed and watched sport on TV until finally it was time. As soon as the light was fading he was away. He said his goodbyes to Terry, who seemed genuinely sorry to see him go.

"Look after yourself mate. I hope it works out for you."

"I'll be OK Terry. I'll see you again when it's all cleared up. Don't forget, if the cops come round you haven't seen me. Now I've gotta go."

He looked around cautiously to make sure no one was watching, carried his bag out to the car and placed it in the back. He unlocked the driver's door and climbed in, still conscious of how stiff and sore his left leg was. At least the car was an automatic so that was one less problem. He adjusted the seat and the mirrors and was at last satisfied.

He gave a last wave to Terry and roared off. After a minute he had taken the turning to the main road and was out of sight.

Terry walked back to his front door, still wondering what this was all about. As he turned to close the door behind him he noticed a police car coming along the street.

It stopped in front of his house.

Chapter 15

At first light on that same hot Saturday morning all available police personnel in the area had converged upon Forster Lookout, a few kilometres outside Mannum. The lookout, normally a quiet spot used only by tourists to view the majestic Murray River from the towering cliffs, had the previous day witnessed the dramatic confrontation between police and criminals which was almost unknown in the history of the area.

At daybreak Chambers re-commenced his search. He deployed his team on both sides of the river. On the Forster Lookout side searchers walked along the cliff tops and scanned the river below. Others went down the hill to the ferry and searched areas around and behind the ferry. This bank was very thinly populated, with only a handful of holiday cottages, and there were few places to hide given the sparse nature of the vegetation. The search turned up nothing.

On the other bank the situation was quite different. The small village of Walker Flat nestled by the water at the opposite ferry terminal. The village and all its surrounds were thoroughly searched and the small population questioned, but nothing was uncovered.

Along from the village, on the narrow peninsular, were beach houses extending a mile or so, many with lawns sweeping down to the river, where you could sit at the water's edge and view the magnificent towering cliffs on the other bank. The searchers diligently walked the entire area between the river and the main road to Mannum but again nothing was discovered.

Meanwhile a police boat had travelled up the river from Mannum and had scoured both sides of the river and all the surrounding inlets, and still there was no sign of Andersen or a body.

By mid afternoon Chambers had to admit that either Andersen had somehow escaped, against all the odds, or his body was somewhere at the bottom of the river. Whether he should bring in more boats to drag the river was a question he would have to consider, but there seemed to be little point in maintaining the search on foot.

He called off the search and ordered everyone back to Mannum Police Station for a debriefing, where the team again reviewed which areas had been searched. They were joined by the staff of the two unmarked police cars which had sat all night and all day observing Tony Andersen's house in Mannum and the shack he owned on the deserted Mannum to Purnong road. The crews of those vehicles again insisted that they had seen no sign of Andersen. The crew stationed by the shack had reported no movement by anyone at all and no visitors.

"What about Andersen's house?" asked Chambers. "Did you see anyone else around there?"

The reply came from Vincent DeLonghi, who was one of the team seconded from Adelaide to help Chambers in his surveillance. "It was a quiet night. We sat outside the house all night and saw only one vehicle, about one am."

"Did you check it out?" "Yeah. It was a guy who drove in from the main street and past us. He came back about ten minutes later so we pulled him over."

"What was he doing at that time?"

"He said he'd just been dropping a mate home who'd had too much to drink, so we had a look in his vehicle and let him go."

"Did you get his details?"

"Yeah, we took his licence details and the vehicle rego", he looked in his notebook, "a guy called Terry Mathews. He lives just a few streets away."

Chambers thought for a minute. "The name doesn't mean anything to me. Does anyone else know him?"

"I do boss." The voice belonged to Andy Cole who was a sergeant at Mannum Police. He had been with the force for most of his life and knew almost everyone in the Mannum area.

"He used to be a bit of a lad when he was younger, quick with his fists in the pub and partial to a bit of joyriding in nicked cars. He's been quiet for years though; he seems to have calmed down. One interesting thing though."

"What's that Andy?" asked Chambers.

"Well he used to be a big mate of Tony Andersen. In fact, as far as I know, they still get together for a beer at The Criterion."

Chambers was interested. The Criterion bar on the main street was a favourite haunt of Tony Andersen. Was it just a co-incidence or was Terry Mathews involved somehow?

"Thanks for that Andy. I might just go and have a word with young Terry; see what he's got to say for himself."

He looked around at the sea of exhausted faces and added.

"I think we'll call it a day there guys. Thanks all of you for the effort you put in, even if we didn't find him. I don't see any point in searching further. He's either dead or he's somehow left the area. Don't forget to book your hours in; I guess the overtime will come in useful."

The meeting broke up and the searchers left for their various homes. Chambers caught up with Andy Cole before he left.

"Andy, before you go, could you do me a favour?"

"What's that Brian?"

"I fancy having a chat with Terry Mathews. I've got his address here. How would you like to go over there with me and check him out?"

Although Cole had been looking forward to a cold beer at home he knew better than to knock back Chambers when he wanted a favour. Besides, he and Chambers went back a long way, and he was curious to see if Terry Mathews was up to no good.

"Yeah I'll come along. Let's check him out then you can buy me a beer."

"You're on Andy. Let's go."

In Chambers patrol car they headed down the hill, turned at the river along Randell Road and drove to the other side of Mannum where Terry lived, a journey of only a few minutes. By this time the light was fading.

Terry watched the police car pull up outside his house, grateful that Tony had just left. They obviously hadn't seen him. The two policemen walked up his driveway and rang the doorbell. Terry opened the door with as much cheery confidence as he could manage.

"G'day officers, what can I do for you?"

The bigger one said "good evening Sir. I'm DI Chambers of Mannum Police and this is Sergeant Cole. We would like a word with you. Can we come in?"

This is a bit formal, thought Terry but he smiled and said "Sure come on in. What's all this about? I haven't been speeding have I?"

"No Sir, it's not about you. We are interested in a friend of yours."

"Really! Who's that?"

"Tony Andersen."

"Tony, what do you want with him?"

"That's our business. When did you last see him?"

"Ah let me see" said Terry, scratching his chin. "It probably was last Wednesday. A few of us usually catch up for a beer at The Criterion on Wednesdays."

"And you haven't seen him since? Say yesterday or today?"

"No, not at all."

Chambers put on his most patient smile. "You see sir, one of our officers reported that he stopped you outside Tony's house in the early hours of this morning. What were you doing there?"

Terry thought hard. He had better stick with the story he had invented at the time. "Sure I was up in that part of town but I was just giving someone a lift home. I may have driven past Tony's house but I wasn't going there."

"Mmm, who was this person you gave a lift to?"

"I can't remember his name. Just some guy I met in the pub and had a few beers with. He had had a few too many so I took him home."

"What number was the house?"

"I don't know. He just told me when to stop. He got out and I turned around and came home."

"OK, so you've had no contact with Andersen since Wednesday?"

"No, none at all."

"Do you have a mobile phone?"

"Yes why?"

"Could I see it please?"

"Sure, here."

Chambers took the phone and navigated to call history. Only one call since yesterday, another mobile number that was logged at 1150 pm.

"What's this call here sir?"

Terry looked. It was the call from Tony with his name clearly displayed.

"Oh that. I'd forgotten."

"That's very convenient isn't it? You had a call from Tony just before midnight and you forgot."

"Well he sounded pissed. I had no idea what he was talking about. Why are you asking me all this?"

"Just a routine enquiry. We want to talk to Tony about a certain matter but we can't find him. And it seems you spoke to him only last night. And shortly afterwards you were seen driving past his house. What does that tell us?"

"I've already told you. I had this garbled call from Tony while I was in the pub but I couldn't understand him. Soon after I gave this bloke a lift home and went to bed. What's wrong with that?"

"And that's your story is it Terry? Do you mind if we have a look around the house?"

"Course not. Go ahead; I've got nothing to hide" said Terry, very glad that he had put away the blankets used by Tony but also concerned in case he had left anything behind.

The two policemen searched all through the house accompanied by Terry but saw nothing suspicious.

"All right Terry" said Chambers, "that's all for now, but don't leave the district; we may want to talk to you again."

"Well that's rich. You grill me but you won't tell me what it's all about."

"Don't push it Terry or we may continue this conversation down at the station. If you see Tony or hear from him again let us know."

The policemen let themselves out and went back to the car. "What do you think?" asked Chambers.

Andy Cole shook his head. "I don't believe a word of what he says. He's had some sort of contact with Andersen and it's just too much of a co-incidence that he was on his street soon afterwards. What should we do? Pull him in and question him some more?"

"No Andy, not yet. If he sticks to his story there's not much we can do about it. The real significance is that we now know that Andersen was still alive several hours after he fell off the cliff. No wonder we can't find a body. At least we've got his phone number. I'll organise a tap on it and make sure we are fed details of all calls on Tony and Terry's phones. Maybe we'll find out where Tony is and what he's up to. I'll sort that out first thing in the morning. But that's enough for one day. Let's go and have that beer.

*****

Terry watched them leave and sat on his sofa deep in thought. He knew the police could trace phone records and now they had his number and Tony's. What if Tony phoned him again? The police would be back. And how was he to phone Tony and warn him? The police would know if they checked the phone logs. As he pondered there was a knock on his front door. Who is it now he thought, and why didn't they use the doorbell?

He opened the door cautiously to see a grinning Tony.

"Hi, I'm back."

"Tony, what the hell are you doing back here? The cops have just left."

"Yeah I know. I saw them as I was leaving. I thought I'd wait around and find out what they were up to."

"They're looking for you. They quizzed me about last night. I gave them the same story but I don't think they believed me. And they've got your phone number from my phone, so if you use it again they'll be able to track you."

"Bugger. OK I'll ditch it and get myself a new one. I'll ring you when I've got one. Anything else I should know?"

"No that was about it."

"OK mate, this time I'm definitely going, but I'll turn this off", pointing to his phone.

"I don't want the buggers to know where I am do I? See ya mate."

"OK Tony, take care of yourself."

For the second time Tony got into his car and started off on his long trek.

***

While Tony Andersen was making his escape from Mannum John Foster also was a busy man.

Following a long exhausted sleep, he had much to do. He contacted Peter Carney in Surrey to tell him what had happened to Debbie. To his surprise Carney was very concerned and informed him that he would immediately fly to Adelaide, and to expect him in the next day or two, just as soon as he could get a flight.

Foster also had two long emails to send urgently. One was to his editor, enclosing a story for publication in The Sun. The other was to DI Patel in Southampton, England to inform him of the activities of the Andersen brothers and to attach the picture of Greg Andersen. Patel had been attempting to track down the Australian who seemed to be responsible for a series of robberies and murders of young emigrants to Australia. Now thanks to Foster he had a name and a photograph to help him. That should give Patel a better start to seek out Andersen.

Finally he drove out to Mannum to see Debbie at the hospital. She was sitting up in bed and smiling. The only sign of her ordeal was a thick bandage around her thigh. He told her about the contact he had made with her boss.

"You know what? He's flying straight out here. He said to expect him in a day or two. What a boss you've got. Not many would go to those lengths."

Debbie smiled. "Well, actually, he's a bit more than a boss."

Foster was downcast. "Oh. You don't mean? Now I understand why you haven't got a steady boyfriend."

"Are you jealous?"

"As it happens, yes."

"Well don't be. And don't jump to conclusions. He's actually my uncle as well as my boss. In fact, I think I'm his favourite niece."

"But isn't he Italian?"

"He sure is. Don't you remember? I said there was an Italian side to the family. My mother is Peter's sister."

Foster relaxed. "That's a relief. Where will he stay?"

I expect he'll get himself a hotel room. He knows that I've only got one bedroom and that you guys are in the other flat. Speaking of which. The doctors say I'll probably be allowed to go home tomorrow, but I'll need someone to give me a hand and look after me for a few days. Do you know anyone who might be suitable for the role?"

Foster smiled. "I'll have to think about that one."

Chapter 16

The afternoon was drawing to an end when Tony Andersen finally set off on his long journey to North Queensland.

He had done this trip several times before and knew that the journey was more than 2500 kilometres and would require about thirty hours driving time. It might be possible to reduce that but the combination of narrow outback roads, wandering animals and the ever-present speed cameras made fast driving an unattractive proposition.

Besides, he didn't mind spending time behind the wheel. To him it was a peaceful time. He normally left early in the morning and made the journey comfortably in three to four days, depending on how he felt after ten hours of driving.

This time it was a little different. He knew there were only three or four hours of daylight left and he was still a little stiff and tired from his ordeal at Forster Lookout. But he had to get away as far as possible from Mannum now that the police were searching for him, preferably across the state border where he would be less likely to be bothered.

He normally took the scenic route through the Riverland towns of Waikerie, Renmark and Mildura before heading along the Sturt Highway across the plains to Hay, where he would head north across New South Wales through Bourke and on to Queensland.

Today he was loath to drive through the Riverland as he expected that that was where the police would be most alert. It would be safer to head quickly back to Murray Bridge, only twenty minutes away, then onto the South Eastern Freeway where at least he could cover some ground quickly and hopefully not be so conspicuous on the busier roads. Where the freeway ended after Tailem Bend he would take the short cut through Pinnaroo and Ouyen, from where he could make for Balranald and rejoin the Sturt Highway through to Hay.

He did not have the hours of daylight or the energy to drive all the way to Balranald tonight but he estimated he could get past Ouyen with little or no night driving, a journey of some three to four hours.

He drove back up Mannum's main street cautiously on the lookout for anyone who might recognise him. Going up the hill he passed the Mannum police station and even though he was nervous he had to smile; the police station was quiet and peaceful with not a patrol car to be seen. This next short drive through Murray Bridge onto the freeway was the most dangerous part of the journey, especially if any of those patrol cars were stationed along it. Once he was on the freeway itself he would be safer.

Consequently he drove very cautiously to Murray Bridge, through the town and on to the short suburban road to the freeway, carefully observing all the road signs and speed limits. In less than half an hour he turned onto the freeway and headed off to Tailem Bend, relieved that no-one had taken any notice of him.

On the freeway he again kept to the speed limits. He spotted one police patrol car sitting at the side of the road with his speed camera and smiled as he cruised past at a legal speed. Soon he reached the end of the freeway at which point the road divides. One section becomes the very busy Dukes Highway to Melbourne while the less busy Mallee Highway heads through Pinnaroo and Ouyen to northern Victoria.

Tony turned onto the Mallee Highway for the two hour drive to Pinnaroo and then over the border into the state of Victoria, where he would be away from the attention of the South Australian Police Force. The sight of the police car made him remember that he needed to phone his brother Greg in England, to tell him what had happened. He decided to chance a quick stop and pulled off the road onto the gravelly shoulder. He rummaged in his bag and found the special mobile phone that only he and Greg used. Of course the battery was flat. He rummaged again in the bag and realised he didn't have a car charger with him. He only had a mains charger so the call would have to wait until he could use that, and that wouldn't be until tomorrow in a motel.

He was annoyed with himself for forgetting the car charger but on the other hand he was relieved. It wouldn't be a pleasant conversation with Greg. It was best left until he felt a little better.

He continued with his journey and made the border with no incidents and relaxed a little for the final two hour stretch into Ouyen, where he arrived at dusk.

Although he had been driving for only four hours he was very tired; the events of the last two days were taking their toll and he was ready for some sleep. He decided not to check into a motel in case he was noticed but instead to find a quiet clearing and sleep in the car. It wouldn't be the most comfortable night but it was better than being spotted. Although he was now technically away from the jurisdiction of the South Australian Police they may have already contacted their Victorian colleagues.

He found a suitable clearing and turned into it. As he switched off the car he was aware of how peaceful and quiet it was, the silence broken only by the occasional passing truck. Gratefully he prepared himself for sleep.

*****

Sunday dawned warm and sunny. Tony blinked and for a moment wondered where he was. He hadn't had his best ever night's sleep, tossing and turning in the back seat of the car. He promised himself that tonight, being far away from home, he would check in to a low cost motel and get a proper night's sleep. His destination was the New South Wales town of Bourke, one of the most remote towns in the State, which had given rise to the expression "back O'Bourke" meaning outback. Despite its importance as a regional hub the town had less than three thousand inhabitants. He should be safe there.

As it was some nine to ten hours drive he made an early start. He splashed some water on his face and was away. It wasn't long before he needed some breakfast and he stopped at the first roadhouse he spotted. Half an hour later, replete from his burger and chips and a mug of tea, he was away again. He quickly came to Balranald where he joined the Sturt Highway which took him across the desolate Hay Plains from Balranald to Hay, a distance of over 130 kilometres with few signs of habitation.

He had made good time to Hay. Although it was late morning he was still pleasantly full from his big breakfast and elected to press on to Hillston, another two hours drive away. He left Hay by the Mid Western Highway across to the tiny town of Goolgowi where he turned onto the Kidman Highway which would wend its lonely way north all the way to Bourke, some six hours drive away.

This section of the road was tolerably green, located as it was in the Murrumbidgee River Irrigation Area, but he knew from previous trips that after Hillston it was very desolate with few signs of life. Again he made good progress on the relatively empty road. In a little under two hours he was approaching Hillston. Although it was a small town of little more than a thousand people it was important to the traveller. The next stretch of road heading to Cobar was remote and largely uninhabited. There was nowhere to refuel for some two hundred and fifty kilometres. Now he was hungry and resolved to fuel himself and the car at the first opportunity.

He stopped at the first roadhouse he came to, looking forward to lunch, but as he wearily heaved himself out of the car a voice behind him said "g'day". He turned round to see a policeman looking at him. He was deep in thought and hadn't noticed the patrol car parked up a little way.

There wasn't much he could do but try to talk his way through this. He smiled and said "g'day, how are ya?"

The policeman looked friendly enough but what did he want? He pointed to Tony's car.

"Your car's a bit old. Where are you heading?"

"I'm going up to Bourke" Tony replied quietly.

"Is your car OK for that?"

"Sure, I've done it before. No worries."

"OK, I guess you know then that there's no fuel stop before Cobar so you'd better fill up while you're here."

"Yeah I will, as soon as I've had some lunch."

The policeman smiled. "The tucker here is pretty good. Mind how you go. We wouldn't want to have to come out and rescue you. Have a good day."

"You too" muttered Tony, very relieved to see him strolling back to his patrol car.

Despite the friendliness of the country policeman Tony was still concerned. What if he realised later who he'd been talking to? Then they'd be looking for him. He ate a hurried lunch, another burger and chips, topped up the car and quickly headed off.

As he knew, the road between Hillston and Cobar was long, flat and straight. He saw little but the occasional kangaroo or emu and was amused at the odd tumbleweeds. The biggest problem on that road was boredom and he was very relieved when some three hours later he reached Cobar.

At Cobar he refuelled the car and bought a cold drink. By this time he had been on the road nearly nine hours and was feeling very tired. Still, only two hours to go and he would be in Bourke, but a rest was called for. He detoured slightly off the Highway into Louth Road, found a spot with a shady tree and closed his eyes.

He slept for only half an hour but it was enough to give him the energy needed for the remainder of his drive. He headed out of Cobar for the last stretch to Bourke.

Two uneventful hours later he was pleased to see Bourke ahead and it was still only early evening. No more driving, at least for today, and the promise of a good night's sleep. He had a soft spot for Bourke. Like his native Mannum it was a small town located by a river, in this case the Darling, one of Australia's longest rivers and part of the enormous Murray-Darling river system. The water made a stark contrast to the arid country he had just passed through.

He knew a good, inexpensive motel where he had stayed before, the Darling River Motel on the corner of the Mitchell Highway and Warraweena Street, and made his way there.

He checked in for one night to a basic but pleasant room.

He wanted to eat and knew a Chinese restaurant just down the road. It was a few minutes' walk but as he had been sitting all day he elected to stroll down. Before he went he plugged in his mobile phone charger. When he came back he would have to phone Greg with the bad news, not a call he was looking forward to.

An hour later, pleasantly full from the Chinese food and a few beers, he made his way back to the motel.

His head barely touched the pillow before he was sound asleep. He didn't even have time to reflect that there were still two full days of driving ahead of him.

*****

On the same day that Tony Andersen was making his tedious journey from Ouyen to Bourke, back in Mannum it was party time. A Sunday BBQ was held in the garden of Jim Preston's house at Murray Bridge. Preston was the hero of the moment. His identification of Tony Andersen at Adelaide airport had been the key piece of information in the investigation. DI Chambers, who was also present, owed him a great deal.

Preston, who hadn't seen Alan Warner since meeting him on the flight from Sydney to Adelaide, wanted to catch up with him again before he returned to the UK.

Alan and Carol were now inseparable and had decided, after considering many possible options, to return to the UK and attempt to rebuild their lives there.

Debbie and Foster were also there, Debbie still with a thick bandage on her leg and hobbling with the help of a crutch loaned by the hospital, Foster acting as chauffer and live-in housekeeper. Foster had decided to stay in Australia as long as his visa would allow, and to pursue his investigations.

Peter Carney, tired, jet lagged and straight off the plane from England was delighted to find his favourite niece in such blooming health despite her ordeal at Forster Lookout.

As Preston busied himself with the sausages John Foster noticed that Alan Warner was standing on his own, apparently deep in thought. He wandered across and tapped Alan on the shoulder.

"Penny for them Alan."

Warner blinked. Hi John, I was just thinking about all that's happened."

"Yeah I guess it'll be a while before you come to terms with it all."

"I suppose so. I'd love to know just what it was all about. What was Tony going to do? I don't get it."

"No it's still a bit of a mystery, but I don't think you would have survived long with him."

"Maybe, but I'd still like to find out. You know we had sort of become friends. Funny isn't it?

Foster paused for a moment.

"Alan, there's a name for this. It's called the Stockholm syndrome and it's used to describe a situation where someone who is kidnapped starts to relate positively to his captor."

"Is that so? I haven't heard of that one before. But why did they kidnap me?"

"How do you mean?"

"I'd already given them the money and they knew I had no more so it couldn't have been about blackmail. If they had wanted me out of the way why not just kill me. It doesn't make sense does it?"

Foster scratched him head.

"No, I can't totally work it out either. But the main thing is that you're safe now. Carol tells me you've decided to go back to England."

Warner frowned. "Well that's what Carol wants to do."

"And you don't?"

"You see I kind of like Australia, at least the bits I've seen. But it's more than that. I want to find Tony and work out what was going on. Maybe even rescue him before he gets in too deep."

"He's in it pretty deep already" remarked Foster. "Robbery, kidnap and murder. It doesn't come much deeper."

But Warner wasn't convinced.

"Well, robbery yes; kidnapping – did he really kidnap me or was he hiding me as he claimed? And it hasn't been proved yet that he has murdered anyone."

Foster persisted.

"But there's a lot of circumstantial evidence against him He's a violent dangerous thug."

"He may be John, but there's also a lonely frightened little boy in that hulk of a body. When I was with him it was like being with a younger brother who's a bit simple."

Foster grinned. "Rather you than me. What are you going to do?"

"I'd like to hang around for a while if they'll let me stay on. They must find Tony eventually and then perhaps I can talk to him and make some sense of all this."

"What does Carol think?"

"She thinks I'm crazy and wants to go home as soon as possible. Before we go we should catch up with you and Debbie in Adelaide."

"I'd like that. Maybe when she's thrown away the crutch. Anyhow I don't know how much longer my paper will let me stay here following this story before they order me back to England."

"How do you and Debbie feel about that? You're quite an item now."

"We are trying not to think about it. You know, one day at a time. I'd like to stay here with her but whether I could get a job, or even permanent residency, who knows?"

"You'll have to marry her. Then they'll let you stay" said a soft voice behind him.

He turned and saw Carol standing there looking very happy.

"You're trying to marry me off are you Carol?"

"It might do you some good she replied. "It seems to me that you're half way there already. Anyway, why are you monopolising my Alan? I want him back."

Foster laughed. "He's all yours. Think about *your* wedding instead of trying to marry me off."

"We'll start planning it as soon as we get back to England."

"When will that be?"

"As soon as I can persuade this man here that it's time to go. He has some crazy notion he wants to hang around for a while."

Alan gave her an odd look. "It's not a crazy notion. I just want to find out what was really happening and see the loose ends tied up".

"Yes OK, I know that you're safe and well and that's all I care about."

"Sausages are ready" yelled a voice from the other side of the garden.

Warner looked around, relieved that a conversation he didn't want to pursue had been neatly interrupted.

"Let's join the others."

*****

On Monday morning the town of Bourke was already hot and sunny. Tony Andersen wanted an early start. He had enjoyed a good night's uninterrupted sleep and felt much better. The eight or so hour's drive ahead of him to Blackall would be a breeze.

He gathered together his few belongings to stuff into his bag when he noticed his mobile phone on the floor, plugged into its charger and now fully charged. Damn, he had forgotten to call his brother Greg last night. He had to call him as soon as possible; what time was it there now?

He scratched his head for a while. He knew from his regular calls to Greg that England was nine hours behind at this time of year. As it was only six in the morning in Bourke it would be around nine in the evening in England. Perfect!

He took a deep breath and carefully pressed the button.

Greg Andersen had been sitting all day worrying. He lived in a little flat in a not very attractive part of Slough. It wasn't much to look at but it was cheap and gave him good motorway access to most parts of the country.

Today had not been a good day. He sat at his breakfast table and opened up his copy of the Sun. The front page put him completely off his meal. There, under a headline AUSTRALIAN MURDERERS FOILED were pictures of himself and Tony.

The accompanying story made little sense to him except that Alan Warner was alive and Tony was dead or missing. He had spent the whole day reading and re-reading the article and trying to make sense of it. He and his brother were now exposed and who knows what had happened to Tony. He tried to phone him on their private mobile phone but there was no answer.

He spent the whole Sunday brooding, not knowing what to do. He daren't go outside. Anyone who read the morning Sun could recognise him.

It was late in the evening when the phone rang. It was the special phone only he and Tony used. Better be careful.
"Hello" he said cautiously.
"Greg, is that you?" came a familiar voice.
"Tony! I thought you were dead. Where the hell are you?"
"I've been hiding at my mate's place. You remember Terry?"
"Sure I remember Terry. What are you doing there?"
"Well I can't go back to my place can I? I'm a wanted man around these parts. Terry has sorted out a vehicle for me and I'm on my way to North Queensland. I've got mates up there. "
"What will you do in North Queensland?"
"Greg, we could wait a while till the heat dies down, and then start the business up again, couldn't we?"
"Never mind all that. What the bloody hell happened with Warner?"
Tony gulped. Here goes. "Well there's been a bit of a problem."
"What sort of problem?" enquired Greg menacingly.
"He's – er – he's escaped."
"Escaped! How could you let him escape?"
"But Greg, I didn't have much choice. We were followed."
"Who followed you?"
"That bloody pommie reporter. And he had the police with him. They ambushed us when we stopped at the lookout."
"What bloody lookout?"
"Forster Lookout at Walker Flat" Tony mumbled.
"What the hell were you doing there?"
"Well, Alan and me were on our way to Sydney, just like you said, and he wanted to see the view before we left. We were only stopped for a few minutes and the cops arrived."

"What happened?"
"They tried to arrest me but I had a gun."
"God you didn't bloody kill someone did yer?"
"Course I didn't, but I bloody nearly killed myself. I fell off the cliff into the river."
Upset as he was Greg nevertheless was beginning to see the funny side.
"Tony, you're not making this up are you? It sounds more like Benny Hill than Lee Child."
"What child, and who's Benny Hill?"
"Oh don't worry. What happened next?"
"I managed to get to the other bank and got Terry to come and fetch me. I stayed the night at Terry's. He got another car for me and now I'm on the run. The police are looking for me."
"Tony, what a bloody shambles. Where are you now?"
"I'm heading up to North Queensland to hide out with a mate for a while."
"Shit, I'd better keep my head down for a spell. Phone me again when you're safely up there. And don't do anything else that's stupid."
"No Greg, look I'd better go."
Tony rang off very relieved. It had gone better than he expected. If Greg had thought he was dead maybe he was relieved despite the cock up. Well at least he had put him in the picture. Now he could get on with his journey.

From Bourke he turned onto the Mitchell Highway which would take him four hundred kilometres to the small settlement of Augathella where he would pick up the Matilda Highway for the final stretch to Blackall, another two hundred kilometres.
He had ordered an early breakfast which was served to his room. He had made it a large one as there would be

very few services until he reached Charleville some four hundred and fifty kilometres away.

After breakfast he headed off, careful to keep to the speed limit to avoid drawing attention to himself, although there would be very few police cars on this lonely road.

He had a quiet and rather boring drive along the highway. Soon he had crossed over the border into Queensland through the small township of Cunnamulla and onto Charleville, which he reached in the early afternoon.

He bought some lunch at a roadhouse there and once again carried on along the Mitchell Highway until it ended at Augathella. There he turned onto the Matilda Highway and pointed north for the final two hours to Blackall.

He made good time and reached Blackall in late afternoon. He was far from any major city and as safe as he could be. Besides, only one more day's driving and he would reach his mate's property near Charters Towers.

Neville would put him up for a few weeks until the heat died down. He felt bold enough to check into a motel again. After a steak and several beers for dinner he had an early night and looked forward to the end of his journey the following day.

The forecast for the next day was for extreme heat. Today's route was mostly through very arid country with few towns of any consequence. The few very small towns were typically located on the banks of a small creek or river, of which there were many in the area. Paradoxically the region can be hot and arid but it can also be wet and flooded. Tony was glad that at the moment it was dry.

He ate a hurried breakfast and was on the road early before the heat became extreme.

He continued his journey along the Matilda Highway and in just over an hour passed through the town of Barcaldine. Although it boasted a population of less than fourteen hundred souls it was the biggest town he would pass through until he reached Charters Towers. At Barcaldine he crossed the Capricorn Highway, so called because it follows the Tropic of Capricorn in an east west direction, and continued north through the empty country ahead of him.

He made sure he had food and more importantly water in his car as it would be some time before he touched on any significant settlement, Hughenden, over three hundred and fifty kilometres and four hours drive through some very inhospitable territory.

He pressed on taking little rest and passed through the tiny settlements of Aramac and Muttaburra. In the heat of the day he saw little sign of people or even animals but simply miles and miles of hot arid countryside. It seemed that the whole world was sheltering from the heat. Finally, in mid afternoon, he was relieved to reach Hughenden.

Hughenden sits on the banks of the Flinders River, sometimes dry, sometimes flooded. It is also a major crossroad where Tony had to turn onto the Flinders Highway for the final two hundred and fifty kilometre drive to Charters towers. With only two and a half hours to go he was on the home run. Even so the road was busier than those he had traversed over the last two days. He watched his speed and kept an eye open for police cars.

As he approached the outskirts of Charters Towers he was more relaxed, even elevated. Now he could hide out of sight for a while at Neville's property until the heat died down. He was so pleased he relaxed his guard and saw at the last minute a police patrol at the side of the road, and a policeman standing alongside waving at him to pull over.

He couldn't believe it; so near to his destination. Nevertheless he had little choice but to pull over and see what the cops wanted him for.

He stopped and wound the window down. "G'day" he said, trying to sound more confident than he felt. "What's the problem?"

The police officer seemed neither friendly nor hostile. He looked up and down the car and finally spoke.

"Have you come far, driver?"

"Just from Hughenden today" replied Tony trying to think quickly.

"And where are you heading?"

He thought quickly again. He wouldn't tell him that his destination was right here.

"I'm off to Townsville."

"OK driver, this is a random breath test stop. Have you had any alcohol to drink recently?"

Tony could have kissed him. Just a routine RBT patrol. The beer he had had at Hughenden would be well and truly through his system by now in this heat. "No" he said. "None."

"Just blow into this mouthpiece" the officer recited as he handed him the little machine.

Tony gave a long puff and handed the machine back. The officer took the reading from the machine and looked back at Tony, seemingly a little more friendly.

"That's OK driver. You're all clear. On your way. Have a good day and take care."

"Thanks. See ya" said Tony as he drove quietly away. Further down the road he turned off and headed for his destination.

Neville had a small property of a few acres of scrubland just outside the town. It wasn't very pretty but it offered Tony the seclusion he needed. He swung into the long dirt driveway and pulled up outside the house, to see a figure coming cautiously out of the front door.

He's wondering who it is, thought Tony. He got out of the car and waved.

"G'day Neville, it's me."

"Tony you mongrel, why didn't you tell me you were coming. It's been a while. What are you up to?"

"Oh just the usual. The cops are taking a bit of an interest in me back home so I thought I'd go walkabout for a while."

Neville laughed. "So nothing's changed then. Still riding on the edge eh. Come on in and we'll have a beer."

Over a much needed cold beer, and then another, Tony told Neville as much as he thought he needed to know. He asked if he could stay for a few weeks. "I'll pay my way of course."

"That's fine Tony. Stay as long as you like. It's good to have a bit of company occasionally."

After a few more beers Tony went to bed more relaxed than he had been for some time.

Now he could chill out for a while, maybe even do some fishing.

Chapter 17

John Foster was frustrated. In the three weeks since the events at Forster Lookout life had become very quiet. He had imagined himself playing an active role in hunting down the Andersen brothers, Greg in England and Tony in Australia. He was to be disappointed. In England DI Patel, of Sussex Police, had received the pictures of Greg

Andersen from Foster but had so far been unable to locate him.

Meanwhile, in Australia, all efforts to establish whether Tony Andersen was dead or alive had come to nothing. If he was alive he had simply disappeared. If he was dead where was the body? He had totally vanished.

Detective Inspector Brian Chambers, who had been so close to apprehending Tony Andersen, had to admit he had absolutely nothing to go on. There had been no reported sightings and no body. Reluctantly Chambers had shelved the case for a while until new evidence turned up.

All of this left Foster in a precarious state. He was in Australia to report on the hunt for the people who were robbing and murdering young British men. It was now generally accepted that the Andersen brothers were responsible for many, if not most, of these crimes. Now that the Andersens had vanished and no new crimes were coming to light Foster was a man without a purpose. He had nothing to report to his editor at the Sun Newspaper in London. Every day he expected a call to order him back to Britain for some new assignment.

Normally that wouldn't have bothered him too much, but right now he didn't want to leave South Australia. He had been living with Debbie Simmons, the only casualty from the pursuit of Tony Andersen. She had been hit in the thigh by a stray bullet fired by Andersen. She was not seriously hurt but required some patching up and had been limping around on a crutch loaned by the hospital.

Foster had cheerfully moved in to look after her but already she needed little looking after. Now, with bandages and the crutch gone, there was little to show for her ordeal except some occasional pain and stiffness in the leg. She was already back at work in her job of assisting newly arrived mining engineers to settle into their new jobs in the Australian mining sector.

They still had a great time together, both in and out of bed, but on the occasions when she had accompanied her clients to their remote locations he felt redundant and without purpose.

Today was one of those days. Debbie was away with a client and would not be back until late the following day. He had already telephoned DI Chambers but as expected there were no new developments. He spent the day on mundane routine chores, cleaning the flat, doing some shopping and spending a bit of time working out at the local gym.

The late summer weather was still warm and when evening finally came he sat out on the veranda with a Cooper's beer in his hand wondering how much longer he could sustain this pleasant but non productive lifestyle.

His thoughts were interrupted by his mobile phone playing it's ringtone of a quirky little jazz number. He brightened up; that would be Debbie. As he picked up the phone and looked at the screen he was downcast again; it was his editor, Mervin O'Grady. Here it comes, he thought; the end of the party.

"Hi Mervin, how are you?"

"Hello John, I'm not bad. Overworked and underpaid as always. What about you? Tired of the idle life in sunny Australia yet?"

Here we go, he thought. "I admit it's a bit quiet at the moment but we are on the lookout for new leads in the story."

"Yeah. I'm not sure you're going to find out too much more. But never mind: I've got something to keep you out of mischief for a while."

"You're bringing me home are you?" said Foster trying to sound more cheerful than he felt.

"Getting homesick are you? No, your sentence isn't over yet. As you are already there you can make yourself useful. It'll save me having to find the money to send someone else out there."

Foster was intrigued and more than a little relieved. He accepted that he and Debbie would have to part eventually but please not just yet.

"So what's this about Mervin?"

"Have you heard of Francis Ventrice?"

"Yes, he's the new boss of UKIP isn't he?"

"That's right, head of UKIP, or to give it its full title The United Kingdom Independence Party. He's not that new actually. He's been in the job for a few years now."

"Now I remember. Two or three years ago wasn't it? He led a leadership battle against Nigel Farage and won. I must admit I don't know much else about him."

"Well John you are just about to get to know a lot more. Have you heard of Our Nation?"

Foster laughed. "No, what on earth is that? It sounds like the title for a hymn."

"Very funny. No it's actually a political party in Australia. It's fairly new but they already have a lot of support."

"So what have they got to do with anything?"

"It's like this. Now that UKIP are enjoying such enormous success in the UK, Ventrice has become something of a cult figure. Our Nation wants that kind of success. Their policies are very similar to UKIP's and they have invited Ventrice to do a lecture tour in Australia and to exchange ideas. He arrives in two weeks time."

"And you want me to report on it?"

"A lot more than that. You will be embedded with the tour in its entirety. You'll be the official press rep for The

Australian and The Sun. We want all the info you can dig out on the policies and the politics and the man himself. We want to know what makes him tick; his strengths and weaknesses."

"You don't want much do you Mervin?"

"If it's any comfort I think you are just the man for the job. Play this one right and you could make a big name for yourself. It won't do you any harm at all coming close behind your kidnapping story."

Foster was flattered but mystified. "Why is it such a big story?"

"There are a lot of influential people here who are seriously concerned about the rise of UKIP. Now that the Tories are losing seats to them they are running scared. Members in the lower house are afraid for their seats and even the mighty in The House of Lords are concerned that the Tory Party could be wiped out. It doesn't get much more high profile than that."

"Wow, it's a big one all right. Whereabouts is he going?"

"Everywhere! The tour starts in Brisbane, then on to Sydney and Adelaide, down to Melbourne and across to Perth. And there are one or two little detours on the way. I'll send you some links for reading material and then you can follow up your own. I'll also send you contact details for the people in Oz who will organise your transport, accommodation, press passes and all that stuff. Get stuck into this John. It could make you a star."

"Sounds like I'm going to be a very busy boy."

"It sure does. Don't let me down on this one; I recommended you for the role. Do your research and we'll talk again in a few days time."

"Right Mervin, thanks for the chance. I won't let you down."

Foster put the phone down feeling energised again. And he could stay in Australia for a while yet, another month or two by the sound of it. Debbie will be thrilled, he thought. It's amazing; as one door closes another opens.

Chapter 18

Geoffrey Blaines had a problem. It was on his mind for much of his time and it frequently kept him awake at night.

He pondered on the injustice he suffered. After all, his plan, which had been several years in the making, was perfect. Francis Ventrice would leave for Australia imagining he would become an international political superstar. He would not have thought for a moment that he would be returning to England in a box, courtesy of a lone assassin.

The only problem was that he still hadn't found a suitable lone assassin. Ventrice' tour of Australia was due to start in just under two month's time. Three weeks later it would be over and he would have missed his chance.

Sir Marcus Tomelly had reluctantly agreed to the scheme and had discussed it with his colleagues in MI5 and ASIO. Both agencies had agreed that they would be happy to see the end of Ventrice but they declined to be party to the actual deed, declaring it was not a job for a respectable security service.

As Tomelly had forecast they agreed to provide a degree of logistical assistance and intelligence but the actual execution of the plan was solely the responsibility of Blaines and his co-conspirators.

Part of the intelligence provided had been a list of names in Australia and Europe of men who might be suitable for such a role. Blaines had investigated all of them but had not found anyone he thought could handle the job.

He had arranged a constant feed of stories in the media about violent crimes but those also had yielded little success. He became despondent. He had imagined that finding an assassin would be the easy part. There must be lots of men able and prepared to kill if the price was right. He came to realise that the combination of talents he required was quite rare. He needed someone who could be trained to fit in Ventrice' entourage without exciting any comment, calm enough to carry out the deed and smart enough to escape. Moreover he needed someone who could be trusted to retire afterwards and never speak of it again.

The problem vexed him and with only a few weeks to go he was starting to imagine that his beautiful plan would come to nothing. His thoughts were interrupted by a knock on the door as his personal secretary, Michael Robinson, entered the room carrying a file.

Blaines looked up. He had imagined several times that Robinson had many of the skills he was looking for. He had served in the army for years, was calm under pressure, an expert marksman and very handy with explosives. The problem was that he was happily married with two growing children in good schools. He would not have wanted to retire and disappear from London. Besides it might look suspicious if he did.

"What can I do for you Michael?" he enquired.

Robinson looked excited. "Geoffrey I've had an idea. I may have found your man, or more correctly men."

"What do you mean, men? I thought we were looking for a lone assassin?"

"Well we haven't found one have we? But these two have a lot going for them. For a start they are Australian and know the territory very well. Not only that they have been running a people smuggling racket which involves extracting cash from gullible young guys, shipping them to Australia and then robbing them – sometimes murdering them."

"How do you know all this?"

"They have just been blown. Their last operation went sour and was foiled by the Australian Police, oddly enough with some help from a British journalist."

"What good is that to us Michael? Haven't they been arrested?"

"That's the beauty of it. These guys are brothers. Greg Andersen, the older brother, has been masterminding the operation from here in England and his brother Tony has been dealing with the victims in Australia. He knows how to get rid of people there. The list of people he has been accused of eliminating is quite long and the methods varied. They have managed to escape the police and they are both on the run, one here in England and one in Australia."

Blaines was struggling to take it all in.

"So, tell me if I'm right. All we have to do is find these two, wherever they are, train them up and get them into Ventrice' tour party. Doesn't that sound like a tall order Michael?"

"It's not easy but do you have a better idea? They are on the run and can't operate their business again. If they are caught they'll get life. They should be amenable to a suitable retirement package for one last job."

"But how would we get them into Ventrice' group?"

"Again it's perfect. Before they operated this scam they had years in the personal security business. We simply get our mole to organise extra security for Ventrice on his tour and bingo, our men are in. Have a read of this file. It'll show you what they are about."

"OK I will. But wouldn't they be recognised?"

I thought about that. This is just the kind of assistance we could request from MI5 and ASIO. They need to be disguised and given new identities. Surely they could organise that much?"

"You'd think so wouldn't you? Well done Michael. I'll have a read of this file and see if I think it's feasible."

*****

Blaines read the file carefully several times and came to realise that what Michael Robinson said made sense. If they could find only one of the brothers it ought to be possible to sell him on the plan and contact the other. After all, surely it was only a matter of time until one of them was picked up.

He explained his problem to Sir Marcus Tomelly, who on this occasion was able to help. In Britain MI5 had instructed all police forces to inform them of any sightings of Greg Andersen. The same message regarding Tony Andersen had gone out from ASIO to the various Australian police forces.

Now it was up to the police forces of these two countries to find his man. Blaines would be biting his nails for a while longer as he watched his deadline approach.

Chapter 19

In Southampton the weather was grey, cold and windy, with a promise of more rain on the way. DI Joe Patel stood staring out of his window, deep in thought, as the public hurried by with their collars up.

Following his conversation with John Foster three weeks earlier he had devoted more time to his string of robberies of young men in Australia. It had taken some of Foster's research in Australia for Patel to realise that his series of robberies was more serious than it had appeared. He had thought that the victims, although living in his patch, had been perhaps a little gullible and careless and had paid the penalty by being robbed when they arrived in Australia. He was unwilling to commit major resources to what looked like unfortunate but petty crime.

However, Foster had alerted him to an issue he was previously unaware of; that some of these young men were being murdered, not just robbed, and it appeared the same criminals were responsible.

Now he had received from Foster some much stronger evidence, a name and a photograph. The ring leader was a tall Australian named Greg Andersen, although he never used that name with his gullible victims. He would assume a new identity, get a new pay as you go mobile phone and set up a website.

When he had processed a few victims the website and phone number would disappear, to be replaced by new ones a few weeks later. When Patel did the calculations of just the few victims he knew about he realised it was a very profitable business. Add in the victims from other parts of the country away from his jurisdiction and it was indeed a significant money spinner.

Foster admitted that until they could pick up the Andersens none of this could be proven, but the accumulated circumstantial evidence was compelling. The recent death of Charlie Winter, run down by a large vehicle on a lonely country road and the kidnapping of Alan Warner had both happened in the locality where Tony Andersen lived and his disappearance when Warner had been freed added to the certainty, as did Warner's ability to identify Greg as the man he had spoken to in England and Tony as his kidnapper.

Patel had revisited the victims he had previously interviewed and they confirmed that the man in the photograph, Greg Andersen, was the man they had spoken to, but with a different name and mobile phone number.

He noted the different phone numbers and requested copies of the call logs from the telephone companies. The pattern was, as expected, that the phone would be used for only a few weeks and then discontinued.

His original idea had been to monitor the internet for new sites promising similar deals to those of the Andersens and send in undercover officers to check them out. But now there was a flaw in that scheme; since Foster had printed his exposes a few weeks before, the trail had gone cold. No new web sites had appeared and Andersen seemed to have vanished.

Ever resourceful Patel decided to try another approach. He scoured the various mobile phone logs for a pattern and eventually he found one. The logs revealed that the base station for most of the phones was located in Slough. He obtained from the phone companies maps of the areas covered by the towers and worked out that it was a mostly mixed business and industrial area with a few blocks of flats. Andersen must live in one of those flats.

Now that the case had been upgraded from multiple robberies to robberies and murders he felt more confident about deploying resources. In addition his superiors were showing a much closer interest in the case and his requests for more resources were quickly auctioned. Accordingly he had some of his staff cruise around that part of Slough to see if they could find any trace of Andersen. For a while there was nothing and Patel wondered if he were wasting his time and resources, but eventually his luck turned.

One of his detectives, patrolling an area he had visited several times before, noticed a tall well built man emerging from a corner shop carrying a small bag of groceries. Despite the unkempt beard the man now sported he knew it was Andersen. As Andersen appeared to be on foot the officer parked his car and hurried after him. Andersen turned the corner, walked a short distance up the adjoining street and stopped outside a small block of flats. He took out a key, opened the door and went in. The officer continued past the flat and noticed there appeared to be only four flats in the small block.

He walked up the street a little way before turning and walking back past the flats, making a mental note of the names of the occupants as he passed. Then he left to avoid arousing any suspicions.

Back at the police station he researched the block and contacted the rental agency, who confirmed they were the letting agents for all four. The agents stated that all four flats were currently rented out; two of them to students, one to an elderly lady who had been there for several years, and one to a middle aged man by the name of William Hebblestone.

Patel was delighted. Hebblestone must be Andersen. He sent various officers to walk past the block and observe. They quickly formed a pattern of who the inhabitants were and confirmed that Andersen must indeed be Hebblestone in number three.

Ready to mount a raid, Patel applied to the magistrate for a search warrant and informed his superior of what he was going to do. Presently his phone rang. It was his boss Keith Lawson, an old hand with many years in the force, for whom Patel had great respect. Patel picked up the phone, noted the caller ID and said "Hi Keith, how's it going?"

"Fine Joe, fine. I just wanted a quick chat with you about something. Could you pop up to my office?"

"Sure, I'll be right up" said Patel, curious as to what this was all about.

He knocked on the door and a big voice said "come in". Patel entered and Lawson waved him to sit down. He looked concerned.

"Joe thanks for coming up so quickly. I've got a rather delicate matter to discuss with you."

"What would that be?" asked Patel cautiously.

"Well, you know your interest in this Greg Andersen character? It appears that other people are interested in him too."

"What other people?"

"I received a routine memo last week to the effect that if there were any positive sighting of Andersen it was to be referred to Special Branch."

"That's odd. I wonder what they want with him. He's just a petty criminal, albeit a nasty one."

Lawson frowned and continued.

"I don't know either Joe. But the upshot is we've been told to back off and leave him alone."

"Why is that? What do they want with him?"
"I don't know any more than you, but orders are orders. I'm afraid you'll have to stop at this point."

*****

Patel was still standing at the window, looking out but seeing nothing, deep in thought. Now he knew why his superiors were showing a much closer interest in the case and why his requests for more resources were quickly auctioned. He had no choice but to go along with his orders and the planned raid to pick up Andersen had been cancelled.

He still had his officers take a surreptitious walk past the flat but they reported no sightings and no sign of movement at all.

Patel contacted the letting agents who informed him that Mr Hebblestone had given a month's notice of vacation and had left immediately. The flat was now empty and they had no forwarding address.

At this point Patel almost gave up. He had one last possibility. He emailed John Foster in Australia to see if he knew or suspected anything.

Foster didn't, and apparently Tony Andersen had also disappeared.

Patel sighed and elected to go back to his other cases. He wondered if he would ever know what had happened to Andersen and why.

Chapter 20

Greg Andersen nursed his sore head. He vaguely remembered walking from the corner shop back to his flat. As he fumbled in his pockets for his key his world went black. On waking up with a headache he found himself in what he assumed was some sort of cell, a smallish white washed room containing a single bed, a toilet and two chairs.

What the hell am I doing here, he thought, and why? It must be the cops. But surely they would have just arrested me? No need for this strong arm stuff. Who then? He suddenly had a chilling thought. Had one of his past victims somehow caught up with him? If so what did he want? It was a slightly nerve-racking prospect. He wasn't likely to be too friendly.

As he was pondering on the not very pleasant choices awaiting him he heard a metallic scratching sound as his cell door opened. He stood up quickly to react to what was coming. Two men in dark suits entered his cell. Andersen was confused. They didn't look threatening; they merely entered the room and stood looking at him.

The short one smiled and said "good afternoon Mr Andersen."

Play for time, he thought. "What did you call me?"

"Mr Andersen. That's correct isn't it?"

"Nah, you've got the wrong bloke. My name's Hebblestone."

"Yeah, and I'm Michael Bublé", growled the tall one.

"I don't know what you mean" said Andersen trying to appear confused.

The short one smiled again. "Come on Greg; we know perfectly well who you are so why don't you just admit it?"

"Let's just say I was this guy Greg Whatever, which I don't admit to; what do you want with him and who the bloody hell are you?"

"OK Greg, we'll play it your way for a while. Let's just say we have an interest in the business you've been running."

"What business? I don't run any bloody business."

"Oh you're very good. But you see, despite the hat and the heavy beard you've grown, we still recognised you. You're famous Greg. Your picture's been all over the front pages of the Sun recently."

"I keep telling you; I don't have any business; you've got the wrong man."

"If you don't have a business what do you do for a living. You're a long way from home. Funny, you have an Australian accent just like Greg Andersen."

"There's more than one bloody Aussie in this country you know. I don't do anything for a living. I'm just here for a holiday, tourist you might say."

"Oh right! An Aussie tourist is living in a little flat in a crappy part of Slough. It's a very upmarket type of holiday you've got here. Your landlord tells me you've been here over a year. Slough isn't normally regarded as a must-do tourist attraction."

"Well it's just a cheap base really."

The tall one barked out an angry reply, "Yeah, it's just the base from where you go and find your victims. Come on Greg, get real. If we were interested in your victims you'd be in front of a magistrate by now. Cut the crap; admit who you are and we'll tell you what we want from you."

The short one smiled again and said in a soothing voice, "Look Greg, we are being very patient but don't push it. My colleague here has a much shorter fuse than I have."

Andersen thought quickly. This is classic good cop, bad cop stuff. They know who I am so why aren't they just arresting me? What the hell do they want and who are they?

He looked up. "Who are you and what do you want?"

The short one looked pleased. "That's better Greg. Now we can get down to business."

"You still haven't told me who you are. Are you the cops?"

"In a manner of speaking. But not your conventional police force. You can call me Bill and my colleague here is Ben."

"Yeah. And I guess I'm the little bloody weed am I? Should I believe a word of this?"

"You'll come to believe. You see you don't have a lot of choice. We know all about your little business with its robberies and" he paused for effect, "its murders. No, don't interrupt. If we were concerned about such things you would have been handed over to justice by now. We have different interests shall we say."

"I don't get it. You talk in riddles."

"Let's just say Greg that we have a proposition for you that may be considerably to your advantage. But we shouldn't discuss business on an empty stomach. Lunch calls. We'll have something sent to you and resume this conversation after lunch. I'm told they do an excellent all day breakfast here. You must be hungry. It will give you time to reflect on the position you are in and make you more co-operative."

With that the two men turned, left the cell and bolted the door.

Andersen sat on his bed in a state of confusion. What the hell was going on and who were these guys? He figured he had no option but to listen to their proposition. Presently the cell door opened again and a burly guard placed a tray on the floor and without a word made a quick exit.

Andersen was certainly hungry and the meal, as predicted, was a full English breakfast; eggs, bacon, sausage, black pudding; even hash browns. It came with a mug of tea and Andersen wolfed down the lot gratefully. With a full stomach and with some of his fear and confusion gone he noticed his headache was slipping away.

Presently the cell door opened and the two "policemen" re-entered. The short one, Bill, opened the conversation.

"Good afternoon Mr Andersen, or is it still Mr Hebblestone?"

"Very funny. All right, you know who I am so why am I here? You're not going to arrest me so what the hell do you want from me?"

The unexpected response came from Ben. "We'd like you to perform a little service for us. It could just be the way out of the mess you're in."

"You guys are still talking in riddles. Are you going to get to the point – if there is one?"

"You are in one hell of a mess Greg. We could hand you over to the police on charges of robbery and murder."

Andersen relaxed and pointed his forefinger towards Ben as if to prod him.

"But I haven't murdered anyone. And you can't prove I have."

Ben shrugged. "Actually you may be right there. But your brother has, on your instructions. That's called being an accomplice to murder. It carries a very long sentence."

Andersen was still unperturbed. "Come on, I don't know what my brother has been doing. Besides, he's dead so you're not going to get much out of him. You'll have to do better than that."

"I like your spirit Greg but you know that's bullshit just as much as we do. Your brother would appear to be alive and well after all. True at the moment he's in hiding, but it's only a matter of time before he's found. Even smart men make mistakes, and you have to admit Tony isn't very smart."

"Why the interest in me and my brother? If you want to charge us go ahead. We'll deny everything."

"Look, even if we didn't charge you, your livelihood is fucked. Do you seriously believe you could resume your business? Every cop in the country knows about your little scam and is on the lookout for any re-appearance."

"What's it to you whether our business is OK or not? You're still not making any sense."

With an air of resignation Ben said "Tell him Bill".

Bill once more assumed his patient smile.

"Now Greg, just calm down and listen. We're here to help you. We have a business proposition for you; a very lucrative one."

"Go on."

"That's better. We want a small operation carried out, for which you and your brother seem eminently suitable."

"But if my brother is alive he's missing, somewhere in Australia. You said that yourselves."

"Don't worry about that. This operation will take place in Australia. Let's get comfortable. Sit down on the bed there and we'll grab these chairs."

When they were seated Bill continued.

"That's better. Now let's have a nice friendly chat. A colleague of ours is about to embark on a tour of Australia."

"So what? Lots of people do that."

"But this person is special. You will be a member of his entourage for his forthcoming lecture tour of Australia."

"Entourage!"

"Don't play the dummy Greg. You know what I mean. You and your brother will be a part of his security team during the tour. You see, we have heard rumours that our friend will meet with a very nasty accident at some point while he's down under."

Andersen thought he understood at last.

"What and you want us to stop it?"

Bill's smile widened even further.

"On the contrary dear chap. We want you to arrange it. You and your brother seem to be rather good at that sort of thing."

Andersen shivered. These smooth talking policemen were leading him to a very dark place.

"I still don't follow. What kind of accident are you talking about?"

"Well he might just drown in a boating accident, or slip over the edge at a lookout. You know the kind of thing of course. We don't mind too much how it happens so long as it is permanent."

"So you want me to kill somebody or you'll charge me with murder. Doesn't sound like much of a deal to me. And why do you want him gone?"

Bill's smile had vanished.

"You don't need to know the details. Let's just say he is a major threat to the established order of things and a correction is required."

"So you get me to do your dirty work for you then you let the Aussie cops pick me up? Count me out."

Ben lost his patience and stood up.

"Why don't you just shut up and listen. We're doing you a big favour here."

"It doesn't look like any bloody favour to me."

Bill's smile returned.

"Gentlemen, please, let's sit quietly while I outline the deal. First, Greg, this will be a carefully planned operation. You and your brother will be given new false identities and you will be admitted to our friend's inner circle by our contacts. You will have the details of every event and of his leisure breaks while on tour. Together with our representative you will plan exactly where, when and how the incident will take place. When the job is done you will be given a totally new identity with which to start a new life."

"And then what? Come back here to have you guys pick on me again. You're still not very convincing."

"I haven't finished yet. Your new identities, plus the generous settlement you will get, will enable you to retire to a place of your choice. You'll never have to work again. In fact we don't want you to work again. No one will know who you are or where you are."

Andersen was suddenly less belligerent.

"What's this 'generous settlement'?"

"I'm glad you asked that Greg. This is a most important operation and is very well funded. If you accept our offer you will immediately be given £250,000 and you will be kept in our safe house and trained, until your new identity is ready. Then we arrange your flight to Australia where you will be placed in another safe house with your brother until he also has been trained in his new identity."

"How do we find Tony?"

"I'm sure you will be able to contact him when our deal is done."

"Mm, but 250 grand won't go far if we have to spend the rest of our lives on the run."

"I agree. But that's not all. When the task is successfully completed two million pounds will be placed in your bank account. I think you will agree that's a very satisfactory retirement package."

Now Andersen was interested. This was money on a scale he and Tony could only dream about.

"You're kidding me; two million quid?"

"On the contrary my dear chap. We are deadly serious, if you'll excuse the pun."

Andersen thought quickly. Are these two a pair of nutters or is this a serious offer? I'll string them along and see.

"OK, suppose I say yes? What happens next and how do I know you're on the level?"

Bill resumed his smile.

"That's better Greg. As I said earlier you will stay here as our guest while we acquaint you with every aspect of our friend and prepare you a new identity. During this training period you will learn how serious we are and exactly what you have to do. As to our financial credentials; as soon as you agree to join us we will open a bank account in your name with an initial balance of £100,000. Thereafter it will rise over three weeks to £250,000 as you prove yourself capable of doing what we ask. You will have internet access to it at all times and you can set your own password, so that we have no control over it."

"Does that mean I have to spend the next few weeks in this cell?"

"No of course not. You will have a very pleasant room in this house and you will be free to move around it and the grounds – within reason. We wouldn't want you to take the money and run would we?"

Andersen was hooked. After all, if he could pull off just one more murder and retire how good would that be? Besides Tony would, as usual, carry out the actual deed and he himself would be the brains behind the operation.

"How do I know you will live up to the bargain with the two million when we're done?"

Bill put on his best trusty bank manager look.

"You'll have to trust us on that one I'm afraid. Just as we have to trust that you and your brother won't go to ground in Australia leaving us poorer by a quarter of a million pounds plus everything we will invest in you in the next few weeks. Some of the training you are about to receive will cover how you escape and how we set you up in a new profitable life. After all, it's in our best interests that you should retire quietly and not give us further trouble. What do you say?"

Andersen finally smiled.

"OK, it's the best offer I've had all day. I'm in. When do we start?"

"Excellent, welcome aboard. You won't regret it. I'll send a steward who will show you to your room. Your personal effects from the flat are already there and we will settle your accounts there and give notice."

"You seem pretty certain I was going to agree."

"My dear fellow, when you look at your options what possible other decision could you have taken? You're an intelligent business man after all. It's late in the day. Enjoy your room and its facilities and we will start your briefing in the morning. Good bye for now."

With that Bill and Ben left the cell and closed the door. Andersen reflected that he hadn't asked them their real names or who was behind this plot; not that they would probably tell him the truth.

He wondered whether he was now working for some branch of the British Government or the Australian Government or even some private individual with a big grudge.

Ah well he mused; it's going to be an interesting few weeks.

*****

Geoffrey Blaines and Michael Robinson left the safe house with a feeling of a job well done.

Blaines smiled and said "Well Ben, how do you think that went? Oh and congratulations on your bad cop role; most convincing."

Robinson too thought things had gone quite well.

"Well Bill, I think we've found our man; intelligent and ruthless enough to get the job done but stupid enough to accept the story we've given him. I was surprised though that he picked up on the flowerpot men."

"Yes perhaps these Australians are a little more cultured than we give them credit for. Anyway Michael, that's a job well done. I think we deserve a drink now."

The two men made their way to the nearby Red Lion, happy that their plan was moving along nicely. The Red Lion turned out to be a genuinely old country pub with low beams and timbered walls. They sat in a quiet corner with two pints of real ale. Robinson held up his glass and said "Congratulations Geoffrey; it all seems to be going along swimmingly."

Blaines however looked as if he were deep in thought. After a while he looked up.

"Oh yes Michael, very well indeed. However I think we need a backup plan, a plan B if you like."

"What's the problem? What did you have in mind?"

"It's like this. A lot is riding on these two Australians. If they chicken out at the last minute or stuff up in any way our plan is ruined. I think we need someone else over there to keep an eye on them and make sure things go as they are supposed to."

"Have you got someone in mind?" Robinson asked cautiously.

Blaines looked Robinson straight in the eye and put on one of his patient bank manager smiles.

"As a matter of fact I think I have. He's the person sitting opposite me right now."

"I'm not sure I follow you. What would I have to do and why me?"

"Come on Michael; remember your years in the army before you joined me. You're an expert marksman and you know quite a bit about explosives. Also you are one of the few people who know about this project. Why take the risk of involving more people?"

Robinson was beginning to feel uncomfortable. "You still haven't said exactly what it is you want me to do."

"Don't look so worried my boy. If all goes well it's just a liaison role. You basically follow the tour around and become the communications link between Greg Andersen and our mole. After all you know both of them already. Andersen will have some contact with the mole who is the tour organiser, but there's no need for him to know that he's one of our team. He will take his day to day instructions from the tour organisers but he will confer with you, and you alone, about how, where and when the deed will be done. Andersen already knows you as Ben and there's no need for him to know any more than that."

Robinson was still uncomfortable. "OK so I deal with the mole and find out the precise details I need about Ventrice' comings and goings and work out a plan with Andersen. That sounds fine but what if things don't go well, you know, if the Andersens don't deliver for whatever reason?"

"That's where Plan B comes in. Someone has to work out how to finish the job and do it. You're perfect for the role. You know the key players and your army training has given you all the skills you will need."

By now Robinson was looking a little pale and anxious.

"You want me to carry it out? That's a big leap from helping you to plan it. And surely if I did it I would be the prime suspect?"

"Who would suspect *you*? You never left these shores. You would travel to Australia on a false passport issued by our friends at MI5. No-one knows you there and Andersen only knows you as Ben. Anyway the chances are that the Andersens will do the job for you and there's nothing for you to do. Let's just say you are our insurance policy."

"That's all very well for you to say Geoffrey but you're not the one at the sharp end. I take all the risks and what's in it for me? The Andersens do all right if they succeed. What do I get; a pat on the head?"

"Now you're seeing things in a much more sensible light Michael. You know we would look after you. Let's discuss some possibilities."

An hour and two more pints of real ale later the pair left the Red Lion and headed for their respective homes. Robinson was still a little apprehensive regarding his enhanced new role in this drama, but excited by the personal and financial possibilities it offered him. Blaines was in a happy and mellow mood; both his Plan A and Plan B appeared to be in place.

Chapter 21

The transformation of Greg Andersen proceeded at a brisk pace. His appearance had to be changed, especially since his photograph had appeared in British and Australian newspapers.

His hair, naturally light brown to blonde, was darkened and restyled. He was told to keep the beard he had grown since the publication of the photos but it too was restyled and much neater. The colour of his eyes was changed by the simple expedient of tinted contact lenses.

A tailor was commissioned to measure him and produce several bespoke suits and shirts that would be worn by an up-market body guard and suitable shoes were provided.

A voice coach, who would only admit to being called Frank, appeared several times to tame Andersen's rough Australian accent.

At first Greg had complained. "But aren't I supposed to be an Australian bodyguard? Shouldn't I have a bloody Aussie accent?"

Bill was amused. "Greg, we aren't trying to make you less Australian. It's just that to fit in with our friend and his retinue we need to polish you up a bit. You don't have to sound like me, just a bit less like an Australian bushman."

Greg laughed. "OK for a minute I was afraid you would want me to drink warm pommie beer as well."

"We wouldn't attempt that yet. Drinking real ale is a taste we Englishmen acquire as we mature. We'll leave you to your ice cold chemical brew. You'll get plenty of that over there."

When the transformation was complete and Greg appeared in his new outfits Bill was very pleased.

"Your own mother wouldn't know you now" he declared.

While the physical appearance issues were being worked through, Andersen finally learned the details of the job he had to do. Bill had waited for a while, to get to know Andersen better before he revealed too much real detail.

When he became convinced that Andersen could be trusted with the role he sat him down with a drink. "Greg" he started, "Have you heard of Francis Ventrice?"

Andersen thought for a moment. "The name doesn't ring a bell."

"What if I were to tell you that he is the leader of UKIP, The United Kingdom Independence Party?"

"Oh Yeah, now I remember. I've seen him on TV. I don't take too much interest in politics. What's he done?"

"It's not so much what he has done, more what he is going to do. He is going to meet with an accident while touring Australia."

Andersen smiled. "So 'our friend' is this Ventrice character then. Why him? Who has he upset?"

"Let's just say that he is a huge risk that has to be eliminated. You don't need to know any more."

"It's pretty high stakes you are playing here Bill. We are going to need a foolproof escape plan. If I'd known it was this high profile I might have wanted a bigger reward."

Bill's smile had been replaced by a dark look. "You have already been promised a very substantial sum and there are some significant resources who will help you to escape. We have a deal, as you say in your country. Should you mention any of this to anyone else or attempt to change this deal, you will live to regret it. But not for long. Do I make myself clear?"

Andersen gulped. "Only joking Bill. You know I'm your man. Tell me more."

Andersen learned the details of Ventrice' tour. It was a hectic schedule with little time taken out for personal recreation.

With Bill he had discussed how and where the demise should take place. Bill had casually suggested the Sydney Harbour Bridge Climb might be an opportunity, one of the few outings Ventrice had requested for himself, but Andersen wasn't convinced.

"For one thing it's too public and for another it would be too difficult to arrange. All the climbers in a group are attached together with the group leader. It would be impossible to have one member slip and fall off."

They combed the rest of the itinerary but no obvious ideas presented themselves. Ventrice wasn't particularly interested in water sports or boating so there were scant opportunities on that front. His major passions outside of politics seemed to be photography and wine appreciation. Indeed, one of the few days off he had permitted himself was while the tour was in Adelaide. He had requested a day tour of the Adelaide Hills and the famous adjacent Barossa Valley wineries, so that he could indulge his two hobbies.

"You're from Adelaide aren't you?" asked Bill. "Does that give you any ideas?"

"It's a possibility" replied Greg practicing his newly acquired 'posh' accent. "There are some remote spots up there. Let me think about it."

Meanwhile other people had been busy. The backroom staff at MI5 had been hard at work building a credible new identity around the Andersens. With co-operation from the Australian Security Intelligence Organisation, generally known as ASIO, a new personal security company had been established in Australia and a credible history and references created. The principals were two

Australians, Trevor Buckingham and John Whiting. Identities were created for them complete with passports and driving licences, which would be finalised with photographs of the remade brothers.

While the training was happening Greg contacted his brother Tony on their private mobile phones and explained the plan to him without revealing the name of the intended victim, not that it would have meant much to Tony. He wasn't sure if Tony really had got the picture but he seemed happy enough with the idea of one more big job and then a nice retirement with lots of money.

"I could buy a beaut house in Mannum with river views. I'd like that" he said to Greg.

Greg had to accept that Tony, despite his occasional violent outbursts, often resembled an innocent child.

"Look Tony" he explained gently, "we won't be able to go back to Mannum. We would be too well known there and the cops wouldn't leave us alone. But don't worry; I'll find somewhere nice for us."

"You mean we'd have to live in another state? Queensland maybe?"

"No not Queensland. Not anywhere in Australia."

Tony had to grapple with this idea.

"But Greg, I've never lived outside of Australia. I might be scared."

"Don't worry; there are lots of nice places. People tell me Spain is a lot like Australia. Maybe we'll go there."

"Oh would I have to learn to speak Spanish? That would be hard."

"No mate; most people there speak English so we'll be OK. As I said don't worry; I'll sort out somewhere really nice for us. Do you fancy a big house with a pool?"

"Yeah Greg, that sounds great. I know you'll look after me. You always have. What should I do now?"

Don't do anything and keep yourself out of sight. I'll be coming back to Australia soon and then I'll tell you where to meet me. I think it will be somewhere in Brisbane. Then I'll give you the right training and we'll be ready. Just think; one more job and we've cracked it. Until then keep your head down."

Chapter 22

On Friday April 22 two men left Heathrow Airport to fly to Australia. They left at different times and on different airlines but their destination was the same.

Greg Andersen, in his new identity of Trevor Buckingham, took a morning British Airways flight which went nonstop to Sydney apart from a refuelling stop at Singapore. He arrived in Sydney on a cool morning with a promise of rain. His instructions were to take the shuttle bus to the domestic terminal and there to catch a connecting flight to Brisbane. The last thing he really wanted was more flying after the twenty one hours he had already endured but it was only just over an hour to Brisbane so he was stoical.

In the arrivals hall he was pleased to see a man standing among the throng of taxi drivers holding a sign which read 'Trevor Buckingham'. He walked over to him, smiled and said "Hi, I'm Trevor". The man's expression was impassive. "Can I see your ID?" he said in a quiet voice.

Anderson produced his passport in the name of Trevor Buckingham. The driver looked at it, looked at Andersen and seemed satisfied.

"OK let's go" was the only response. He led Andersen out to the car park where a Toyota sedan with dark windows was waiting. The driver opened the luggage compartment and motioned to his passenger to put his luggage in.

As they drove out of the airport Andersen attempted to enliven the sparse conversation. "What was all that ID thing about? You would know what I look like wouldn't you?"

The only reply was a quiet, considered "You can't be too careful".

That went down well, thought Andersen. I'll try another approach.

"Where are we going?"

"I'm taking you to a safe house."

"Whereabouts?"

"It's less than a half hour drive. That's all you need to know."

"It's a bit cloak and dagger isn't it?" asked Andersen.

He received no reply and gave up. He settled back and watched the suburbs as they passed through. Not knowing Brisbane very well he had no idea where he was going.

A short while later the driver turned the car into a wide driveway with high timber gates, which opened as they approached. Inside was a two storey house, modern but with no distinguishing features, with a high brick wall around it.

The car stopped at the front door and the driver got out and removed the luggage. "This is your new home. Enjoy."

Andersen tried one last attempt at humour. "You don't expect a tip do you?"

The driver grinned slightly, got back into the car and drove away without a word.

Andersen watched him go and said out aloud "I wonder if they're all this friendly."

A voice behind him said "Don't mind him. He's under orders to keep quiet."

Andersen turned around. The front door had opened and a short, chubby, cheerful looking man stood there.

"Who are you?" was all he could think of to say.

"I'm Hugo. I'm the manager of this facility. Come in Trevor, you must be very tired."

He picked up the suitcases and motioned the weary traveller to follow him. Inside the house was cool. Andersen could hear the gentle whirr of air conditioners as he entered the large hallway. Brisbane was certainly warmer than Sydney had been.

Hugo waved towards the wide staircase. "Come on, I'll show you your room. You can have a rest then I'll give you the grand tour."

He followed Hugo up the stairs and was shown into a very large bedroom, more like a suite than a bedroom. Hugo pointed to the small kitchenette. "Help yourself to a snack if you're hungry, and there are drinks in the fridge. Dinner will be a while yet and will be in the dining room downstairs; shall we say seven o'clock? That'll give you time to have a rest and freshen up."

"Thanks, this looks great" said Andersen, genuinely surprised and delighted at what was on offer.

Hugo withdrew and Andersen headed straight for the fridge. Ah, some cold beer. He opened one gratefully. He downed his drink quickly and lay down on the bed. Within seconds he was asleep, exhausted by the long journey.

***

Another man left Heathrow on the same day. Michael Robinson was leaving on an early evening flight with Cathay Pacific to Sydney via Hong Kong. He had never been to Hong Kong before so he had organised a one night stopover to have a quick look and to break up the long tedious journey. He had never experienced a flight of that duration.

He too travelled with fake ID, courtesy of Blaines' contacts in MI5. He had become Paul Schofield. Apart from a restyling of his hair and some new clothes it was judged to be unnecessary to change his appearance further. After all, he was there as an observer and the only people he would have any contact with were The Mole and Greg Andersen, both of whom knew him already.

His flight to Hong Kong arrived at one o'clock in the afternoon. He had booked a taxi to take him into Kowloon. As he entered the arrivals hall he looked for his name in the crowds of drivers who were holding up name placards. At first, in his tired state, he was disappointed. No sign of a placard with the name Robinson. Suddenly he realised what he was doing and had to smile. He looked again, this time for Paul Schofield, and soon spotted it.

Forty minutes later he was disembarking at his hotel, The Eaton, in the middle of the Kowloon shopping district on Nathan Road. The drive along the harbour side had been impressive; although he had passed more blocks of densely packed, high rise flats than he had ever seen in his life.

His room at The Eaton was pleasant and cool, if not particularly large. He didn't care. He gratefully sank into the bed and was immediately asleep.

When he woke it was late in the afternoon. He had a shower and changed. He had only a limited amount of time in Hong Kong and he intended to make the most of it. He wanted to visit the famous Night Market on Temple Street, which was just around the corner, one of the reasons why he had picked this hotel. It opened all evening so he had plenty of time. He went first to the Tin Hau Temple, also on Temple Street, where he marvelled at the exotic decorations, intricate carvings and the smoky atmosphere from the many incense sticks and coils.

He enjoyed the market; stall after stall was selling clothing, souvenirs and all manner of electronic gadgets.

He took in the atmosphere and admired the goods on offer but bought nothing. Nor did he take any photographs. He was determined that there should be no evidence that he had ever been there.

When he had seen enough he strolled back to The Eaton where he enjoyed a superb Nasi Goreng in the outside T garden bar and restaurant. Another beer later and he was ready for bed; the long trip had caught up with him.

He was awake early next morning, for which he was quite grateful. He had only the morning until his taxi was due to pick him up and take him to the airport for the next leg of his flight to Sydney.

He felt a need for some exercise and, according to his tourist map, there were several parks located on steep hills just behind Nathan Road. After a quick breakfast he set off and found one of the walkways which led him up the hills by Kings Park, through winding steep paths with thick rain forest –like vegetation. On reaching the top he discovered the Yau Ma Tei Service Reservoir Rest Garden, in effect a small flat area at the top of the hill where you could stroll the paths and admire the views or be more energetic on the running track. He marvelled at the tranquillity and the small number of people there considering what a crowded city Hong Kong is; it was a welcome respite from the thronging crowds on Nathan Road. He stayed there for a while enjoying the peace then made his way back to Nathan Road. He still had time available so he wandered along amazed at all the shops and the sheer quantity of shopping that was happening.

Eventually he sated of crowds and shopping and made his way back to the hotel, where he showered, changed, checked out and quietly waited for his taxi in the ground floor foyer.

He reached the airport in plenty of time to check in for his flight, which left at seven pm just in time to arrive in Sydney soon after seven am when the night flying curfew was finished.

He had managed to get some sleep on the flight but he was still tired and stiff from nine hours cramped in an aircraft. Sydney was still cool and threatening rain, which surprised him as he had believed it was always warm and sunny there. He had a tense moment at the immigration counter as the official examined his new passport and the entry card he had filled in, claiming that he was here as a tourist for a few weeks.

He needn't have worried. The official handed them back with a smile. "Thanks Mr Schofield; enjoy your stay."

He hurried out into the arrivals hall and found the shuttle bus to the domestic terminal, where he checked in for his short flight to Brisbane.

On landing in Brisbane he had a similar experience to the one enjoyed by Greg Andersen on the previous day. He was met by a driver who spoke very little and drove him to the safe house. Robinson was tired and happy to sit there without any conversation.

He was greeted at the front door by Hugo who gave him a welcoming smile. "Welcome to Brisbane Mr Schofield. Your colleague is already here. I'll show you up to your room. You can freshen up and maybe join us in the lounge for a pre-dinner drink. That's the room over there on the right."

Schofield had a quick catnap followed by a shower. Feeling tolerably human again he made his way down to the lounge to see if there was anyone around. He walked in and noticed just one person, Greg Andersen, sitting in the armchair with a beer in front of him, engrossed in the sports section of a newspaper.

"Good afternoon Trevor" he boomed.

Andersen looked up. "Well if it isn't my old mate Ben, or should I say Paul now?"

"Very funny. Don't use that name again. Remember I'm Paul Schofield and you are Trevor Buckingham."

"Yeah, yeah, yeah, don't worry; I've got it. Can I get you a beer?"

"That would be great Gre – er – Trevor." Both men laughed.

"What do you make of this place?" asked Robinson, now with a beer in his hand.

Andersen shrugged. "Not much to say really. We seem to be the only people here apart from Hugo and he hasn't said much yet. The place is nice enough and we are certainly being looked after. Hugo is good company, better than the miserable sod that drove me here."

Robinson laughed. "Yes I think I must have had the same driver. So when does your brother get here?"

"He's due in tomorrow if he can follow the instructions I've given him."

"Good, then we can start to get organised. We've only got a week or so to get him properly briefed and disguised."

Andersen looked thoughtful. "He'll be OK. He can be a bit dim but he doesn't have to do much; just stand around and look tough really. He's good at that."

"I hope so. It's too late to change our plans now."

"Don't worry; he'll be fine. He's as fresh as a daisy. We are the ones with the jet lag. Still we should be over in a day or two."

"That would be nice" said Robinson. "I seem to feel tired all the time, and then I'm awake at night."

"It's like that for all of us mate. Let's have another beer and then find Hugo and see when we're gonna have some tucker."

"What's tucker?"

"Dinner you goose. Didn't they teach you anything at that fancy English school?"

***

While Greg Andersen and Michael Robinson were enduring their long flights Tony Andersen was pursuing a slower journey, but just as long.

Greg had phoned Tony and explained the plan to him. It had been kept very simple so Tony would not be confused. He was to leave Charters Towers on Monday and drive down the lonely Gregory Highway to the small town of Emerald. He would see little traffic and should be quite safe.

There were few towns along the way; Belyando Crossing, little more than a roadhouse, and the small town of Clermont. It was some 500 kilometres and Tony should be able to cover it in about 5 hours or so, which would get him to Emerald in the early afternoon.

At Emerald he would pick up the Capricorn Highway, so called because it runs east west tracking The Tropic of Capricorn for some 600 kilometres from Rockhampton in the east to various remote mining towns in the west.

Tony however would only have to drive the 280 kilometres to Rockhampton, where he should – carefully – spend the night in an anonymous motel.

On the second day he was to take the Bruce Highway from Rockhampton down to Brisbane, some 650 kilometres south, which he could comfortably cover in one day. The road, although busier than the outback roads he had previously taken, did not go through many large towns; most had been bypassed by the Highway. Nonetheless Greg asked Tony to wear his large stockman's hat all the time. It would not look out of place there and would help to conceal his identity.

Tony took it all in then asked "but where do I go in Brisbane? It's a big place and I don't know it very well."

"It's easy Tony" smoothed Greg. "Just follow the Brisbane Highway past the Sunshine Coast and Brisbane's northern districts and you'll see signs to the airport. Then come off the Highway at the exit for Kingsford Smith Drive. It's easy."

"But how will I know where that is Greg?"

"Look, it'll be obvious, but buy yourself a map just in case. Drive along Kingsford Smith Drive and you'll see a Toyota Aurion, black with dark windows, parked at the roadside." He gave him the registration number. "Got that?"

"Yes Greg I've written it down."

"OK, there will be two guys in the car. One will bring you to us in the Toyota and the other will take your car."

"What will happen to my car?"

"Don't worry about the car Tony. After this job you'll be able to afford whatever car you want. Now, one last thing, and make sure you write this down."

"OK."

"Write down this mobile telephone number." He gave him the number. "If you get any problems, even if the police pick you up, phone this number. When it answers just say 'this is Tony. I need help'. Got that?"

"Yes Greg. And what happens then?"

"You'll be asked where you are and what the problem is, then someone will sort it out for you. You shouldn't need it but it's just if anything goes wrong. Are you OK with that?"

"Yep I'm fine; just leave it to me. What happens when I get there?"

"Don't worry about that for now. We've got nearly two weeks before we start the job. Plenty of time to prepare you."

"OK Greg, I guess that should be enough."

"Right mate, we'll see you at the house on Tuesday arvo. We can have a beer and some tucker."

"OK, it'll be good to see you again Greg. I've missed you."

"Me too Tony; just remember be careful and keep your head down."

"I will. Bye."

Tony put the phone down and thought about what Greg had said. It was another long drive but he was used to that. He was looking forward to this next adventure and Greg would look after him.

He had been living with Neville in Charters Towers for almost a month. The lack of anything to do and the constant hiding was beginning to get to him.

Chapter 23

In Adelaide the events at Forster Lookout three weeks earlier were moving towards a form of closure.
A BBQ lunch was taking place on Saturday, on the veranda of Debbie Simmons' flat in Norwood.
The event was to say farewell to those who were returning to England, Peter Carney who needed to go home to his business and Carol Mannering and Alan Warner, who had finally made the decision to go home.
Warner had wanted to stay on for a while to confront Tony Andersen. He still didn't fully understand why he had been kept a prisoner for so long and what Andersen's intentions really were. However, as there had been no sightings of Tony Andersen in the intervening weeks and both the Andersens had gone into hiding, Carol had finally been able to convince Alan that enough was enough and it was time to go home and pick up their lives again.
Detective Inspector Brian Chambers was also present. He too wanted to farewell Alan and Carol, who had been key players in one of his most baffling cases. For him it wasn't over yet as they were still working to establish the whereabouts of Tony Andersen and arrest him.
John Foster was perhaps the most cheerful person present. He had told the others of his extension in Australia to cover the Francis Ventrice tour and was obviously overjoyed at the prospect as was Debbie.
Peter Carney was happy for his niece Debbie and could see how smitten she was. But the thought he kept to himself was that it was only another month or so and then the lovers would face the same problem again.
Carney's thought were interrupted by Debbie as she asked, "Peter, we're a bit quiet in Adelaide at the moment aren't we?

"Yes there's not a lot happening right now" he conceded. "I thought you'd be glad of the rest. It would give your leg a chance to heal properly."

"You know me uncle; I'm not the sort of girl to sit around and rest."

"What are you plotting?" asked Carney, pretty confident that he knew the answer.

"It's just that John is going to be following the Ventrice tour around Australia for three weeks, so I thought I might go with him."

"So you want three weeks holiday then?" asked Carney trying to keep a straight face.

Debbie bit her lip. "Well I could come back to Adelaide if anything urgent popped up, so the business wouldn't suffer."

"I guess that would work" said Carney. OK, I don't think anyone is scheduled to come to Adelaide in that period anyway."

"Thanks Peter, you're a darling."

"When you I refuse you anything? Besides, when the next batch comes through you're going to be very busy."

"Congratulations Debbie" said Carol. "Things seem to be working out well for you and John right now."

"Yes, it's lovely isn't it. But what are you guys going to do back in England?"

"I don't really know" admitted Carol. "I guess I'll go back to my nursing job and Alan can go back and work for his dad again. The trouble is there's no money in these things and this job of Alan's in Australia was supposed to help us get out of the rut we're in."

Alan agreed. "I suppose dad will have me back but the business isn't doing all that well and he can't afford to pay me very much. Also I quite like what I've seen of Australia and I don't really want to leave. But then you all know what the visa situation is like at the moment so I don't have any options."

"I've got an idea" said Carney. "I could do with some help in my business in England. It's all getting a bit too much for me to handle on my own any more. When we're back in England give me a call and we'll have a chat."

Warner was shocked. "Peter that's fantastic. But why me?"

"Alan, I like what I see. You're obviously a young man who's prepared to accept a challenge and to take risks to get ahead. I like that. Besides, I think you're not a bad judge of people either, which is what I need."

"What makes you say that?"

"I think you've handled your ordeal well. You formed a working relationship with Andersen and you can even see his good points."

"I didn't have much choice."

"Maybe not, but you made the best out of a bad situation."

"I guess I did, but I don't have much of a business background and I have no idea how you operate."

Carney laughed. "Don't sell yourself down. You've been through the process yourself and you've experienced firsthand what can go wrong if it's not done properly. That's a valuable, if painful, training exercise you've had."

"Well I guess if you put it like that. I'll definitely be in touch once we're home. And thanks again."

Carney was beginning to feel embarrassed and was relieved when Brain Chambers interrupted the conversation.

"Sorry to break this up folks but I've got to go. A policeman's work is never done you know."

"What even on a Saturday?" said Warner.

"'I'm afraid so. The job never ends and I've still got quite a backlog thanks to you guys."

"I didn't mean to cause you problems" said Warner quietly.

"Only joking Alan. But I have got a lot on right now and I need to go, so it's time to say goodbye. I hope things work out for you in England."

"Thanks Brian" said Warner. "And you will let me know what happens with Tony Andersen?"

"Yes I will, although I suspect John here will know before I do." He grinned and looked at Foster. "Anyhow I must go. Look after yourselves. You too Peter. I have to say it's been one of the most interesting and surprising cases I've had."

**

The following day John Foster and Debbie made two trips to Adelaide Airport. The first, in the morning, was to take Carol and Alan for their domestic flight to Sydney where they would change to a British Airways flight to go back to England.

For the two girls it was an emotional parting. Over the last few weeks they had bonded strongly but now it was all over.

For the second visit they took Peter Carney, who had booked an evening direct flight to Kuala Lumpur from Adelaide with Malaysian Airlines.

This parting was less traumatic for Debbie as she knew that Carney had regular trips back to Australia, but she wondered if she would ever see Carol again.

Chapter 24

Tony Andersen's journey from Charters Towers to Brisbane had been long but uneventful.
As instructed he left Charters Towers on the morning of Monday April 25. He completed the 480 kilometre lonely journey to Emerald, arriving there mid afternoon, where he joined the Capricorn Highway for the last stage of the day, the 270 kilometre drive to Rockhampton.
Rockhampton was a much busier place than any he had experienced since leaving South Australia seven weeks earlier. He felt more conspicuous than he had anywhere else and was greatly relieved when he had found a basic motel on the outskirts and had checked in for the night.
Next morning he woke up early in a state of excitement. Today was the day he would be re-united with his brother. Greg would look after him then. He was determined not to be late so he was on the road early after a quick breakfast.
The journey was straightforward; the Bruce Highway ran close to the coast for over 1600 kilometres all the way from Cairns in North Queensland, through Rockhampton and on to Brisbane. It was much busier than the roads he had travelled on to date and he took Greg's advice to wear his big hat at all times to make him less obvious to any curious observers.
He enjoyed a smooth uneventful journey, stopping only for lunch. By mid afternoon he was approaching Brisbane airport. He watched the exits carefully. He had to ignore the exit for Brisbane airport and carry on a short distance to the exit for Kingsford Smith Drive where his escort should be waiting.
He breathed a sigh of relief when he saw the exit sign, even though this was an area he had driven through on

several occasions. He cruised along Kingsford Smith Drive heading back towards Brisbane City keeping his eyes open for the black Toyota. He was in luck; he found it parked in one of the few shady spots along the road. He parked just in front of it and got out of his car. He walked slowly and carefully towards the Toyota and checked the number plates as he came near. Yes it was the right car.

More boldly he walked up to the car, saw two men sitting in the front seats and waved. The men got out. One was a youth wearing jeans; the other a thick set man in a dark suit, who didn't seem very friendly. He looked carefully at Tony, appeared to be satisfied and simply said "so you're here then. Get your gear and my little mate here will take your car."

"OK" said Tony quietly. He walked back to his car, packed the few loose belongings into his bag and walked back to the Toyota, which already had the luggage compartment open. He placed his bag in it, closed the lid and opened the front passenger door.

"Haven't you forgotten something?" asked the big one.

"What's that?"

"Your car keys."

"Oh yeah, here" he said holding them up. The youth in jeans grabbed them without a word and walked back to Tony's car.

"OK let's go" said the big one. "I've been hanging around here long enough."

Tony looked with some nostalgia as he watched his car drive away. Although it was only an old Holden it had served him well for the last few weeks, carrying him across three states and along outback roads with no trouble at all. He forced himself to look away.

"Where are we going?" he asked.

"Don't you worry about that. We'll be there in twenty minutes."

Tony shut up and watched the streets go by. He tried to figure out where he was but his knowledge of Brisbane was very slim once he had left the area around the airport.

The driver was nothing if not accurate. Twenty minutes later they reached the house with the timber gates and high walls.

As the car pulled up the front door opened and a short man emerged.

"Hello Tony" he said. "I'm Hugo. Grab your things and follow me."

At least he seems friendlier than the driver, thought Tony. He followed Hugo into the hallway where he at once recognised the tall man standing there.

"Greg, is it you? Geez you look different. Is that what the poms have done to ya?"

The two big men embraced and Greg laughed. "This is my new look for our next job. You'll be getting a new look too. It's good to see you again mate."

Tony was very tearful. "It's great to see you too. I thought you'd be mad at me for what I've done. I really cocked up that last job didn't I?"

"Tony, don't worry. You've actually done us both a big favour, even if you didn't intend to. One more job and we're rich men and we can retire. Come and sit down and we'll have a beer and talk."

***

They had just less than two weeks to effect the transformation of Tony and create his new documents.

They decided the most effective way to change his appearance was to do something about his shock of unruly blond hair. As Greg put it, "we have to get rid of the Boris look." Tony wasn't sure what Greg meant but he smiled anyway.

His hair was trimmed back to a stubble and what was left was dyed black. The result was to make him look much more menacing, especially when they had found him a dark suit, white shirt and tie to complement his new appearance.

Tony looked at himself in the mirror and exclaimed "geez this get-up is bloody uncomfortable and I look as if I'm going to a funeral."

Greg laughed. "Well that's OK because that's what we are going to be doing."

Tony was confused again. "What do you mean?"

"Don't you worry your head about it mate. You look great, just the right image for an expensive minder."

Tony was embarrassed. He wasn't used to compliments.

"I won't let you down again Greg" he said quietly.

"No I know mate but remember, from now on I'm Trevor Buckingham and you're John Whiting. So, who am I?"

"You're Trevor" said Tony brightly, enjoying this new game.

"Well done mate; now let's use those names from now on. The Andersens have disappeared and when we finish this job we leave the country with our new identities."

"When are we doing the job Greg? Er sorry I mean Trevor."

"Not for a while yet. I haven't worked out exactly where. When we are in Adelaide is a possibility and that's over three weeks from now. We need to look at the tour schedule together and work out the best way to handle it."

"Yeah" said Tony thoughtfully. "I guess we know the ropes there a bit more."

Sometimes he's not so dumb, thought Greg.

"You could be right. We know our way round there and where all the quiet spots are. Anyhow we can look over the schedule together and see what we can come up with."

Tony was thrilled to be part of the planning process.

"Just who is this guy; and what's he done so that we have to get rid of him?"

"He's a pommie politician mate. And he's causing lots of grief back in his own country. He's made a lot of enemies, fortunately for us."

"Why is it fortunate for us?"

"Don't forget; this is our retirement package. You haven't forgotten the big house with the pool have you?"

"Of course not Greg. I just wondered."

A few days later Tony was pronounced ready. His photo documents now matched his new appearance and he had learned his role.

Even for Tony it wasn't very difficult. He just had to stand around looking confident and in control and keep quiet. Let Greg do all the talking and organising.

Ventrice would have one of his own minders with him but he had been briefed that the two Australians were there only to assist as they knew the territory better.

The scene was finally set. In four days time they would be joining the Ventrice entourage for the start of the tour.

Chapter 25

John Foster had six weeks until he was scheduled to join the Ventrice tour. He was pleased that he also had time to keep up to date on what was happening, if anything, with the hunt for the Andersens.

This was a story that was to take an odd twist for him. He had contacted DI Joe Patel, in Southampton, England, to ask him how the search for Greg Andersen was going and received a discouraging response.

Patel told him that he had finally discovered Greg Andersen's address but that the suspect had fled and there had been no further sightings. Patel thought it wise not to mention to the press that they had been warned off by the security services.

Foster was disappointed but he filed a follow up story anyway, explaining what little he knew under the headline KILLER DISAPPEARS. The publication of his story in The Sun provoked an immediate reaction. Next day, just as he was heading off to bed Foster received a phone call from his editor, Mervin O'Grady, in London.

Normally Mervin saved money by communicating via email so a phone call was an event in itself.

"Hi Mervin" he said as breezily as he could, desperately hoping his new assignment wasn't going to be cancelled. "What's new?"

"Hi John, I've got something rather interesting for you."

"What's that?" asked Foster cautiously.

"It's about your story on the disappearance of Greg Andersen. I've been warned off."

"What do you mean, warned off?"

"I had a phone call from *my* boss. He has been contacted by the security services and has had a D-notice slapped on him. How strange is that?"

"That's really odd. Did they tell you anything else?"
"No, they just warned us off publishing anything about Greg Andersen and his disappearance."
"That's it then is it?" said Foster morosely. "No more follow up stories."
But Mervin was an old hand and not so easily put off.
"Not exactly John. I've been told not to publish stories about Greg Andersen or to draw any attention to him. They didn't say anything about Tony Andersen and his disappearance."
"So we keep on looking over here?"
"Exactly; I know it's been quiet of late but you never know what might happen. He's bound to turn up sometime. When he does, send me a story and I'll decide just how much we can get away with. Just forget about Greg for now."
"Is the Ventrice job still on?" asked Foster anxiously.
"Yes John, no change there. It should be easy enough for you. And you can keep your eyes peeled for any news of Tony while you're at it."
"Yes, I can do that. Anything else; I'm ready for bed?"
Mervin laughed. "No that's it. Don't forget it's morning here. I'll let you know what's happening by email, unless I want to keep it confidential, in which case I'll phone you. Bye for now."
"Goodnight Mervin" said Foster and gratefully took himself off to bed.

PART 3 - Execution

Chapter 26

Francis Ventrice looked out of the window as the plane approached Brisbane Airport. Although it was barely morning, this Sunday in early May was hot and sunny. Ventrice had slept well on the journey from Bangkok and was looking forward to his first day in Australia. One of the many benefits of business class flying he thought.
Four of them were in the small business class cabin; Ventrice himself, Alice and Grace, and a large quiet man, Edward Hopkins.
Hopkins had known Ventrice for much of his life. They met at university where Hopkins appeared to be more interested in playing rugby and improving his skills in Tae Kwon Do. Despite the time he spent on these activities he still managed to gain a respectable degree in Finance and Accounting.
 For a few years their paths diverged as Hopkins followed his career while Ventrice steeped himself in the family business.
When Ventrice eventually took over the reins of the business he knew exactly who he wanted as his number two. Hopkins was quickly recruited and had been with the company ever since, successfully guiding its financial path. He also fulfilled another equally useful role in the business, that of discreet minder for Ventrice. On several occasions, while doing business in less salubrious areas, Ventrice had been assured by the quiet bulk of Hopkins alongside him. The few hard men who tried their luck with him soon found that they had underestimated his ability to move quickly and effectively, courtesy of his

martial arts skills. Generally they were left alone and Ventrice took comfort from having the gentle giant beside him.

Naturally Ventrice wanted Hopkins by his side during the Australian tour. His tour organisers had also proposed that they hire two local security guards for the duration of the stay on the grounds that they knew the territory better.

Ventrice, although not totally convinced, agreed to go ahead with the idea figuring that too much security was better than too little. Privately he doubted he would need anyone other than Hopkins but better safe than sorry. They were due to meet the Australians the following day.

The flight had been pleasant but long. They flew Thai Airways and had an overnight stop in Bangkok. The twins knew the city well and had taken him to places not frequented by the average tourist. He found it fascinating but was glad to have Hopkins alongside.

As the plane taxied to the terminal Ventrice made a last check of his appearance. They were due to be met by two senior figures in the "Our Nation" party and he wanted to create a favourable initial impression. He wore a lightweight dark suit, white shirt and tie. He wasn't too sure what the dress code might be in this hot, tropical city but he reasoned that his outfit should be acceptable anywhere.

He needn't have worried. The two men who met them were elderly and obviously old school, dressed conservatively in suits and ties despite the bright sunshine.

After initial introductions the party was whisked away in a large Lexus limousine to the Next Hotel right in the middle of Brisbane city centre. Their greeters left them to check in and freshen up, after inviting them to be their guests for dinner at the hotel restaurant.

Ventrice was keen to check out the hotel's facilities and it wasn't long before all four of them changed into shorts and T-shirts and were sitting under an umbrella by the rooftop pool admiring the sights of Brisbane and sipping their first local beer.

**

The remainder of Ventrice' entourage made their way to Australia but not quite in the style of Ventrice and his close associates. They too travelled by Thai Airways via Bangkok but there was no stopover for them other than the few hours to refuel. They travelled in economy class which was a far cry from the luxury and space awarded to the others.

They arrived in Brisbane on Saturday, the day before Ventrice, and were checked into the same hotel, albeit in standard rooms. Ventrice, Hopkins and the twins had three adjoining suites.

This small group consisted of Phillip Gardner, the tour organizer, Peter Breckenridge, a UKIP MEP, and Asha Gillespie, a small lady of Middle Eastern descent. Asha was an accomplished researcher for UKIP and had been exposed at various times to the media to demonstrate that the party supported the rights of both women and ethnic minorities.

The decision had been made months earlier to restrict the number of attendees to keep costs to a minimum. Ventrice had his right hand man and his two PAs, a term which occasionally caused a few raised eyebrows among party members. Ventrice volunteered to fund the airfares and accommodation for his small inner circle himself. The other three were funded by UKIP and Our Nation. The arrangements seemed to suit everyone and Ventrice was once more shown to be squeaky clean in how he used the Party's money.

The two groups had arranged to meet for lunch on the following day, Monday, when they would be introduced to their opposite numbers and organisers within Our Nation. While Ventrice and his inner circle enjoyed the hotel pool and a few drinks the economy class contingent had two days to rest and recover from the horrors of the long flight and to get over the jet lag as best they could.

One of them had a meeting to attend on the Sunday afternoon. While Ventrice and his inner circle were lounging around the hotel pool Phillip Gardner slipped away quietly. He left the hotel, walked a few yards along the Mall and turned into George St. Less than a block down George St he found what he sought, The Villager Hotel, a small pub in an older style building.

He ordered a beer at the bar and found himself one of the tables outside on the pavement. He sipped his beer and watched the endless parade of taxis along George St as he waited for the man he had come to see. It was a very warm and humid day. As he sipped his drink he had difficulty staying awake. He was drifting away when a familiar voice disturbed his quiet with "Can I get you another one of those?"

He looked up to see Michael Robinson smiling at him. "Hi Michael" he said as he struggled to be alert again, "why not?"

Robinson returned from the bar with two beers and seated himself. "So Phillip how was the flight?"

"Endless" he replied, "and now I can't seem to stay awake, except in the middle of the night."

"It'll pass. It usually takes a few days."

"How come you're not affected?"

"Don't forget I've been here for two weeks. I'm well over it."

"Yes of course. How is your training going?"

Robinson was careful in his response, being only too aware that Gardner was not totally supportive of the plan.

"Everything's in place. You'll meet our guys on Monday evening at the tour opening meeting."

"Great." said Gardner, trying to sound more enthusiastic than he felt. "Where are you staying?"

"Just at a small hotel a short walk away" Robinson answered vaguely. "It's best if I keep out of sight as much as possible."

"I guess so. You still intend to go ahead with this plan then?"

"Absolutely, nothing has changed. I gather you're not convinced yet?"

"You know what I think; that it's a high risk and pointless scheme. I thought you might have been able to push that point of view to your superiors."

"We've talked about it but the boss still wants to go ahead."

"Then he's an idiot."

"This idiot, as you call him, is a well respected senior government figure and he has maintained you in well paid comfortable employment for several years now. You take his money so you follow his orders."

"That may well be true, but there was never any suggestion that I'd be a murderer."

"That's very harsh Phillip. It's a necessary reaction to a threat to our nation. Besides you don't actually have to be part of it."

"That's easy for you to say isn't it? But I know what's going to happen, who is responsible and I did nothing to prevent it."

Robinson had picked up on something that alarmed him. "What do you mean, you know who is responsible?"

"Come on Michael. I know that your boss is Geoffrey Blaines."

"Well I can't confirm or deny it" said Robinson pompously. "What makes you think that?"

"I've seen you with him often enough and overheard some of your conversations."

"So now you've been eavesdropping on me."

Gardner was now fully awake and alert, his tiredness gone.

"Michael, do you really think I'd carry on with this madcap scheme without taking out some personal insurance. If the finger gets pointed at me I want to be able to deflect it."

"So you're not with us then? Does that mean you are going to actively work against us?" said Robinson menacingly.

"That's not what I said. I don't agree with this plan, as you know, and I hope that Blaines acquires some common sense and cancels it, or that the scheme simply doesn't work. I'll continue to help you plot Ventrice' political death but not his actual one. Besides, Ventrice always has his sidekick with him. Are your guys going to be able to get past him? And have you got a really detailed sensible plan yet?"

"Well no" said Robinson hesitantly, "but we will be working out how and when over the next few days."

"Good luck to you. I still think it's harebrained. If I were you I would be looking for my escape path when the shit hits the fan."

"You worry too much. Let's have another beer and enjoy the sun."

"My round I think" said Gardner and made his way to the bar.

Robinson thought over what had just been discussed. Was Gardner going to be an active threat or would he just sit on the sidelines hoping the plan would be cancelled, as he claimed? He would have to keep an eye on him and make sure he didn't do anything foolish.

Gardner returned with the cold beer and they turned the conversation around to the general delights of Brisbane and its warm sunshine.

Chapter 27

Among the passengers boarding the Monday morning flight from Adelaide to Brisbane were John Foster and Debbie Simmons. Foster was heading to Brisbane to join the Ventrice tour. Tonight was to be the opening night of the tour where the various parties got to know each other and Ventrice was to make an opening address.

Foster had convinced Debbie to come along. Not that she needed much convincing. Her love affair with Foster had become ever more intense since the events at Forster Lookout a few weeks earlier.

She had negotiated time off work for the three weeks of the duration of the tour with an agreement that if anything urgent popped up she would return to Adelaide to deal with it. Foster's hotel rooms for the tour were paid for by his employers, the Murdoch Press, so Debbie's costs were minimal.

Foster had managed to get her assigned to the press contingent as his assistant and photographer which meant she could accompany him to all functions open to the press.

The two hour flight from Adelaide was uneventful. They caught a taxi from the airport to the Next Hotel in Brisbane City Centre, only twenty minutes away, and by early afternoon were checked into their room.

Like many days in Brisbane it was very warm, sunny and humid. From their hotel window they could see the rooftop pool glinting, several floors below them.

"Come on let's go for a swim" said Debbie, "We've got stacks of time before the meeting."

"OK, we may as well grab our opportunities while we can."

Debbie changed into a tiny black bikini which showed off her magnificent body.

"Now that you are dressed like that I can think of much more interesting things to do than swim" remarked Foster.

"Down boy. Plenty of time for that later. Let's go."

They made their way to the pool which was not crowded at that time of day. Only a few sun lounges were occupied. They pulled two lounges together, angled them to catch the sun, and settled in. "Swim first then we'll have a drink" announced Debbie as she made for the pool. The water was pleasantly warm without being too hot and they enjoyed swimming several lengths. When Foster stopped Debbie swam up to him.

"Hey, do you see who's over there?"

"Over where?"

"At the far end there. The guy on a lounger by himself."

Foster looked. "You mean the guy with the blue shorts and sunglasses? So what?"

"You're not very observant for a reporter are you? Isn't that Francis Ventrice?"

Foster looked again. "I think you could be right. What's he doing on his own if it is him? They say he always has his minder with him."

"Well surely there must be times when he wants to be alone. He probably doesn't sleep with him you know" said Debbie with a sparkle in her eye.

"Yeah I guess. So the great man has arrived. He looks a bit different in the flesh from what I expected."

"I imagine many people are like that. I think he actually looks rather handsome. Time I got to know him better" she said enigmatically.

"What do you mean?" asked Foster but his words never reached her as she was already strolling along the poolside, hips swaying delightfully.

As she strolled past Ventrice' lounger she feigned surprise and put on her best Australian accent. "Hey, say aren't you that pommie politician?"

Ventrice looked up, seemingly annoyed at the interruption to his privacy, but on seeing Debbie his expression changed to one of total delight.

He smiled. "That's the first time I've been called a pommie politician. Lots of other things but never that."

Better not overdo the strong accent, she thought. "You are Francis Ventrice aren't you?

"I guess I must be. I didn't think I was very well known so far from home. And who are you?"

"I'm Debbie Simmons" she replied as she stuck out her hand. "Pleased to meet you."

"Well Debbie Simmons" he teased, "and what might you be doing here?"

"Actually I have to confess. I'm one of the people covering your tour. I help out with the press corp."

"Lucky press corp."

Debbie tried to think of a suitable response but was interrupted by the arrival of a large thick set man carrying two drinks." He glanced at Debbie and said "Everything OK Francis?"

Ventrice looked up at him. "Everything's fine. Look this is Debbie Simmons. Debbie is one of the tour group. Debbie meet my assistant Edward Hopkins."

Hopkins seemed to relax and said "Hi Debbie".

"Hi" said Debbie. "Do I call you Edward or what? It sounds a bit formal."

Hopkins laughed. "It does seem a bit formal in this setting. Just call me Ed."

"Well how do you like Australia so far Ed? Actually I guess you get asked that all the time."

"No that's OK. It's great so far. I just love your weather. But where are my manners? Can I get you a drink? We're just about to have one?"

"What about your boyfriend over there?" Ventrice asked innocently.

"Oh that's OK. He's not my boyfriend. He's my colleague on the paper. Yes I'd love a drink thank you. Could I have a glass of chardonnay, very cold?"

"No problem" said Hopkins and headed back to the bar.

"Have a seat" said Ventrice, pointing to the lounger next to him. "You must tell me all about yourself."

Debbie sat down. "Not much to tell really. I'm actually from Sydney originally but I do temp jobs wherever they crop up – like this one. It's a nice little earner for three or four weeks."

"So you don't work for a newspaper then?"

"Not really. For this job I'm working for The Australian, just helping out their reporter, the guy over there. You know, a bit of PA type work. Sometimes I do a bit of photography as well."

Ventrice glanced over towards Foster. What's she playing at, thought Foster.

Their conversation was interrupted by the return of Hopkins bearing a glass of chardonnay. He handed it to Debbie and sat on the lounger on the other side of Ventrice.

"Thanks Ed. Very cold. Perfect," cooed Debbie.

"So you're interested in photography?" asked Ventrice. "That's one of my hobbies too. I hope to take some great pictures while I'm here."

"Well there are lots of beautiful sights here."

He smiled broadly. "Yes and I think I am looking at one of them right now. Perhaps I could show you some of my pictures sometime?"

"We'll have to see how things work out, won't we?" said Debbie. "After all you have a very busy schedule Mr Ventrice."

"Mr Ventrice? I haven't offended you have I Debbie?"

"No of course not – Francis. I'm sure we will be seeing a lot of each other on the tour. I would very much like to see your work."

Ventrice seemed very pleased and was about to reply when he was interrupted by Hopkins. "Francis, don't forget we have a meeting shortly. We ought to be getting ready."

"Yes that's a pity" said Ventrice. "I was so enjoying our conversation Debbie but I'm afraid duty calls. I'll make sure we meet again."

"I understand Francis, and thanks for the drink."

"Will you be coming to the cocktail party tonight?" asked Ventrice.

"Yes I'll be there" said Debbie cheerfully. "Any excuse for a free drink."

Ventrice laughed. "Maybe I'll see you there then. Bye for now."

Ventrice and Hopkins picked up their belongings and made off to their meeting as Debbie strolled back to where Foster was lying attempting to appear nonchalant.

"What a nice man" she exclaimed as she sat down."

"What was all that about?" asked Foster moodily.

"Don't be grumpy John. I thought we were here to report on Ventrice. Now I've got to know him. That's quite a coup isn't it? Besides he's quite sweet."

"You need to watch yourself" said Foster as he relaxed a little. "He's got quite a reputation with the ladies."

"I think I can look after myself, don't you."
Foster had to agree. Besides it couldn't do any harm to his stories if he could get close to the man.
"I'm sure you can. But I thought you loved *me*. Another swim?"
"Don't be churlish. Let's have another swim then we'll go back to the room where I'll take off this wet bikini and show you how much I love you."
"How do you expect me to swim straight with that thought in my head?"
"Come on, one more swim before you split your shorts."

Chapter 28

The large convention room at the Next Hotel was a hubbub of activity. Prior to the main cocktail party the UK contingent had met there with officials of Our Nation and had been properly introduced. As befitted the occasion Ventrice took pains to meet with all the Our Nation party members and impressed them with his charm and his ability to remember names. He and Hopkins were also introduced by Phillip Gardner to the two Australian security staff who stood uncomfortably in the background.

Gardner beckoned them come forward. "Francis, these are your local security officers. They come highly recommended. I'd like you to meet Trevor Buckingham and John Whiting."

Buckingham smiled, looked Ventrice straight in the eye and said "Welcome to Australia Mr Ventrice. It's our job to take care of you." The other man, Whiting, merely shook hands, smiled weakly and looked at the floor.

"Pleased to meet you gentlemen" said Ventrice cheerfully as he shook hands. "It makes me feel very safe and secure to have you on board. However I'd like you to stay in the background and just keep an eye on things. I don't want it to look as if I'm surrounded by bodyguards. You do understand don't you?"

Gardner replied for them. "We've already talked about that Francis. They will be very discreet and mostly invisible. Tonight they'll be up there on the mezzanine floor where they can observe the whole event without being seen themselves. I'm taking them up there now."

Gardner wasn't a small man but he certainly looked it as he led the two giants away to their watching post.

"Well what do make of them?" said Ventrice to Hopkins.

"Buckingham seems pretty switched on. The other one looks more like dumb muscle."

Ventrice grinned. "That's rather the impression I got. Ah well, as long as they know their stuff and generally keep out of the way. Let's go and meet some more people."

At eight o'clock the event was opened to the press corp and other invited guests. The initially sedate atmosphere quickly became noisier as the drinks flowed.

Ventrice worked the crowd extensively and even he was beginning to forget names as he moved about. Then he spotted one person whose name he wouldn't forget, Debbie Simmons, standing wearing a long red dress with the same man she was at the pool with. He wondered if the man really was just a work colleague.

He quickly manoeuvred himself over to her. "Hi Debbie" he exclaimed. "So glad you could make it. Are you going to introduce me to your colleague?"

"Francis this is John Foster. He's with the Murdoch Press."

"Pleased to meet you Francis" said Foster.

"Delighted" said Ventrice, "but didn't I detect an English accent there. You're a long way from home."

"Yes I am. I actually work for The Sun in London, but I'm covering this tour for The Sun and The Australian."

Ventrice laughed. "You'll have to write your stories in two different languages for those readerships. I hope you will be saying some nice things about me. The Sun can be so tiresome at times."

Foster decided he quite liked Ventrice too. He was a refreshing change from most politicians.

"Fortunately we've got translators. I write one story and send it to both papers. They each then package it up for local consumption."

"It keeps the costs down" said Ventrice wryly. "I approve of that. Anyway regretfully I must keep circulating. That's *my* job. Look after this lovely lady John."
As Ventrice melted into the crowd Foster looked at Debbie. "Well he certainly is a charmer."
"Are you just a little bit jealous?" whispered Debbie.
Foster straightened his tie and stood more upright. "Come on, let's get another drink."

The crowd was silenced by a message over the PA system. "Ladies and Gentlemen, please welcome the leader of Our Nation Party, Mr Harold Fleming."
A large, red-faced man stood up to address the crowd. "He looks more like a farmer than a politician" whispered Foster.
Debbie giggled. "Well that's probably because he is. Didn't you read your briefing notes? He owns a large station in outback Queensland. You know Australia has a long tradition of farmers turning to politics."
"Perhaps they think they're the landed gentry" replied Foster as Fleming began his speech.
He had a voice that matched the size of man he was. He doesn't really need a microphone, thought Foster.
"Ladies and Gentlemen, I will be mercifully brief. I would like to introduce you to our guest of honour, Mr Francis Ventrice. As you all know, Francis has helped to take the popularity of his UKIP party to ever greater heights. I believe there is much we can learn from him as our party follows a similar course. Without further ado I give you Mr Francis Ventrice."
The crowd applauded and Ventrice took his place at the microphone. He was relaxed and composed as he took a moment to scan his audience.

"Ladies and Gentlemen" he began. "First let me tell you that I am honoured to be invited to your beautiful country. I have long admired the energy and can-do spirit of Australians. This address tonight will be very brief. After all the purpose of the evening is for us all to get to know each other before the first public meeting takes place tomorrow night."

"Your party leaders have seen, as we in UKIP also have, that we share a common concern about what is happening to our countries, and we have come to the same conclusions. The traditional parties have let us down time and time again. We need a new voice."

His voice had risen to a crescendo. "Ladies and Gentlemen, we *are* that voice and, starting tomorrow, we will make ourselves heard. But tonight". He paused for effect and said in a much quieter tone, "Let's have another drink and get to know one another. Thank you."

Ventrice left the podium to thunderous applause.

"He's a showman all right" said Foster. I wonder what he's got in store for us tomorrow night."

The waiters were back circulating in the crowd carrying trays of Australian bubbly and orange juice for the abstainers.

Debbie and Foster helped themselves to another bubbly. Foster looked around. "You haven't noticed where the men's room is?"

Debbie pointed to the far left corner. "It's over there down a short corridor."

"Just hold my drink will you. I won't be long."

As Foster threaded his way through the crowd Debbie was aware of a large man approaching her; Ed Hopkins.

"Hello Ed" she beamed. "Is it all going well for you tonight?"

"Yes it's fine. Look Debbie I've got a message for you – from Francis."

"Really, what is it?"

"Well you know that it's a busy time for him tonight and the whole of tomorrow but he would like to meet you again. He's asked me to ask you if you would like to have dinner with him at the hotel on Wednesday evening. Will you still be around?"

"Yes I will. We are flying down to Sydney on Thursday morning. Tell him I'd love to."

"Great, he said to see you in the small bar about seven thirty. Is that OK?"

"That's fine. Thanks."

"Super, he'll be very pleased. Sorry I must go. More mingling with party officials I'm afraid."

Gardner wandered off as Foster returned.

"Wasn't that Ventrice' minder?"

"Yes, Ed. He's a nice guy."

"He looks more like hired muscle to me."

"Don't let appearances deceive you John. He's a charming and intelligent man. He just looks like a gorilla. It's probably useful for the role he's in."

"Mm, what did he want?"

"I've been invited to dinner at our hotel on Wednesday night."

"What with him?"

"No silly, with Francis. Ed was just passing on the message."

"That's a bit rich isn't it? Couldn't he have asked you himself?"

"Come on, he's a busy man and he's the star of the show."

"You turned him down of course?"

"No, I've accepted."

"You've accepted! What about me?"

"You'll have to eat alone that night. I'm sure you won't starve."

"Who else will be there?"

"Just me I suppose. John I do believe you're getting jealous again."

Foster looked down at the floor. "It's not that. Well just a bit. You and him alone. Isn't that living dangerously?"

Debbie put her arms around him. "Come on John. It's a respectable hotel in the middle of the city and I know what I'm doing. I've coped with more determined men than Francis Ventrice. The better we get to know him the more interesting your stories will be."

"I guess" said Foster. "But just watch yourself."

"I'll be OK John. Come on, one more drink and we'll head off to bed."

"Best offer I've had all day" he grinned.

Chapter 29

The day after the first public meeting in Brisbane Ventrice slept in late. The meeting had finished very late and he was exhausted. However he was also elated. His speech had connected with the crowd and was favourably reported. He lay in bed with a morning coffee and scanned the two morning newspapers he had been given; The Brisbane Courier Mail and The Australian. He noted that there were very few newspapers in Australia compared with the UK. He supposed it had something to do with the smaller population.

But he didn't mind. His coverage had been generally favourable. One analyst in The Australian had compared his speech to one of Adolf Hitler's but the rest had seemed favourably impressed.

He switched on the TV and was delighted at the coverage there also, including a video of part of his speech. It was all going well. He could relax and enjoy the rest of the morning and have some lunch. In the afternoon he had a long session with Our Nation officials which was necessary but would probably be a little tiresome. Still he had the evening to look forward to.

His dinner date with Debbie was at seven thirty and he was very excited about it. She had seriously impressed him. He wanted a closer look at that lovely body and to take her to bed, but he also knew she was a confident and intelligent woman. Best play it carefully he thought. She'll need to be coaxed into bed and I don't want to frighten her off by moving too quickly. Still he had a plan in his head. Over the next few days he would draw her in ever closer for the ultimate moment.

These thoughts excited him. He couldn't have Debbie right now but there were other options. He picked up his bedside phone and dialled the number of the suite next to his where the twins had been installed.

Grace answered. Ventrice smiled. He didn't really know whether he preferred Grace or Alice but then who needed to choose when he had both.

"Hi Grace" said Ventrice. "What are you up to?"

"Nothing much Francis. How are you this fine morning?"

"Oh, happy but restless. I think I need some relaxation. I've got a nice big bed here. Why don't you both join me?"

"That sounds great Francis. We'll be right along."

Ventrice had barely put down the phone when the connecting door was opened and the twins walked in looking very eager. Ventrice admired the two young bodies clad only in flimsy negligees. "Good morning ladies. Good to see you as always. Come on in, but I do think you're a little overdressed for what I have in mind."

The girls looked at each other and giggled. They threw off their negligees revealing two beautiful naked brown bodies and climbed into bed on either side of him.

**

While Ventrice was enjoying his morning exercise his two Australian security men were sitting several floors below in a quiet corner of the hotel coffee shop.

Presently they were joined by a third man, known to them only as "Ben".

"Morning Ben" said Buckingham wryly as Michael Robinson sat down. "Morning Trevor, morning John, how are you this morning?"

"Fine" said Buckingham. Whiting just smiled weakly.

"OK, to business guys. You've had a couple of days to observe Ventrice. Have you had any further thoughts on how to deal with him?"

Buckingham looked around as if he were frightened he would be overheard. He seemed satisfied.

"As a matter of fact we have. In fact, more than that we've got a plan. I had a chat with Ventrice yesterday and he's given me an idea. One thing he really wants to do while we are in Adelaide is to look around the wineries, sample some wines and take some of his precious photographs."

"OK, but how does that help us?"

"Well Tony here has a lot more detailed knowledge of the Adelaide area than me and he's come up with a good option."

Perhaps he's not as dumb as he looks, thought Robinson. "Go on."

"We'll take Ventrice out for a tour of the hills area and show him the splendid photo opportunities at the Whispering Wall."

"What on earth is that?"

"It's actually a large dam along the Gorge Road. Its circular shape lets people talk to each other from opposite ends and they can hear quite clearly what the other end is saying."

Robinson was becoming impatient with the tourist chat. "But what's that got to do with our plans?"

"Patience Ben" replied Buckingham. "The dam is very high with a sheer drop to the valley floor. Ventrice wants to see it on his way to The Hills wineries and take some photos. If he were to fall over the edge it would be fatal."

He paused and smiled.

"And your Ventrice problem would be solved."

Robinson could see the possibilities but what about the problems?

"If it's a tourist spot wouldn't there be lots of people there?"

"Yes, later in the day. We've convinced Ventrice that the best photo ops are very early in the morning. It should be empty then. There is a bigger problem though."

"I thought there might be. What is it?"

"Well Ventrice never goes anywhere without that sidekick of his – Hopkins."

"Couldn't you deal with him as well?"

"Well we could I guess, but it's a risk. He apparently is a very capable guy. And we want it to look like an accident don't we?"

Robinson scratched his chin and looked concerned.

"That would certainly be the preferred option. It gives us all a better chance to get away. So what needs to happen?"

"We just need to make sure that Hopkins doesn't come along on this trip."

Robinson thought for a minute.

"We can work that out. Just leave it with me and I'll make sure Hopkins is in no fit state to join you."

"How will you do that?"

"Don't worry about the details guys. I've got contacts in the tour party. We'll take care of Mr Hopkins. Otherwise it seems a good plan."

Buckingham was happy. "It's all down to Tony here. Didn't I tell you he was a really useful guy?"

"You did Greg, or should I say Trevor. Congratulations Tony. I'm impressed. Let's see. That's only six days away. You guys finalise the detail of your plans. I'll make sure Ventrice doesn't change his mind and I'll organise some airline tickets in case we have to get out quick. How does that sound?"

"Perfect" replied Buckingham.

**

Francis Ventrice was sitting in a quiet corner of the hotel's smaller bar. He wanted to be there a few minutes early both to collect his thoughts and to have the visual delight of the approach of Debbie Simmons.

His day had had its ups and downs. Following his analysis of the press reports of his speech the night before, he spent the rest of the morning in bed with the twins. Exhausted by the two eager younger women he had another nap and woke up ready for lunch.

As he looked forward to lunch he was reminded that lunch would be with the leaders of Our Nation, followed by a meeting to analyse the night before and to plan the strategy for the next public meeting in Sydney. He knew it was necessary and he had to make the best of it. He regarded some of the Our Nation leadership as worthy but dull and he wasn't expecting a riveting afternoon.

As it turned out some of the party's younger members were present and the discussions were more interesting and animated than he was expecting. One young lady, introduced to him only as Emily, he found particularly interesting. Tall, elegant, attractive and intelligent, he was immediately drawn to her. Perhaps she could offer more than political discussion; she could be an interesting challenge.

But Emily would have to wait. He was already planning a campaign of conquest of Debbie Simmons. Two, in parallel with his very demanding schedule, could be considered to be over-egging the pudding. He would have to place Emily on hold until he could see the outcome of his plans for Debbie.

Now he sat in the hotel bar sipping on his gin and tonic, waiting for Debbie to arrive.

She arrived practically on time looking stunning in a white mini length dress which showed off her beautiful tanned legs. This one is a stunner, he thought as he stood up to greet her.

"Good to see you" he said, I was afraid you might not come."

"Well here I am" replied Debbie. "You don't think I would stand you up after accepting your kind offer?"

"I just thought you might be put off by my sending Ed across to ask you. I don't normally do things like that but I couldn't get a minute to myself."

"Certainly not. I know how busy you must be. You can make up for it by buying me a drink."

"Of course, how remiss of me." Ventrice mused that he was behaving more like a schoolboy than a man of substance. She was really getting to him. "What would you like?"

"What's that you've got there?"

"Just a common or garden G&T. I would have had some wine but I haven't decided what to eat yet."

"I'll have one of those as well then. It's been a hard day" she said with a pained expression.

"Why, what have you been doing?" asked Ventrice looking concerned.

"Lounging around the pool mostly" she said with a big grin. "Still you work up a thirst you know."

Ventrice was smitten. Not just beautiful and intelligent but a sense of humour as well. He beckoned over a waiter and ordered a G&T for Debbie and another for himself.

While they waited for the drinks Ventrice related what he had been doing during the afternoon, omitting any reference to Emily. She was duly sympathetic. "I guess in your job you have to take the lows with the highs."

Ventrice was about to reply when the drinks arrived. He signed the docket and turned to Debbie.

"Now young lady, you are going to educate me."

"Why Sir, I don't know what you mean" said Debbie coquettishly.

Ventrice laughed. "No, I've been looking at the menu and there are several dishes we don't often see in England. I'd be delighted if you would guide me through."

"Sure, anything in particular?"

"What are Moreton Bay Bugs?"

"Oh, they're lovely. They are like a small lobster or crayfish. Maybe more like a langoustine."

"And chilly bugs?"

"That's the same thing but in a chilly sauce."

"I like the sound of that. I enjoy most seafood. What's this Barramundi?"

"Now you're talking "said Debbie with her eyes gleaming. "It's one of my favourites. It's a local fish, a very meaty fish. Absolutely delicious. I recommend it."

"Debbie you've convinced me. It's going to be a seafood evening for me. I'm having the chilly bugs followed by the Barramundi. What about you?"

"Actually I really love both of those. I think I'll have the same. You can order the bugs as a shared dish for two."

"Good, that's settled. Now for a nice white wine to go with it. I seem to remember you're partial to an ice cold chardonnay."

"Yes, that's fine by me, but what about you?"

"Well I don't drink much Australian wine at home but, hey, when in Rome as they say."

"Except you're in Brisbane, but I get the idea. Would you like to choose one? You have a reputation for being a bit of a wine buff."

"You know" said Ventrice, "I think you know a lot about me whereas I know very little about you. So what is the Debbie Simmons story?"

Over dinner Debbie told Ventrice all about herself, or at least what he needed to know. She told him she worked part time for her uncle, based in Adelaide, who ran a sort of employment agency, but that she wasn't needed full time so she took on other odd jobs like this one. She explained that she met the new recruits from the UK and escorted them to their mining jobs in the outback."

"So you've seen a lot of Australia then" said Ventrice. "It's a huge country. I really had no idea of the scale until I came here."

"True, but I mostly work in South Australia and the Northern Territory, which is closer to home." She laughed. "I say close but it's still sometimes a two hour flight north followed by hours in a truck on rough roads."

"It must be fascinating. Funny I was only reading recently about some trouble you had in Adelaide with English tourists. One was murdered and the other kidnapped."

"Yes, Alan Warner and Charlie Winter."

"You know the story then?"

"Know it? I was part of it."

"Really, I'm fascinated. Tell me all about it."

Debbie related the events leading up to the climax at Forster Lookout. She explained that her uncle had asked her to look after visiting reporter John Foster and Warner's fiancée, Carol Mannering. She carefully avoided any mention of her passionate affair with Foster.

Ventrice was impressed. The more Debbie explained what had happened the more he recalled the story he had read.

"Wasn't someone hurt or killed in the shootout" he asked.

"It's a bit overstated to call it a shootout. Tony Andersen, the kidnapper, fell off the cliff into the river and it's a big drop. We thought he would have been killed but the police now think he survived and is on the run. The only other casualty was little me."

"Wow, what happened to you?"

"I was shot in the leg by Andersen, but I don't think he meant to. He stumbled and the gun went off."

"That's amazing. You seem to have recovered from it."

"Yeah I'm fine. Just a little scar on my leg."

"That's a shame. Such nice legs too. Show me."

"Really Mr Ventrice" she said demurely. "It's quite high up."

Ventrice smiled. But if you don't show me I might think you were making it all up."

"No it's ridgy-didge. That's real in your language. Tell you what."

She looked around and saw there was no-one close by.

"Look" she said as she slowly pulled up her dress to reveal a scar near the top of her thigh.

"Now do you believe me?"

Ventrice felt a strong stirring as he looked at Debbie's thigh and the edge of her small white panties. He laughed to break the tension. "I never doubted you for a minute" he said as Debbie pulled her dress down. "They did a very neat job of stitching you up."

"So there you go" she said, "this job was probably offered to me as some kind of recompense for my efforts."

After desert and coffee Ventrice realised they had been talking for hours. He knew he had an early start and a busy day in the morning. He decided to play it with cool with Debbie for now but to make sure there would be another opportunity.

"Look Debbie" he said. I must turn in soon as I've got a really full-on day tomorrow. But the day after I've got the day off for a bit of R&R. In the morning I'm doing the Sydney Harbour Bridge Climb with Ed, and then later in the afternoon I'm going to one of the local beaches with the girls. Would you like to come along?"

"The girls?"

"Oh, yes. My two PAs. They're twins. Lovely girls. Bridge climbing isn't their thing but they wanted to go to one of Sydney's famous beaches. You'd love them. Why don't you come along? We've hired a minibus with a driver and we'll have a picnic and some drinks with us. You would really enjoy it. Say you'll come."

"Are you sure you've got room for me?"

"Plenty, there's just the four of us. Ed is coming too. He likes to keep an eye on me. Well?"

"Yes OK, I'd love to."

"Great" said Ventrice. "The minibus is coming to the hotel car park at three o'clock. We'll meet you there. Don't forget your bathers. I did like those black ones you wore at the pool."

Debbie laughed. "You only like them because they're very small. I might want to wear something a bit more respectable if I'm going out with someone of your status."

"Bugger my status" said Ventrice. "See you three o'clock on Friday then. OK?"

"OK Francis, and thanks for a lovely evening." She kissed him on the cheek.

They departed to their respective rooms, Ventrice delighted at how this affair was going and looking forward to further progress. Debbie had mixed emotions. She understood perfectly where Ventrice was heading. She enjoyed his company very much and these liaisons would certainly help John with his stories. All the same she needed to be careful. She was associating with a man who was used to getting what he wanted.

Chapter 30

Thursday was another busy day of travel for all those taking part in the tour.
The Ventrice inner circle, Ventrice himself, the twins, Ed Hopkins, took a late morning flight to Sydney.
Their Australian minders were also present although Ventrice insisted they kept a low profile and travelled in a different part of the aircraft. After a short flight of just over an hour they were met at Sydney's Kingsford Smith Airport by local officials from Our Nation and were whisked away discreetly in a luxurious minibus to their hotel in the centre of Sydney.
Once again the Ventrice inner circle was housed in three adjacent suites, this time with views down to Circular Quay, The Opera House and the Harbour Bridge. The view was enhanced by the sparkling sunshine that greeted them.
"What a beautiful place!" exclaimed Grace. The others had to agree; Sydney was turning on its best for them.
They chose to have lunch at one of the many delightful restaurants on Circular Quay. Ventrice wore a hat and sunglasses in order to appear less conspicuous, but it was obvious that some people knew who he was. A sympathetic waiter, impressed not only by Ventrice but also by the twins, found the four of them a pleasant corner table where they were less likely to be spotted.
The Australian bodyguards were instructed to buy a sandwich or similar and hang around on the Quay – and try not to look too conspicuous.
They sat on a bench eating a burger while the inner circle had a splendid seafood lunch accompanied by fine wines.
"They sure know how to look after themselves" observed Tony.

Greg had been pondering on the situation and how it might affect their plans. "They sure do. But what bothers me a bit is that Ventrice and that guy Gardner, the tour organiser, seem to want to keep us at arm's length. Are they just being a bit overconfident or do they smell a rat?"

"What d'ya mean?"

"Well they act just as if they would rather we weren't there at all. Still, as long as we can make sure that Gardner can't come on the wine tour we should be OK."

"I suppose so" admitted Tony.

"Just think mate. In a week's time Ventrice will be in a box and we'll have the money to party like that."

The assassins sat quietly munching on their burgers, each thinking of the future they would soon be enjoying.

**

John Foster was having a very different day. They had taken a morning flight to Sydney and had been picked up by Debbie's mother Maria, who drove them to the family home in Leichardt, in the heart of Sydney's Inner West Italian community.

Maria was short and had dark olive skin, a typical southern Italian. Initially Foster was amazed that Debbie could be her daughter; they were so different, but then he noticed their facial features definitely said mother and daughter. She must get her height and colour from her father he thought. He remembered that Debbie had said her father was not Italian.

But the more he talked with Maria the more he could pick the family similarities. Like Debbie Maria was friendly, outgoing and intelligent. No wonder Debbie's father had snapped her up.

He finally got to meet him when they reached the house after a thirty minute drive. Russ Simmons, short for

Russell which he never used, was tall, well over six feet, and skinny, with a mop of light brown hair.

He smiled and gave his daughter a big hug and then turned to Foster. "Welcome to Sydney John. I've heard all about you."

"Thanks Russ" replied Foster."I didn't think the news had travelled that far."

"Oh don't you worry. Your story hit the papers here big time. You're both very lucky you didn't come to grief."

"Yes we're very lucky; it could have been nasty."

"Anyway sit down and I'll get some beer and you can tell me all about it. I guess you are a beer drinker with a name like that."

Foster smiled at the by now familiar joke. "Yep, Foster by name but not by choice of tipple. In Adelaide I was drinking Coopers."

"I'm not sure what's in the fridge but I'm sure we can find you something more interesting than Fosters. What about you Debbie? No, don't tell me – a cold chardonnay. I think we can manage that."

"I'll have one of those as well" said Maria. "After all it's an occasion isn't it?"

They chatted over the drinks and between them Foster and Debbie related the detail of their encounter with Tony Andersen in Mannum.

"And he got away?" asked Russ incredulously.

"We weren't sure at first" said Debbie. "If you saw the height of those cliffs you wouldn't believe that anyone could survive a fall from them. But the police are convinced that he did survive it and that someone has helped him to escape."

"And they are pretty sure they know who it was" added Foster. "But he denies it and they've got no evidence so they're waiting and watching"."

"It's creepy isn't it" said Maria. "To think that he might still be around somewhere. I wonder what he'll do next."

"It's the same problem in England" said Foster. "Tony's brother Greg has disappeared and they are looking for him as well."

"Well I guess it's not your problem anymore" said Russ.

"No I suppose not. But I feel like it's a story that's ended prematurely. I would really like to take it to its conclusion, whatever that is."

"Yes I can understand that. You never know he might show up in the near future. In the meantime you've got Francis Ventrice to follow."

"Yes I have. I don't quite know what to make of him. When you meet him he's a very nice guy, full of charisma, but when he starts speaking he seems to turn into someone else. What do you make of him Russ?"

"I think he's just another right wing demagogue with dreams of power. It's just like Our Nation here. They spout all the generalities but they haven't a clue what they would do if they ever were to get any power."

"You're probably right but on the surface he's very charming." He looked at Debbie. "Isn't he Debbie?"

"Oh don't you worry dad. It's just that I met him at the hotel the other day and he invited me to dinner. He's a very charming man."

"And what about tomorrow?" teased Foster.

"I'm going off for an afternoon at the beach with his party, that's all."

Russ laughed. "I gather you don't approve John. I must admit, in my experience men like that are after just one thing. You watch yourself my girl."

"Come on dad. You've brought me up to look after myself. You men think all women are naïve but we're not."

"No I suppose not but all the same stay alert. Anyway can you stay for dinner? Maria has cooked up something quite special."

"Do you think I could come here without having some of mum's cooking? Sure we can but we need to go back to the hotel later. We've both got a busy day tomorrow."

She glanced at Foster and teased him. "Haven't we John?"

"Some of us" said Foster. "While you are lazing in luxury at the beach I'll be writing up details of Ventrice' boring bridge climb.

"Someone's got to do it" said Debbie cheerfully.

**

They chatted and drank and had a splendid Italian style dinner, courtesy of Maria. Foster was very impressed.

"That was fantastic Maria. Can you cook like this Debbie?"

For once Debbie looked embarrassed as Maria replied for her. "She never had the time or the patience to learn how to cook properly. Always her head was full of other things. Pity the man she marries; he'll have to cook for himself or starve."

It occurred to Foster that with looks like hers she didn't need to be able to cook but he kept the thought to himself.

Debbie simply said quietly "No one has asked me yet mama."

Better change the subject, thought Foster. "We need to be going soon. I've got to be up early to cover Ventrice' Bridge Climb. You can have a lie in and prepare for your strenuous afternoon on the beach."

"You're just jealous you weren't invited" said Debbie with a twinkle in her eye. "Besides I'm not sure I'd trust you with those twins around."

"Twins?" asked Russ.

"Yes, everywhere he goes he has these two gorgeous Thai girls with him. He calls them his PAs but well, you have to wonder."

"He's a bit of a character this Mr. Ventrice I think. Maybe John is right. You need to watch yourself."

"It's good to know you're all worried about me. Come on John, call a cab and we'll get you home so you can have an early night before your gruelling day."

"It's been good meeting you John" said Russ. "I hope we'll see you again."

Debbie reached up and kissed him on the cheek. "So do I."

As the taxi took them the short drive to the city Foster was very content. It was nice to feel part of a family again.

"Thanks for a lovely day" he said. "I really like your folks."

"I think they liked you as well."

"Was that true what Maria said about your cooking?"

"Pretty much. Haven't you noticed how often I eat out?"

They laughed. Foster realised that the parting that was inevitably going to happen soon was going to be devastating for both of them.

"I know what you're thinking" said Debbie. "Let's just enjoy it while we can. Cheer up. We've both got a busy day tomorrow."

Chapter 31

It was a mild sunny day in Sydney as John Foster left the hotel for the short walk to The Rocks, the oldest part of central Sydney stretching from Circular Quay across to Millers Point and Darling Harbour.

The place he sought was at the nearer part of The Rocks so he was there in a few minutes, to find the area already cordoned off by the police. Cumberland Street is where the meeting place for the Sydney Bridge Climb is located, in an area just west of the bridge itself.

It was early in the morning but already a small crowd of interested onlookers had arrived. Foster also recognised some of the reporters covering the tour.

They hadn't long to wait. Presently a large Lexus limousine arrived and pulled in alongside the entrance to Bridgeclimb. First out was Ed Hopkins, followed by Francis Ventrice. Ventrice gave a cheery wave to the crowd and headed for the entrance followed by Ed. Two other large men emerged from the limousine and followed Ventrice to the entrance.

Two more bodyguards I suppose, thought Foster as he watched them pass through the entrance doors. Although they had their backs to him he had an odd feeling he had seen them somewhere before. He couldn't think where but the feeling was so strong he decided to hang around until the climb was completed and he could get a better look. After about half an hour, in which the climbers change into their climbing clothes and experienced the pre-climb drill, three figures emerged from The Tunnel for the first stage of the climb. Foster recognised Ventrice and Ed Hopkins. The third man he assumed was the guide; all climbing groups have to have a qualified guide.

Foster assumed that the other two men had stayed behind at the depot. He was correct in his assumption; Ventrice hadn't wanted them to accompany him on the climb, for which the two men were not unhappy as neither was particularly fond of heights.

Foster knew he now had a long wait as the climb itself lasts some three hours. He decided to take a break and found a small café where he had a very welcome hot Panini and coffee, all the more pleasing as he had skipped breakfast to be there early.

He had left Debbie sleeping soundly. He knew he wouldn't see much of her today. By the time he got back she would be getting ready for her trip to the beach with Ventrice. Still he would see her again this evening.

He took his time with his breakfast and read the local newspaper, The Sydney Morning Herald. The coverage of the Ventrice tour in it was not as extensive as the coverage in the Murdoch press. Perhaps that reflects the views of the owners, he thought. Presently he strolled back to the Bridgeclimb entrance and was dismayed to see that the crowd was much bigger. He managed to find himself a spot where he could see the entrance, farther away than he would have liked, but he had his camera with a powerful telephoto lens, which gave him confidence that he could get some clear photographs.

He didn't have long to wait. The entrance door opened and Ventrice emerged. He waved to the crowd and signed some autographs for people at the front.

A small PA system had been set up by the door, courtesy of a local TV station and Ventrice was invited to speak to the crowds. "We want to know if you enjoyed our Bridge Climb Mr Ventrice."

Ever the showman, Ventrice stepped up to the microphone. "Ladies and gentlemen" he began. "Let me tell you that I have just had one of the most amazing experiences of my life. The climb itself is exhilarating and the views of your beautiful city and harbour from the top are exceptional. I take my hat off to the people who made this possible and I would like to personally thank Charlie here, our guide, for conducting us safely around the bridge and for being so nice about it. Give the people a wave Charlie."

An embarrassed Charlie, still in his climbing suit, stepped forward from the entrance and gave the crowd a wave and a smile.

Ventrice continued. "Thank you Charlie. And now folks, if you don't mind I intend to see some more of your beautiful city before our presentation tonight. Thank you all for your interest."

With that he moved to the waiting limousine, closely accompanied by Ed Hopkins. He smiled and waved once more before getting into the car amid cheers and applause. Ever the showman, thought Foster. Now where are the other two?

Almost immediately the two large men came through the door and made a beeline for the back seat of the limo. Foster was too intent on taking his photographs to study them intently; that could come later when he had a bit of free time and could see a bigger image on his laptop. But the feeling was still with him that he knew them from somewhere.

Meanwhile he might as well enjoy a stroll around The Rocks and some lunch. He had nothing much else to do. Ventrice was having his beach afternoon and the press had been politely asked to keep away and give Ventrice some privacy. Not that anyone had been told which of Sydney's many beaches they would be aiming for. Debbie would be with Ventrice enjoying the beach. He still wasn't sure how he felt about that. He could see the logic in having Debbie close to Ventrice as an informer on the inside but he was also concerned that the woman he loved was being actively chased by a rich and powerful man.

**

At three o'clock Debbie was waiting in the hotel entrance. She was looking forward to a trip to the beach and to meeting the twins, who were a big hit with the photographers. She also enjoyed the company of Ventrice and Ed was a nice guy so she was expecting a pleasant afternoon. She had her tiny black bikini on under her shorts and T-shirt. I might as well keep Francis happy she reasoned.

Almost on time a small minibus arrived. The Ventrice party must have been warned that the bus was imminent and arrived at the same time. Ventrice looked around and seemed happy and relieved when he spotted Debbie sitting in the palm studded foyer.

He came over to her and took her hand. "I'm so glad you could make it. Come and meet the girls."

He led her to the bus which the twins were already examining and introduced them. They both gave Debbie a hug and started asking her girly questions about Sydney and the shopping there. Debbie was relieved. She had wondered whether they would be friendly or not. It seemed that they cheerfully accepted her company.

She said hello to Ed and joined the others in the bus. The driver, a short, cheerful, olive-skinned man, who Debbie judged to be Turkish, like many Sydney taxi drivers, watched them board and took his place at the wheel.

He turned round to face his passengers with a big smile. "I wanted to welcome you. It is not every day I get to drive such a well known person. I am honoured. I did not also expect to have three such beautiful ladies in my bus. The beach you want to go to is only about twenty minutes away and the afternoon peak is not yet upon us, so please relax and it should be an easy trip."

He turned around, started the vehicle and eased it out into the afternoon traffic. Almost immediately they were moving onto the famous bridge and heading for the North Shore. From the northern side of the bridge, on the very wide freeway, the view back to the city encompassing the harbour, the bridge and the Opera House, was spectacular.

Soon they left the freeway and headed off on the Mosman Road. "Which beach are we heading for?" asked Debbie, who had initially thought they were going to Manly.

Ventrice replied. "We've been told there are two nice beaches up past Mosman, Obelisk Beach and Cobblers Beach. We'll try Obelisk first and see if we like that. If not we'll go on to Cobblers. They are both quite close. I didn't want to spend the day stuck in a bus. Are you OK with that?"

Debbie smiled. "Yes, that's fine. I had assumed we were heading for Manly that's all."

"We thought of Manly but decided it was too far with the weekend traffic."

"No that's cool. Obelisk should be fine" said Debbie and turned back to watch out of the window. She thought it was an interesting choice for a politician to make as both beaches were frequented by topless and nude bathers. She wondered if Ventrice knew that.

Very shortly they had arrived. The driver stopped at one of the paths which led down to the beach.

"I'll be parked just up the road" he said. "Phone me when you want to be picked up."

He handed Ventrice a business card and got back in the bus. Ventrice and the girls were carrying bags which looked suspiciously like a picnic and Ed carried a heavy looking Esky. Debbie could guess that the Esky had cold drinks, very nice ones she assumed knowing Ventrice as she did. She wondered guiltily if she should have brought something.

Ventrice seemed to have read her mind. "I had the hotel pack us a few nice things" he said looking at Debbie. "Let's go and find ourselves a good spot."

They walked down the path and found that the beach was not particularly crowded. It was midweek and by now the summer heat had peaked and the weather was turning to autumn. Still it was a pleasant warm sunny day and they had a choice of several suitable spots.

Ventrice chose a place where they were not too obvious to passersby, dropped the lunch basket and promptly removed his shirt and shorts. He had a good body and Debbie admired the way he looked in his designer swimmers. Ed kept his shirt on. "I burn easily" he explained. "It's the curse of my Scottish ancestry."

The twins removed their T-shirts and shorts, revealing they wore only small bikini bottoms underneath. They ran around like excited children. They must have known it was a topless beach, thought Debbie as she removed her clothes to reveal the tiny black bikini.

Ventrice looked at her and laughed. "So you decided not to come in something more respectable then."

"I don't have anything with me that's more respectable I'm afraid. Do you approve?"

"I certainly do" he replied. "Although it would appear that, small as it is you appear to be overdressed by the standards of this beach."

"Well I'm not going to go naked. And just think what it would do to your reputation if you were photographed with a naked lady. Aren't you taking a bit of a risk in choosing this beach?"

Ventrice appeared unconcerned. "I learned long ago that being seen with beautiful women, in whatever states of dress or undress, tends to enhance my reputation rather than destroy it. After all, I am just having an innocent picnic am I not?"

Debbie laughed. "Innocent is not the word I would have used to describe you Mr Ventrice."

"Oh, Mr Ventrice is it now? You've gone all formal on me again. I hope I haven't offended you. Please wear whatever makes you feel comfortable."

"Just joking" replied Debbie. "But since this is a topless beach I may as well join in the spirit. It'll be good to keep my tan nice and even."

She took off her bikini top to reveal a pair of perfect breasts, evenly tanned. She noticed the effect she had on Ventrice.

He recovered quickly and quipped "you must have done this before to have such an even tan."

"Let's just say that my flat in Adelaide has a nice private balcony. Anyway what about a swim? You too Ed. Take that shirt off and let's have a dip. You can always put it back on after."

Ed looked up and smiled. "You're quite a salesman Debbie. OK let's do it. My first swim in Australian water."

They ran to the water and joined the twins who were already splashing about in the shallows. Ventrice was quite a strong swimmer and was quite happy swimming up and down until the twins shouted "what about the picnic Francis?"

"You're right of course" replied Ventrice. "It's time for something nice. I'll race you back."

He ran back to their spot and was the first to get there. The twins and Debbie sauntered back, accompanied by Ed who seemed not inclined to run. Once back Ed was careful to put his shirt back on.

"Let me be mother" said Ventrice as he opened the picnic basket. "Ed how about you fix us some bubbly?"

In no time at all they sitting on the sand enjoying the finest food the hotel could muster, accompanied by bottles of expensive Australian bubbly.

"This is the life" exclaimed Ventrice. Let's have some photos. Alice, Grace, you stand over there with your backs to the water. Debbie you stand between them."

Debbie did as she was asked and posed between the twins, noting that she was at least six inches taller than them. Ventrice was like a child with a new toy. He arranged the girls in several poses and ran off a series of shots. "Perfect" he exclaimed. "You three really look good together."

No one had noticed that behind them, further along the beach, a professional photographer with a Turkish brother was also taking pictures of the group with a large telephoto lens.

They spent the rest of the afternoon eating, drinking and frolicking in the sea. They stayed until the sun was starting to go down, bringing with it the oncoming chill of the evening.

They packed up their belongings, dressed, phoned the driver and headed back to the drop off point. Ventrice walked alongside Debbie."Thanks Debbie, it's been a really nice day. Will I see you again?"

"I'm around for the whole tour" she replied. "I've enjoyed today too. Thank you very much."

"Look Debbie, tonight I have to meet one or two people and tomorrow I'll be very busy all day with the Sydney event. But on Sunday I'm having a small cocktail party in my suite in the afternoon. I would love you to come."

"That sounds like fun. Any interesting guests?"

"Just one or two special people" Ventrice replied vaguely. "Come up about two o'clock and be prepared to write off the day."

Debbie wondered about this vague sounding invitation but decided to take the risk. "OK I'll be there. It sounds intriguing."

They got into the minibus and returned to Sydney city centre. At the hotel Debbie left the others with a cheery farewell. "Thanks for a great day guys and Francis, good luck with your event tonight."

Ventrice was pleased. His scheme was maturing nicely.

Chapter 32

John Foster was enjoying a lazy Saturday morning. He knew he would be having a late night as he had to cover the Sydney event in the Ventrice tour. He was lying in bed with Debbie beside him.

She was reading a magazine. He started to peruse the morning papers to see if there was anything interesting. First he tackled the Australian. It was a paper he had come to enjoy as it reminded him of some of the more serious British newspapers.

The only mention of the Ventrice event that evening was a piece he had written himself and was mainly there to remind the public of the event. He noted that so far there had been no hostile press. Ventrice was being treated gently by the media, in contrast to some of the comment he was subjected to in the British Tabloids.

He put down the Australian and picked up one of the tabloids. What a difference. The front page headline read "Pommie Politician's Staff Frolic Topless". He was immediately interested. He looked harder at the picture and couldn't believe what he was seeing - Debbie standing between the twins topless.

"My god, look at this. Debbie what have you been up to?"
"What are you talking about?" she replied. Foster silently passed her the paper.
"Oh my goodness" she giggled. "It's a good photo of us. I wonder who took that."
"Good photo" exploded Foster. "There you are topless on the front page and all you can say is 'good photo'. I thought you were just having a quiet day at the beach."
"We were. It's just that it's a topless beach and everyone else was topless so ...."

"Well you're famous now, or should I say infamous. Look what it says. Ventrice PAs topless with mystery blonde."

"Really, I'm a mystery blonde now am I? I've never been a mystery blonde before."

"You're treating this as a big joke. You expose yourself to Ventrice then you finish up exposing yourself to half of Sydney. Have you no shame?"

"Calm down John" said Debbie icily. "You're getting pompous and upset over nothing. You know better than I do that this type of trivial news is gone and forgotten in a day or two." She laughed. "I guess it's my fifteen minutes of fame."

Foster was still upset. "I'm amazed you are taking it so calmly. You are spotted topless with Ventrice then you tell me you're going to his private cocktail party tomorrow. What about me?"

"What do you mean 'what about me'? Don't forget I'm doing all this for you to help you get the more personal stories."

"You seem to be enjoying it."

"Of course I'm enjoying it. Good food, good wine, good company, but so what? What's your problem John? You're just jealous of Ventrice aren't you? Are you afraid I'm going to dump you and run off with him?"

"No of course not. But did you have to take off all your clothes for him?"

"Oh come on John. It was a topless beach. There were lots of other people around and I still had my knickers on."

"That's all very well. But what will he want next time, knickers as well?"

Debbie leant over and put her arms round him. "Look John, the only person I take them off for is you. You'll have to trust me on that one. If Ventrice comes on too heavy I'll deal with it. He's not going to rape me you know."

Foster began to calm down. "All right, but how are we going to deal with this?"

"Simple, we don't do anything at all. It'll blow over."

"I suppose so, but I don't think you should go to the event tonight. I think the appearance of the 'mystery blonde' might cause a bit of a stir."

"You're right. I don't want to be harassed by the press and I wouldn't want to make things difficult for Francis. I'll stay away from this one. By the time we get to Adelaide it will have blown over."

She gave him a wicked smile.

"Speaking of being harassed by the press, isn't it time you did some harassing. I've missed you. Come here."

**

After an exhausting morning in bed the two lovers emerged to go for a dip in the pool before lunch. Although the weather was only mild rather than warm the hotel pool was heated and they enjoyed waking up with a refreshing swim.

Over a quick lunch in a nearby café they planned their day. Debbie decided that, as Foster was going to be involved in the Sydney event for most of the late afternoon and evening she would keep out of the way and seize the chance to spend the day with her mother.

"Let's hope your parents don't read the tabloids" said Foster with a grin.

"They're not as puritanical as you John" she replied. "They'll be fine. But you've reminded me. I need to phone Francis and tell him I'm going to lay low for the rest of the Sydney stay."

"OK let's go back to the hotel. I've just remembered something I want to do."

"What's that?"

"Yesterday I took some photos of Ventrice' local bodyguards. They looked vaguely familiar. I want to see if the picture is clearer on the laptop screen. Let's go, I don't have much time."

Back in their room Debbie busied herself by phoning her mother, who was delighted to have her daughter for the day, and Ventrice who thanked her for her common sense and said he would easily fend off any questions.

"Don't forget our cocktail party tomorrow" he said. "I'm looking forward to it very much."

"Maybe I should keep away from that, in case it proves to be embarrassing for you."

"Nonsense, it's invited guests only and there will definitely be no press. I'll see you there." He said confidently and rang off.

While Debbie was making her phone calls Foster connected his camera to the laptop and downloaded the photos he had taken at the bridge climb. He navigated to the pictures of the two bodyguards and studied them intently. For a while he wondered why he had bothered. They were two large men in dark suits and short haircuts, indistinguishable from most of their ilk. He wondered again why he thought he recognised them.

When Debbie had finished her phone calls he beckoned her to come over.

"Look at this picture" he said. "Do they remind you of anyone?"

Debbie looked at the screen and shook her head. "Not immediately, no. Should they?"

"I don't know. I just feel as if I've seen them somewhere before."

"Why would you think that? After all you haven't been to many places in Australia, really just Adelaide, Brisbane and here."

"Yes I know but I can't shake off the feeing, particularly the bigger one."

Foster suddenly stopped and looked at Debbie. "Big guy, Adelaide, Mannum. Doesn't he remind you of someone?"

Debbie looked at the picture more carefully. "Well, but for the hair it could be. Surely not?"

"You're thinking what I'm thinking. With different hair he could be a dead ringer for Tony Andersen."

"But why would he turn up here looking very different? I thought he was on the run."

Foster thought. "Maybe he's being clever and thinks he wouldn't be recognised with short dark hair and a suit."

"Doesn't that sound a bit too clever for Tony?" replied Debbie. "Maybe we are putting two and two together and getting five."

"It's possible." agreed Foster. "What about the other guy?"

They both looked again, this time with a dawning realization.

"Are you thinking what I'm thinking?" said Debbie.

Foster looked up. "Yes, I think that's Greg Andersen. What the hell is going on? Why are they in Ventrice' tour party?"

"I don't know. Maybe they are just trying to start over and get back to a legitimate job. After all, they used to be in the security business."

Foster shook his head. "I can't accept that. They are both wanted men. Why do something that puts them so clearly in the public spotlight?"

"Have you got a better idea?"

"No, but I'm going to look into it further."

"What are you going to do?"

"Well I'll be meeting with the tour organisers this afternoon. I might have a word with the guy who's in charge. What's his name? Yeah – Gardner, Phillip Gardner and ask him how they come to be on the tour. I smell a story here."

"I thought you might" laughed Debbie. "It's time for me to go over to mum's. I'll see you later."

"Much later maybe" said Foster. "If I'm in really late I won't wake you, in which case I'll see you in the morning."

"Lovely, give me a kiss and then I must go."

Debbie headed off to her mum's while Foster get himself together for the short walk to the tour venue, Tattersall's Club in the city centre, known affectionately to Sydneysiders as "City Tatts".

He arrived in plenty of time for the press briefing. He showed his pass, signed the visitor's register and went in. He was a little early for the briefing and decided on a quick coffee before it started. He made his way to the bar and ordered a coffee. He selected a table in the corner from where he could see most of the room, an old habit of his, and sat quietly to gather his thoughts for fifteen or twenty minutes until the briefing.

Sipping his coffee he looked around at the people gathered there, a varied selection from young to old. Turning his glance to the far corner he suddenly forgot about his coffee. There trying to look inconspicuous were the two men he had just been studying, who he now believed were the Andersen brothers.

He pretended to be looking at something on his phone as he observed them. He became more and more convinced that they were the Andersen brothers.

As he watched them he saw another man walk up to their table and sit down. He obviously knew them. Foster looked at the man but he didn't know him. The three men were engaged in deep conversation which appeared to be very serious.

Foster tried not to look their way too much in case he was noticed but he managed to take some photos on his phone without them noticing.

At that he decided to leave the bar in case Tony Andersen recognised *him*, and made his way to the briefing room where many of the various media reporters were already gathered.

**

At the appointed time Phillip Gardner stood up and addressed them. He pointed out where the official party would be sitting, which parts of the room should be left for guests and the general public, and finally where the press should gather. He ran through the programme and pointed out that there would be a Q & A session for the press at the end.

He ended with "any questions?"

There were only one or two questions of process. The majority of those present had been through this sort of briefing many times before and knew the form.

One cheeky young reporter yelled "will the mystery blonde be here?"

Gardner looked at him with some disgust and said "no I don't think so. Now if there are any intelligent questions I'll answer them. Otherwise we kick off at seven o'clock. Thank you ladies and gentlemen. Before you go there are some drinks and nibbles, courtesy of Mr Ventrice, at the back. Please enjoy and we'll see you later."

Foster joined the throng at the drinks table and helped himself to a cold glass of white wine and a handful of nuts as he observed the gathering.

He waited until Gardner had gathered up his notes and walked over to him.

"Can I get you a drink Phillip?" he said cheerfully.

Gardner looked at him, obviously unsure who he was. Foster ploughed on.

"I'm sorry. I should introduce myself. I'm John Foster. I'm covering the tour for The Australian and the Sun."

"What the Sun in England?"

"Yes, I'm based in London normally."

"Pleased to meet you John."

"Can I get you that drink?"

Gardner looked at his watch. "No I'm sorry. I've got another meeting to go to. Another time perhaps?"

"Sure, but before you go can I ask you a question?"

"Couldn't you have asked it when we had question time just now?"

"Well it's just that I didn't want to raise it in public."

Gardner looked at him quizzically. "It's not about the mystery blonde is it? I had thought you might be a bit more subtle."

"Heavens no" replied Foster smiling. "Nothing whatsoever to do with mystery blondes. It's about your tour security."

Gardner suddenly looked alarmed. "What about my tour security?"

"It's about the two Australian security men you have in your team."

"What about them?" asked Gardner ominously.

"I just wondered where you got them from. Are they local?"

"What business is that of yours?"

"I'm sorry. It's just that I thought I recognised them from somewhere."

"I don't know what you're driving at Mr Foster but we decided we could probably use some extra help, people with local knowledge."

"So you recruited them here?"

"Yes, so what? They came highly recommended. Why all the questions?"

I'm sorry I won't keep you. Just one more question. Do you happen to recall the name of the company they are with?"

"As it happens yes. A company called QANTSEC. It stands for Queensland and Northern Territory Security. It's spelt without a U, you know like QANTAS. Now, are we done?"

"Yes, thank you Phillip. Can I suggest you keep an eye on them?"

"Why do you say that?"

Let's just say they have a bit of a reputation. Anyhow nice to talk to you. Enjoy your meeting."

Gardner looked as if he wanted to quiz Foster some more but Foster had already moved away and melted into the crowd of reporters, so he picked up his notes and left the room.

Foster noted the name QANTSEC in his phone. Tomorrow he'd do some more research on them.

Chapter 33

On the morning after the Sydney event Debbie and Foster slept in late. By the time they were up Sydney was turning on one of its glorious warm autumn days. They lazed around the pool and Foster told Debbie about the event. When he had finished he added "much the same as the Brisbane event really."

"I suppose they are all going to be similar really" added Debbie. "No uproar over the topless twins and the mystery blonde?"

"There was one question from a silly young reporter but Ventrice batted it away effortlessly. I think your virtue is intact."

Debbie laughed. "I think my virtue was gone years ago. Still I'm glad it hasn't provoked an incident."

"So you're still going to this cocktail party?"

"I think I might put in an appearance. I haven't much else to do today and I guess you'll be writing up your story."

"Yeah, I'm going to be busy. On top of the story I want to do a bit more research."

"What about?"

"The Andersens mostly. I saw them again yesterday and I'm convinced it's them. They were deep in conversation with another guy I haven't seen before. I'd love to know how he figures in all this."

"What do you mean – all this?"

"That's what I don't know. What are the Andersens up to and who are they really working for. It all looks just too innocent. I smell a rat."

"Are you sure you're not just getting paranoid John?"

Foster had to laugh. "Maybe, but I'm going to keep my eyes and ears open. There could be a major story somewhere in all this if I could only figure out what it was."

"Well you do what you have to do. Me, I'm going to a posh cocktail party so I'm off to the shower and then I'll get ready. It starts soon."

"What time do you think you will be finished" asked Foster anxiously.

"I don't expect it's going to be a big event, probably just for the afternoon. Don't worry I'll be back long before dinner. Why don't we have something nice in Circular Quay?"

"You're on. But watch yourself with Ventrice. He's a very slippery character."

"All right. But I'm a big girl and I know how to look after myself."

An hour later Foster was making his way to the hotel lobby where he could compose his story on the laptop and pursue his research. He chose that location partly as a break from the hotel room but also because he could watch the comings and goings of the tour party to see if anything interesting could be observed.

**

Debbie left their room and took the lift to the penthouse floor where Ventrice' suite was located.

She was expecting a hubbub of activity but all was quiet. She nervously knocked on Ventrice' door and it was immediately opened by Ventrice himself.

"Hi Debbie" he said excitedly. "It's good to see you again. Come on in."

Debbie walked in to one of the biggest hotel rooms she had ever seen, with large picture windows looking out across Circular Quay towards the Opera House. She could also not fail to notice that it was empty. There was no one else there apart from herself and Ventrice.

"Have I got the time wrong?" she asked. "I thought this was supposed to be a cocktail party."

"It is" nodded Ventrice. "But if you recall I said it was for some special guests only."

Debbie was suspicious. "Where are all these special guests then?"

"Don't look so disappointed Debbie. The twins will be along in a minute. They're just fixing the drinks."

As if on cue the twins entered from a side door wearing stunning identical short kimonos. Grace carried a silver tray loaded with drinks already poured.

"Ah here we are" exclaimed Ventrice. "Have one of these. Grace's special cocktails are absolutely delicious."

Grace smiled demurely as Alice took two glasses and handed them to Debbie and Ventrice.

The cocktails were indeed superb and Debbie started to relax a little and talked with Ventrice about how the Sydney event had gone.

Very soon Alice appeared with a second cocktail. By the time she reached the end of that one Debbie was wondering what was in it. She was beginning to feel quite light headed.

"When are the other guests coming Francis?" she asked.

Ventrice took her hand and looked into her eyes. "I have to admit there are no other guests. I just wanted to spend some quality time with you. It's awfully tiring dealing with an entourage all the time. I just need a little quiet time, and who better to spend it with?"

Debbie was flattered but suspicious. "What about Ed?" she asked.

"Ed's visiting some old friends who live in Sydney."

"What about your two heavyweights?"

"What about them?" asked Ventrice looking very amused. "It's like being followed around by Tweedledum and Tweedledee."

"I guess it is" said Debbie relaxing a little. "Where are they then?"

"I gave them the day off."

"So it's just you and me then?" said Debbie suspiciously.

"Not at all. The girls are here and we'll all have a lovely time. You remember I offered to show you some of my photo collection? It's all ready to go. We are connected to the big screen there. Would you like to see them?"

"I guess" said Debbie trying to sound more excited than she felt.

"Don't worry" said Ventrice. "I won't bore you totally. Just some of the best ones. And we'll have something to snack on while we watch. I take it you like crayfish and champagne?"

Alice had re-appeared pushing a trolley containing plates of assorted seafood; crayfish, oysters, mussels and a whole salmon. There were several salads and in pride of place was a large ice bucket with three bottles of champagne.

"You know how to look after yourself" remarked Debbie.

Ventrice was enjoying himself. "Special occasions demand special food. Here, have some champagne."

With the champagne on top of the cocktails Debbie was beginning to feel slightly woozy and a little sleepy. I hope I don't fall asleep during the slide show, she thought.

**

Foster quickly composed his story covering the previous night's event and dispatched it to the Sun and The Australian. It wasn't one of his finest compositions he knew, but then the evening had not been greatly different to the one in Brisbane.

He was more interested in following up his research into the Andersens and the mystery man they had met. He examined the website for QANTSEC. It didn't tell him much more than he already knew. It was a small security services company with two principals, Trevor Buckingham and John Whiting. Most of their work took place in Queensland and the Northern Territory with some in South Australia.

There was an impressive list of previous clients and some testimonials. He wondered if it would be worth following up on any of them, then realised it was a job he could delegate to the office juniors at The Australian if he thought it would be useful.

He called a waiter and ordered a coffee while he pondered on what to do next. The hotel lobby was quiet and he had a good view of all the comings and goings. He watched as he sipped his coffee and wondered how Debbie was enjoying the cocktail party.

The sound of the lift announcing its arrival at the ground floor caused Foster to break his train of thought and look around. Three people emerged from the lift. Two of them were a middle aged couple he didn't recognise. They walked over to the reception desk and asked for a street map of the area. Foster assumed they must be tourists.

The third person in the lift he did recognise; Phillip Gardner the tour organiser. Foster immediately wondered why he was not at the cocktail party. Gardner looked around as if to make sure that no one was observing him and walked quickly to the exit on Circular Quay.

Foster, who had been pretending to be engrossed in his laptop, noticed this odd behaviour and decided to follow him. He quickly packed up his laptop and headed out onto Circular Quay. He followed at a discreet distance until he saw Gardner sit at a table at the Sundowners Bar, which was already occupied by another man. This man he recognised; it was the same man he had seen talking to the Andersens the day before.

Once again he had the feeling that something wasn't quite right. Who was the mystery man and what was his purpose? Why was he talking separately to Gardner and the Andersens? None of it made any sense. He found a table at the far end of the bar from where he could see the two men without being obvious himself. If Foster could have heard their conversation his ears would be burning.

**

Michael Robinson looked up as Phillip Gardner sat down at his table. "Hi Phillip" he said. "Can I get you a drink?"

"No thanks Michael, I'm in a bit of a hurry. I've got too much to do at the moment."

"OK so what's this all about? You said it was urgent."

"It was just something I thought you should know about. Yesterday, before the event, I was approached by a reporter."

"That's not exactly unusual for you is it?"

"No of course not, but it was what this particular reporter wanted to talk about; the tour security."

"Why would he want to do that?"

"It gets worse. He was particularly interested in the Australian security men. He asked me where we found them and what the company name was."

"Maybe he's just curious and trying to get another angle to write about."

"Maybe, but he said he thought he recognised them from somewhere. Then, just before he left, he said I should be careful of them and they had a bit of a reputation."

"Really, did you ask him what he meant by that?"

"I didn't get a chance to. He moved away and I was much too busy at the time to follow him."

Robinson was puzzled. "That's certainly a bit odd. I wonder where he got that from. Or is he just fishing?"

"Search me, but it's a little hitch in your plan."

"Maybe, maybe not. You didn't get his name by any chance?"

"I did. It's an easy name to remember; Foster, John Foster."

Robinson looked grim. "You wouldn't believe it. He doesn't work for the Sun by any chance?"

"Yes, he said he was covering the tour for the Sun and The Australian. What's the problem Michael? What does he know to make him say what he did?"

"I don't think it's what he knows as much as what he suspects."

"And what does he suspect?"

"I think he suspects that your two security men are not quite what they claim to be."

"And are they?" asked Gardner anxiously. "It was you who told me to hire them remember."

"Don't worry so much. Look I told you at the time that we would construct an invented company around them to give them more credibility. Apart from that they are what they claim to be. They have been in the personal security business for years."

"But that's not why you wanted them in the tour is it?"

"No of course not. They have a job to do and they'll do it well."

"Well now it seems your men are blown doesn't it?"

"I think Foster is just fishing. He can't be sure. We've altered the appearance of those two men dramatically."

"Not enough apparently if Foster recognised them. Where does he know them from anyway?"

"It's best you don't know the details. Let's just say he did some reporting on a job they were involved with."

"But doesn't that undermine your plan? What if he goes public?"

"He won't do that. He has nothing to say that would stand up and he knows it. All the same I'll keep an eye on him and make sure he's not going to give us any bother. Besides it won't matter in a couple of days."

Gardner was alarmed. "Why not?"

"By Tuesday the job will be finished and all our problems will be solved."

"You don't mean it's going to happen that soon. Why didn't you tell me?"

"Look the less you know the better. Isn't that what you keep telling me? If you know nothing they can't pin anything on you. Just hold your nerve and trust me. Go back to your tour party and behave normally."

"OK I don't want to know any more. I was hoping you would have seen some sense by now and called it off."

"You worry too much Phillip. Just act the shocked innocent and you'll be fine." He gave Gardner a hard look. "But don't do anything stupid. There would be repercussions if you did."

Gardner silently stood up, looked at Robinson and walked away.

As he walked he was in turmoil. Should he follow instructions and let events take their course or attempt to do something to prevent it? Either way he was in for a rough time over the next few days.

Foster watched him leave and waited until Robinson also left. Neither man had looked very happy when they parted. Now he was convinced there was something going on, but what was it?

**

Debbie found Ventrice' collection of photographs more interesting than she expected. He had an eye for a good composition.

He started with what he declared was one of his major pastimes, wine appreciation, and with that an interest in the French countryside. He had shots of vineyards she had never heard of. But the pictures weren't just sterile location shots. He was able to take shots of people in landscapes which seemed to make both the people and the landscape interesting.

"And were they all in France?" asked Debbie when he had finished the collection.

"Yes, you seem surprised."

"It's just that the landscape is so varied. I'd always imagined that with France being such a small country it would all be much the same."

"France may be small compared to Australia but it's still a big country. The difference in climate between north and south is huge."

"I suppose so. I'd just never really thought about it like that. Do you only go to French wineries?"

"No I've got pictures of vineyards all over Europe, but I won't bore you with those. Not everyone has my interest in vineyards. How would you like to see some of the pictures I've taken since we arrived in Australia?"

"I'd like that very much."

Ventrice navigated his way to a different folder and began. Debbie quickly recognised the hotel they had stayed at in Brisbane. Some of the shots were around the pool and often featured one or both of the twins.

"They look good on film don't they?" said Ventrice as if he were reading Debbie's mind. "Pity I haven't got any of you at the pool."

"You don't need me" said Debbie. "Grace and Alice are very beautiful."

"Don't be so modest Debbie. There are many different kinds of beauty. The contrast between your height and colouring compared with theirs would make an interesting study. I'll show you in a minute."

What does he mean by that, thought Debbie.

He showed various pictures of Brisbane and then onto Sydney. Some of his pictures of the Bridge Climb were spectacular and Debbie said so.

"Thank you" said Ventrice. "They don't normally allow you to take a camera on the climb but I was able to persuade them to let me. I'm very pleased with them. Mind you, when you have such a spectacular setting it makes it easier. Speaking of spectacular settings here are some of our day at the beach."

Ventrice had demonstrated his creative side yet again with some eye-catching shots of Obelisk Beach.

"Here's one you should recognise" he said as he moved to a picture of Debbie, flanked by the twins, all topless.

Initially Debbie was shocked but then she was struck by the gaiety and innocence of the picture; three girls having fun frolicking in the shallows.

"It's a good picture Francis" she said, "but I hope you're not going to be showing me to all and sundry."

"Absolutely not Debbie, these are for my private collection. I like to keep my public life and my private life separate."

"You slipped up on that at the beach the other day didn't you?" said Debbie sweetly. "And look at all the fuss it caused."

Ventrice put on an innocent and aggrieved expression. "How was I to know there was a photographer hiding in the bushes. Anyway it's all blown over and we're none the worse for it."

"It's easy for you to say that, but I'm the mystery blonde" she teased.

"Debbie, you have my heartfelt apologies if it embarrassed you. That was not my intention. I've learned my lesson. Am I forgiven?"

Debbie laughed. "Of course you are. I'll be back to being plain old Debbie Simmons this time next week."

"Never that" said Ventrice. "No one could ever describe you as plain. I will treasure these pictures of you. In fact I would like some more."

"We are off to Adelaide tomorrow. It may be too cold there to go to the beach. It's usually a bit colder and windier than Sydney at this time of year."

"I don't see that as a problem. I have my beach shots which I will treasure. Perhaps something a little more elegant and sophisticated?"

"What had you in mind?" asked Debbie cautiously.

You look stunning in that red dress you are wearing. Might I have some shots of you in it?"

"I guess. Where?"

"Why not right here. You could sit on a bar stool at the bar there. My camera is always ready. Make yourself comfortable and I'll get it."

Debbie moved across to the bar and sat on one of the stools. She wondered where this was leading and thought she had a pretty good idea. Still, so far Ventrice had behaved like the perfect gentleman and the view from the bar right across the harbour was magnificent, so she forced herself to relax as Ventrice readied his camera.

"OK" he said, "slightly sideways and chin raised. Perfect, you're a natural. That's a lovely shot. Now, swing round towards me a little. Pull your dress up slightly to show off those beautiful legs. Lovely."

He carried on in the same vein for a while as Ventrice took complete control. She was too busy obeying his commands to worry at all. She wondered if this was what it was like to be photographed by a professional. It wasn't unpleasant and she enjoyed the attention and compliments.

Finally Ventrice declared enough. He connected his camera to the large TV screen and played back the shots he had taken.

Debbie was impressed. Ventrice certainly knew what he was doing and she knew she looked stunning in his pictures.

"Lovely" said Ventrice, "you are very easy to photograph Debbie. You know you ought to be a model. Let's take some of the three of you now. Come on over girls and back to the bar."

The twins got up and guided Debbie back to the bar where they posed her between them. Ventrice was ecstatic.

"Perfect, three beautiful women now. How good does it get?"

Ventrice once again took control and composed his various shots. The twins seemed to understand what he wanted almost before he said it. Debbie sensed they had done this before.

"Fantastic" declared Ventrice after taking several shots. "Let's have another drink while I sort out this batch. Alice served them all cocktails while Ventrice busied himself with his camera and laptop. They all examined the results on the big screen while Alice served yet another cocktail.

Ventrice seemed very happy with the results. "Aren't they wonderful Debbie? You three look so good together."

Debbie was now feeling the effects of Alice's cocktails. Maybe she shouldn't have had so many. Still it had been a fun afternoon so far and she was having a good time being the centre of attention.

Ventrice looked up from his camera and said "It's beach bar time. Are you ready girls?"

The twins took hold of Debbie's hands and giggling led her back to the bar stools. Debbie seated herself on a stool a little unsteadily and wondered what was happening now.

The twins stepped out of their kimonos revealing nothing underneath but tiny panties. They giggled again and sat on stools on either side of Debbie.

"They smiled at Ventrice as he lifted his camera. "Come on Debbie, you're a bit overdressed for a beach bar" he said.

Debbie looked at him. She felt her brain was not functioning too well. They weren't at the beach; they were in a hotel room. And yet the twins were dressed, if that was the word, as if they were back on Obelisk Beach.

The twins took Debbie's hands. "Come on Debbie, it's beach bar time again" said Grace. "Come and join us. We'll help you get out of this dress."

Through her haze Debbie felt the twins gently removing her dress until she realised she was standing there wearing just her matching red panties.

"Francis what's going on?" she asked in a faltering voice.

"Don't worry Debbie" he replied. "You're quite safe. Just some more beach shots like we did the other day. You were happy with those weren't you? And today there are no peeping toms in the bushes. Now just pose as I tell you and we'll all have a lovely time."

Once again Ventrice took control and Debbie posed as she was asked as if she were on automatic pilot. It seemed to her that she was in some sort of dream but it wasn't unpleasant and she relaxed into it. Ventrice took several poses and then quietly said "next set".

The twins giggled, slipped off their panties and stood naked. "Look Debbie" said Grace, "we're on a nude beach now. Come and join us."

"I'm not so sure" slurred Debbie through her growing haze.

"Oh come on. It's lots of fun. We'll help you."

The twins gently eased down Debbie's panties and all three stood naked by the bar. Alice picked up more cocktails and handed them to Grace, Debbie and Ventrice. "Here's to our day at the beach" she said. "Come on Debbie, down in one like us."

The twins downed their drink while Debbie hesitated.

"Come on Debbie" they chorused, "down the hatch".

Debbie did as she was asked. She felt she needed another drink but it seemed to make her more unsteady.

Ventrice again took control and directed the girls into various poses.

Debbie was feeling distinctly unreal and wondered if this was actually happening or whether she was dreaming.

Ventrice' voice was hypnotically pushing her from one shot to another and she hardly knew what she was doing.

She was confused and slightly alarmed and yet she was also enjoying what was happening. She leaned back into Grace and relaxed, wondering what was next.

Alice stood up and walked slowly over to Ventrice, her hips swaying slowly. "Come on Francis" she said, "aren't you a bit over dressed for our nude beach?"

Debbie watched in horrified fascination as Ventrice put down his camera and started to unbutton his shirt while Alice tugged at the buttons on his trousers. She wasn't happy with the way things were developing and tried to stand up.

Grace grabbed her hand and said "what are you doing Debbie?"

"I, I think I should be going" said Debbie, aware that she was slurring her words.

"Don't go Debbie, come and join us" shouted Alice as she eased Ventrice' trousers down.

Debbie tore herself free from Grace and tried to stand up. She glanced towards Ventrice and Alice but her eyes glazed as the room dimmed and she slid into unconsciousness.

**

When Debbie awoke she found herself lying on the sofa under a light blanket. She remembered the dream. Was it a dream? She felt herself and realised she was fully dressed.

She looked up.

Ventrice was sitting in another chair reading a book. The twins were sitting in seats by the window looking out and idly flicking through magazines. Everyone was properly dressed.

When Ventrice was aware of her stirring he put down his book. "Debbie you're back with us. I'm so glad."

"What, what happened" she stammered.

"I think you must have had one too many of Alice's cocktails. They're delicious but quite potent."

"But what happened?"

"Can't you remember? We were taking some beach bar shots and you passed out. We carried you here and let you sleep it off."

"How long have I been here? I mean on the sofa."

"Oh not long. Half an hour or so."

"You were just taking some beach bar photos. Is that all?"

"I'm not sure what you mean. You can see them if you like."

"Yes all right; show me."

Ventrice quickly ran through the shots of Debbie in her red dress, then with the twins and finally the topless beach bar shots.

"And that's the lot?" she asked.

"That's all there is. Were you expecting more?"

"What about the ones with our pants off?"

Ventrice appeared very surprised. I don't know what you mean. Did you dream this one? You kept your pants on. It was just some harmless topless beach shots."

"What about what Grace and Alice were doing?"

"You seem very confused. Just what do you think they were doing? They put your dress back on if that's what you mean."

"They were... Well Alice was.... Oh...." She stopped. "It doesn't matter. I must have been dreaming."

Ventrice seemed genuinely sympathetic.

"Let me get you a cup of coffee. It should make you feel better."

"Yes OK".

As Debbie sipped her coffee she tried to make sense of the situation. Ventrice and the twins were acting as if nothing improper had happened. Had she simply dreamed the rest? Had she just had too much to drink? Was her drink spiked? Had anything happened she wasn't aware of?"

"Can I get you anything else?" asked Ventrice solicitously.

"No that's OK Francis. The coffee has made me feel a bit better."

"Have another one then".

"Yes all right. Then I think I should be going."

"That's a shame but I understand."

She quietly sipped her second coffee still trying to make sense of what she thought she had seen. She couldn't quite accept that she'd simply had too much to drink. It wasn't like her at all. But if it had happened what was the point? Was that the way Ventrice got his thrills or was he building up for something else before she passed out or, oh no, after she passed out.

She finished her coffee and stood up. At least she could stand up. She felt a little tired and overwrought but the unsteadiness had gone.

"Francis" she said, "I really must go. I'm sorry I was so much trouble. Thanks for a lovely day."

"It was my pleasure. Don't blame yourself. We all make the odd mistake. Can I see you to your room?"

"No I'll be fine. Thank you."

Ventrice nodded. "Well I guess we will see you in Adelaide then"

"Yes I suppose you will" said Debbie. "Goodnight."

Ventrice closed the door of the suite as soon as Debbie had left. "Thank you girls" he said to the twins. "I think our Debbie is a lovely lady don't you?"

**

Foster was sitting quietly trying to come up with a theory regarding Ventrice, the Andersens and the mystery man. He had gone over the same ground many times and still had not reached any conclusions.

His thoughts were interrupted by the sound of the room door opening. He looked up as Debbie entered. He was pleased that the event had ended at a reasonable hour and there was still time for him and Debbie to go out to dinner together.

"Hi" he said brightly, "all finished or have you just had enough?"

"Oh I think I've had enough all right. I'm exhausted."

She flopped down on the sofa beside him and gave him a big long kiss.

"What was that for?" he asked. "Not that I'm complaining."

"It's been a very strange afternoon" she said wearily. "I'll tell you all about it in a minute. For now just hold me."

Foster was now concerned but he held her until she was ready to talk. Debbie quietly fell asleep in his arms. He waited and wondered. After what seemed like an eternity to him, but was actually only twenty minutes, Debbie stirred and her eyes opened.

Foster looked at her. "It's not like you to sleep in the day. What happened? Did you have too much to drink?"

"Well you could say that, but I don't feel as if I've got a hangover."

"Well what then?"

"Get me some coffee will you and I'll tell you all about it."

Foster made the coffee and Debbie began She told him how there was only Ventrice and the twins there.

"So he tricked you" said Foster angrily.

"Shh calm down. He was very charming about it. I'll tell you the whole story if you can be patient."

She related the details of the seafood lunch, the pictures of the French vineyards and the pictures of Debbie posing alone and with the twins at the bar.

"He's very good" she added, "Some of the best pictures I've ever had taken."

Foster was suspicious. "There's more isn't there? Come on let's hear it."

Debbie lowered her head. "He then wanted some pictures at the tropical beach bar."

"But you weren't at the beach."

"No I know. But he suggested we pretend that the big bar in his suite was the tropical bar."

"I don't think I'm going to like what's coming next"

She told him how the twins stripped down to their panties and persuaded her to do the same so Ventrice could take some photographs.

"So you sat at his bar topless while he took photos. Don't you think that was a bit stupid?"

"Don't get angry and moral John. It seemed like a bit of harmless fun. After all he didn't see any more than he already had at the beach the other day."

"And he didn't touch you?"

"I swear it. He never laid a finger on me. He just took photos. It was like being with a professional photographer."

"When were you with a professional photographer?"

"Don't be like that. I haven't, but I imagine that's what it would be like, more like a busy professional relationship."

"And that's it?" said Foster looking a little relieved.

"No there's more."

"This sounds a bit ominous Debbie."

"Don't be so quick to judge. This is the really weird bit. I blacked out and I don't know how much of it was real and how much was hallucination."

As Foster sat quietly, trying to contain himself, Debbie told him the chain of events from Alice's cocktails, to the twins removing their panties through to the antics of Alice and Ventrice.

Foster was shocked and angry. "And you did nothing to halt it?"

"That's the funny thing. That's why I don't know if it was real or not. I was relaxed and enjoying it, but then I woke up. I was on the sofa fully dressed and the others were sitting reading looking very respectable. They behaved as if nothing had happened. Ventrice said I'd been asleep for about half an hour."

"Surely there would be some evidence of an orgy like that?"

"No the room was tidy. Everyone was dressed respectably and I felt clean and fresh, not abused in any way."

"But you were topless for some photos. You said so yourself. How come you were dressed when you woke up?"

Ventrice said the twins had dressed me and tucked me up on the sofa. He said I passed out just after the beach bar photos."

"Well he would, wouldn't he? You know if this really happened he raped you."

"Steady on John. Nobody raped me. Ventrice didn't even touch me."

"What about the twins?"

"I don't know. Even if it really happened it still wasn't rape. I'm wondering if one of them spiked my drink and I reacted badly."

"Either way that's sexual abuse at least. Shouldn't you be reporting it to the police?"

"Where would that get me? It would be my word against the three of them. The only evidence is the photos and Ventrice showed me all the ones he'd taken, up to the topless shots, which were pretty harmless."

"But he could have taken more that he hasn't shown you."

"True, but If he had surely he would have hidden them?"

"But we can't just let it go."

"What else can we do?"

"Well nothing I can think of. Did he ask to see you again?"

"No he didn't. And we're all off to Adelaide tomorrow. Let's just forget it."

"As you like" agreed Foster reluctantly, "but be more wary of him in future. You know between your experiences and what I've seen this tour is getting more and more weird."

"Why what have you seen?"

Foster told her about the mystery man and his separate meetings with Gardner and the Andersens.

"What do you make of it?" she asked.

"I really don't know but I'll certainly be doing some investigations in Adelaide. I might even see if Brian Chambers can be of any help."

"That's a good idea. Let's put today behind us and go and have a nice dinner."

"Are you sure you're up to it?"

"Yes I'm hungry, but there's something I need to do first."

"What's that?"

"Get your pants off John Foster and come and fuck me hard. I need you badly."

Foster smiled for the first time in a long while. "Well, whatever they put in your drink, can we get some more?"

Chapter 34

On ~~Friday~~ Monday morning there was a flurry of activity at the hotel as the Ventrice party and the entire press corps, complete with various other hangers on, decamped to Adelaide.

A fleet of taxis ferried the more important people from the hotel to the airport while those with smaller pockets took the train. Debbie and Foster elected to go by train to keep their expenses to a minimum. They knew that while in Adelaide they could use Debbie's car and flat, which would also help them. Foster's employers were scrutinising his expenses very carefully so every little helped.

As it happened the Ventrice party were staying at The Feathers Hotel, away from the city in the leafy suburb of Glen Osmond, only a few minutes' drive or taxi from Debbie's flat in Norwood. The public meeting was to be held in the Combined Rooms at The Feathers.

Debbie and Foster had a mid morning flight and were in Adelaide by lunchtime, after putting their watches back by half an hour. They caught a taxi and half an hour later arrived at Debbie's flat.

They had been away just eight days but so much had happened it seemed longer than that. They managed to salvage a passable lunch from what was left in the kitchen.

"I think we'll eat out tonight. There's not really time to go shopping" said Debbie. "We have to be in Mannum soon and that's over an hour's drive. Was Brian Chambers happy at hearing from you again?"

"When I phoned him last night he seemed his usual busy self but as soon as I mentioned I might have a lead on the Andersens he came around."

"Did you tell him what you've seen?"
"No I thought I'd leave that till we're with him."
"Probably wise, he might not take it seriously otherwise. It still seems like a long shot. I guess we had better be going. Do you need to take anything?"
"Just my laptop. All the evidence is on that."
As they made to leave Debbie's phone rang.
"It's Ventrice" she gasped. "I'd better answer it."
"Good afternoon Francis, how are you? Are you in Adelaide yet?"
"Yes I'm here safely ensconced at The Feathers. It makes a nice change to be out of the city amid the greenery. What about you?"
"I got a flight this morning and now I'm back in my flat. It's nice to be home again."
"Yes I'm sure it is. Look, I rang to make sure you were OK after that funny turn you had yesterday."
"I'm fine thanks. I still don't know what caused it though."
Ventrice coughed. "Well Alice's cocktails do have something of a reputation but not usually like that."
"Well just tell her I'm fine will you. I did enjoy yesterday despite the incident so thank both the girls for me. Now I must go. I have an appointment. I'm making the best of a few days at home."
"I understand that but before you go I wondered if you would have dinner with me on Wednesday. I'm very busy till then. I've got all the preparations for Tuesday evening's event this afternoon and I've got a very full day tomorrow before the actual event."
"It's all work isn't it?" said Debbie.
"Well actually tomorrow is a day off but a busy one."
"Are you doing anything interesting?"
"Yes I'm having a tour of part of the Adelaide Hills and then some wineries, with lunch at one of them. I would

invite you but since that incident at the beach the other day on the beach with the photographer, my security has been stepped up, so it's just me, Ed and The Gorillas."

"The Gorillas?" asked Debbie.

"Sorry that's just the term Ed and I use for our two Australian security guards. I'm sure they are probably really nice people. Where we are going is secret. The press haven't been told and just the four of us and our tour organiser know where we are going and when."

Foster had been eavesdropping on the conversation and scribbled down the words 'find out where they are going' on the back of an envelope.

"That sounds intriguing" said Debbie, "and you can't even tell me?"

"Well I can tell you of course but don't mention it to a soul. We are leaving early around seven o'clock to drive to the Whispering Wall to take some pictures before the tourists arrive. Apparently it's only a short distance from the hotel."

"Yes I know it well. I've taken several people there. It's up The Gorge Road which is close to where you are. What then?"

"Then we are going to drive around the hills and take in some wineries, I'm not sure which, and have lunch at Jacobs Creek. I'm told it's very nice there."

"Yes you'll enjoy it."

"Then back to the hotel to get ready for the event. A full day I think."

"Yes it should be lovely. Have a nice time."

"But what about Wednesday?" asked Ventrice.

Debbie paused for a moment. Did she really want to meet up with Ventrice again so soon?

"You're hesitating" urged Ventrice.

"No I'm just checking my diary. That's fine. Give me a call on Wednesday" she said.
"I'll look forward to it" said Ventrice. "Bye for now."
"You handled that well" said Foster.
"Did I? I'm still not sure about meeting him again so soon."
"That's OK. We can cross that bridge later but it gives me a chance to follow up on something not open to the rest of the press."
"How do you mean?"
"I'm going to follow them and observe, at a discreet distance of course. Can I borrow your car tomorrow?"
"Don't you want me to come along?"
"Well just this once no. You would be too easily recognised by them whereas none of them really know me."
"Ventrice met you remember."
"I know, but only briefly, and he met lots of people so I won't stand out. For that matter, if that guy really is Tony Andersen, it's just possible he might remember me, but again it's unlikely."
"I guess so but be careful won't you?"
"I'll be OK. I'm just a curious press man."
"Be serious John. If those guys really are the Andersens what are they up to? We know what they are capable of."
"You're right of course. I'll be careful. Anyhow we'd better go. We'll be late for Brian Chambers."

**

They enjoyed the drive through the hills to Mannum, despite having done it several times before, and arrived at the leafy Mannum Police Station and hour and a half later.

They walked in the main entrance and as their eyes adjusted to the less intense light inside they spotted a familiar figure at the counter looking very bored.

"Hi Roland" said Debbie, "how are you?"

Roland looked up and his expression changed to pure delight when he spotted Debbie.

"Hi Debbie, good to see you again. It's been a while" he said, and quickly added "and you too John of course. I guess you're here to see Brian?"

"That's right, is he available?"

"I'll just check for you."

As Roland went down the corridor to find Chambers Foster smiled at Debbie. "He doesn't change does he? I think he's in love with you."

"He's a dear sweet boy" said Debbie, "but not my type. Ah here is he is now."

Roland came back with a large red faced man behind him, DI Brian Chambers.

"Hi you two" said Chambers, "You just can't keep away can you? Come on through."

"I'll make some tea" called Roland from behind them as they made their way to Chamber's office.

"You know" said Chambers; "the only time he volunteers to make tea without being asked is when you're here Debbie. Not that I blame him. I was young once too."

Debbie laughed. "You're not that old yet Brian."

"Sometimes I feel it. You know all work and no play and all that. Anyhow what can I do for you?"

"I think I may have a lead on Tony Andersen" said Foster quietly.

"Yes John, that's what I thought you said on the phone yesterday. Tell me, we have half the police in the country looking for him and there have been no sightings, yet you claim you have seen him in Sydney. How can that be?"

"I know it sounds unlikely Brian but please hear me out. As you know I've been following the Francis Ventrice tour for my newspaper."

"Yeah, those mad buggers from Our Nation. They don't make a lot of sense to me. What of it?"

"You may be right, but what if I told you that one of their security team looks a lot like Tony Andersen?"

"There are a lot of big gormless muscles available for hire, not just Tony Andersen. Have you got a photo?"

"Yes but we'll get to that in a minute. His appearance has been changed but I'm sure it's him."

"How do you know it's him if he looks different?"

"Bear with me. First it's not just his appearance. Remember I observed him quite a lot during the Mannum incident and I recognise how he walks and holds himself."

"Have you spoken to him?"

"No I've kept well away in case he recognises me."

"So you don't know if he sounds like Tony?"

"No I don't."

"It's a bit thin mate."

"But what about this? There is a second security guy, recruited from the same firm. And who do you think he looks like?"

"I don't know. James Bond? Tell me."

"He looks like Greg Andersen."

Chambers sat back in his chair, looked at Foster and smiled.

"Come on John, is this some kind of windup. You've seen not one Andersen but two. Never mind that the other one is in hiding somewhere in England. Have you been working too hard?"

Foster sighed. "I know it sounds unlikely, which is why I didn't say too much on the phone. But seeing is believing. I want to show you some pictures."

"OK" said Chambers, "let's see if they are more convincing than what you've been telling me."

Foster opened his laptop and brought up the first of the photos he had taken. "Here, have a look through these and tell me what you think."

Chambers slowly looked through the small collection of photos. He seemed to be lost in thought. Eventually he looked up.

"There is certainly a resemblance there" he admitted, "if you assume the hair style and colour have been changed."

"So you think it could be them?"

"Not so fast. For one thing Greg Andersen is a hunted man in England. How did he manage to get on a flight and enter Australia?"

"I don't know, but he's actually calling himself Trevor Buckingham and the other is calling himself John Whiting. Couldn't you check up and see if anyone called Trevor Buckingham has entered the country recently?"

"I guess I could, but it all seems a bit cloak and dagger don't you think? Just maybe a bit too sophisticated for the Andersens."

"Speaking of cloak and dagger, there's one more thing. What do you make of this?"

Foster told Chambers the story of how, when he attempted to investigate further the disappearance of Greg Andersen, his boss had been warned off by the application of a D-notice.

"Now that is odd" murmured Chambers. "Why would British security be interested in a small time thug like Greg Andersen?"

"That's what I thought. And now he turns up supposedly as a bodyguard for Francis Ventrice. What is going on?"

"You might be completely wrong of course. There could be other explanations."

"Maybe, but wouldn't you like to find out?"

"I sure would. If it is them I want to nail them. Old scores to settle. But at the same time I don't want to cause a diplomatic incident and be thrown out of the force. I've got my pension to think of you know."

"But couldn't we investigate further without passing on what we suspect? Why don't you come down to Adelaide tomorrow evening and attend the public event? You could see for yourself then."

"I suppose I could. In the meantime I'll do some flight checking and see if I can find out more about this security company they both work for."

"Good, I'll see you tomorrow night then. You will come in plain clothes won't you? We don't want to frighten them off."

Chambers scowled. "Are you trying to teach me my job John?"

Then he laughed. "You silly bugger. Of course I'll come in plain clothes, but I might have a few re-enforcements nearby in case I need them."

**

Debbie and Foster motored back to Adelaide at a leisurely pace. They were pleased with the success of their meeting. It would be useful for someone else who knew the Andersens to take a look.

Foster wondered if he should have mentioned the planned day out in the Adelaide Hills tomorrow then he dismissed it. It would give Chambers a day or so to make further enquiries and he might just get a scoop story out of it. The rest could wait until Wednesday.

Chapter 35

Several people were awake early on ~~Wednesday~~ *Tuesday* morning. By six thirty John Foster was sitting in Debbie's red Mazda 3 in the street just up from the entrance to The Feathers. He was deliberately early to make sure he wouldn't miss the tour party.

Unknown to Foster plans were being redrawn in The Feathers. At five thirty Ed Hopkins made his decision and telephoned Francis Ventrice' room. He had spent most of the night in the bathroom vomiting and rushing to the toilet. He assumed it was food poisoning, one of the worst cases of it he had ever had. Now, exhausted and dehydrated and afraid to move more than a few feet from the bathroom he knew he couldn't make the winery tour today. Better tell Francis.

Ventrice took the news calmly, as he took most challenges. He thanked Ed for letting him know and advised him to stay in his room all day, drink lots of water and relax. Perhaps he would be over it by the evening. He promised to get one of his staff to pick up some anti-diarrhoea tablets and bring them to his room.

"Look after yourself Ed and I'll see you this afternoon" he ended.

Although Ventrice had maintained a veneer of calm competence he was concerned. Ed had become his constant companion and it had become unthinkable that he would go anywhere new without Ed's reassuring presence. Still he had his two local security men who claimed to know their way around the Adelaide area. He smiled as he recalled the nickname Ed had given them – the Gorillas.

Certainly Whiting was a gorilla but Buckingham was quite personable. He could still have a good day out with those two keeping an eye on things for him. It was one of the downsides of being famous and important that he always needed a retinue around him.

His preference would have been to have had a quiet day in the hills with Debbie as his only companion. What a day that would be. They could walk hand in hand and see the sights. A nice spot of lunch at a café or restaurant, after which they could take the car to a secluded place and have wild sex in the car or among the trees.

He snapped out of his daydream and realised he was very aroused. No such luck today, he thought, but tomorrow had some possibilities. He recalled his plans for Debbie tomorrow, licked his lips and smiled.

He needed to contact Phillip Gardner and let him know what had happened. After all Phillip was the tour organiser and he needed to know about any variations.

The sound of his mobile ringing wrenched Gardner from a deep sleep. Damn, he thought, I should have put it on silent. He picked it up and looked at the screen. Ventrice. Better answer it.

"Good morning Francis" he said thickly.

"Morning Phillip, sorry to wake you up at this ungodly hour but there's something you need to know before I leave for the day."

"What's that?"

"It's about Ed. He won't be coming with me today; he's sick."

Despite his sleepiness Gardner was now awake and cautious.

"What's the problem?"

"It's vomiting and severe diarrhoea. Ed thinks it must be food poisoning."

"Really; he was OK last night. Are you going to cancel your trip out today?"

"No I don't think so. It's the only chance I've got. I'll have the two local security men with me. They know their way about."

Gardner thought quickly. The local security men. What was it that pesky reporter had said? "They have a bit of a reputation."

"Do you think it's wise to go off on your own with those two?"

Well I don't think they will be exactly scintillating company but I'll manage."

Gardner was unsure what to say. Should he tell Ventrice his concerns? After all it was only rumour. It could just be a reporter fishing for a story. But then it seemed a neat coincidence that Ed was suddenly sick enough to be removed, leaving Ventrice alone with the two Australians. His years of undercover work had left him with an instinct when something seemed wrong. But what?

Then he remembered. What was it Robinson had said? Something about all their problems would be solved by Tuesday. Today was Tuesday. Well if anything was scheduled to happen today, perhaps he could throw a spanner in the works.

His thoughts were interrupted by Ventrice. "Phillip are you there?"

"Sorry Francis, I was just thinking. How about I come along in Ed's place?"

"That's very kind of you to offer Phillip. If you're not too busy I'd love to have you along. I might get some more entertaining conversation."

"All right I'll come. I need to make a phone call and have a shower. When are you leaving?"

"Seven on the dot, so I can catch the place before the tourists arrive."

"That gives me about half an hour. I can make it."

"Oh and Phillip, could you do me a favour? Get one of the staff to go out and buy some anti-diarrhoea tablets and get them to Ed. I promised him."
"Yes no problem. I'll see you at the entrance at seven then."
Gardner had a quick shower. He made a phone call to his number two, Asha Gillespie, explained what had happened and asked her to fill in for him today. She could phone him if she had any major issues. And could she sort out the tablets for Ed?
He knew Asha was competent and the temporary added responsibility would be good for her.
He wouldn't have minded some breakfast but that would have to wait. He grabbed a few biscuits that were in the room. They would have to do until he could get something more substantial. He checked his watch and hurried to the entrance.

***

Well before seven o'clock the Andersens were already sitting in the hire car waiting for Ventrice to arrive.
They had already collected the camera bag and a food basket for a late breakfast from Ventrice' staff and the items were safely stored in the car.
"Ben" had sent them a message to be there at 0645 to have a last minute meeting. He reported that Ed Hopkins would not be with them as he had been suddenly taken ill. "Nothing serious I trust?" Buckingham had asked.
"No just a touch of food poisoning. The poor guy is erupting at both ends. He's in no fit state to go anywhere today."
"How did you manage that?"
"Not your concern. I've got a few tricks up my sleeve you know. Now remember what you have to do. Stick close to Ventrice on the dam wall. Make sure he goes over the

side and then get the hell out of there. You've got your plane tickets and false IDs. The airport is less than an hour's drive. By the time Ventrice is discovered you'll be long gone."

"No one is going to believe it was an accident if we're gone."

"Don't bank on it. People will initially think you panicked and fled. It'll take time for other theories to come out. Just make sure you've got Ventrice' camera bag with you. They'll think he was trying to get some interesting shot and fell off. I need the bag for a minute – have you got it."

Buckingham took the bag from the car and handed it to Ben who proceeded to insert a small package at the bottom of the bag.

"What's that?" asked Buckingham.

"Just a tracking device. It could prove very useful" replied Ben. "Now I'd better get out of here before Ventrice shows up."

Right on cue just before seven Ventrice emerged from the hotel entrance on his own. So far so good, thought Buckingham.

"Good morning Mr Ventrice. How are you?"

"Never better" replied Ventrice.

"As soon as Ed comes we'll be off" said Buckingham innocently.

"Ed isn't coming" said Ventrice. "He's not very well."

"That's too bad" replied Buckingham solicitously.

"Yes, he was looking forward to it. Never mind, Phillip is coming instead. Ah here he is now."

Buckingham tried to keep his expression blank as he looked around and saw Gardner coming out of the door.

"So Phillip is coming instead?" asked Buckingham.

"Yes, that's no problem is it? It's still just the four of us."

"No that's fine" said Buckingham, hoping his voice sounded steady.

"Let's go then" said Ventrice approaching the car. Buckingham thought quickly.

"Make yourselves comfortable. I've just remembered there's something in my room I've forgotten. I won't be a minute."

Whiting stood quiet and confused and Ventrice and Gardner got into the back seat of the car while Buckingham hurried back into the hotel. He eased his bulk into the driver's seat and waited for Buckingham to reappear.

Once in the hotel lobby Buckingham made a hurried phone call to Ben. As he expected Ben was not pleased.

"Bloody Gardner" he said, "I wondered if he would be a problem."

"I don't follow you. What do we do now?" asked Buckingham.

"I don't know. I'll think of something. Carry on as normal. When you get to the Whispering Wall call me again. I'll already be there. I'll work out a new plan."

"Well you'd better think of something pretty damn quick. We'll be there in half an hour or so."

"Don't worry I will. Now get back to them before Ventrice gets suspicious."

Buckingham hurried back to the car and got in. "Sorry about that. Stupid of me to forget my phone. OK let's go."

Whiting cautiously drove the car out of the hotel and headed for the Gorge Road. He took no notice of a red Mazda 3 which followed them at a discreet distance.

**

Robinson swore softly after he heard the news from Buckingham. It could be that Gardner had merely come along to give Ventrice some company but his suspicions were that Gardner had other motives, possibly to foil his plan. It had all been going so well. Perhaps he should have arranged food poisoning for Gardner as well.

Now he was sitting in a secluded corner of the Whispering Wall car park waiting for Ventrice to arrive. Soon afterwards his mission would be accomplished and he would be heading home a much richer man. But now Gardner with his soft conscience could ruin the whole thing.

The two Australians still believed what he had told them and were content to throw Ventrice over the side and make their escape.

If only it could be so easy. That was a plan only for the desperate and the stupid. The real plan he had concocted with Blaines was much more subtle. He had instructed the Andersens to stick close to Ventrice on the dam wall. One of them, probably Whiting, would be carrying Ventrice' large camera bag. What neither of them knew was the nature of the package he had planted in the bag, which was not a tracking device.

It was small but deadly, a carefully calibrated quantity of a very powerful explosive which could be triggered by a phone signal from Robinson's mobile phone.

If detonated while they were on the dam wall it was powerful enough to kill Ventrice and the Andersens and would take out a portion of the top of the dam. The water level was so high that the remains of the three men and their baggage would be cascaded down to the valley below, making any forensic investigation very difficult.

It was a brilliant plan. A rumour would be circulated that the Andersens were in reality trained terrorists who belonged to a group associated with al Qaeda and that this was a suicide bombing. It was all very plausible and who would suspect the involvement of either the UK or Australian governments?

And now Gardner had to turn up. He looked at the dam and wondered if it were realistic to expect the four of them to be grouped together at the dam wall at the same time. The explosive would still do its job but Gardner would die as well. That would be sad. He liked Gardner but now he realised that his mole was becoming a problem and a danger. It wouldn't be a totally bad outcome if Gardner were to be eliminated at the same time. In fact Gardner now constituted a bigger threat than the Andersens.

This thought gave him his idea. The best outcome was for all four of them to perish in the explosion. Failing that the next best outcome was for Ventrice and Gardner to be taken while allowing the Andersens to escape. They could be dealt with one way or another later.

That was it. He had his plan which could be varied depending on the outcome of the groupings. Either way Ventrice would be eliminated, the whole affair could be blamed on Islamic terrorists and he would collect the magnificent payoff he had arranged with Blaines.

He was happy. He forced himself to be calm and waited for his phone call from Buckingham.

He didn't have long to wait. In the distance he saw the white Toyota turn off Yettie Road into the short feeder road known as Whispering Wall Road. He eased himself out of the car and walked quickly to the spot he had picked out in the section of the park devoted to antique machinery. He hid himself behind a large yellow object whose original purpose he couldn't imagine. Still the location offered him a clear view of the car park and the dam, which was what he wanted.

The Toyota drew closer and entered the car park. It stopped at the northern end close to the entrance to the dam wall.

He watched as all four doors opened and the men alighted. He observed them through his binoculars. The only man who seemed happy was Ventrice. Both the Andersens appeared preoccupied while Gardner was looking around nervously.

**

Robinson was not the only person watching the occupants of the Toyota. John Foster had trailed it along the Gorge Road, up to Williamstown and onto the oddly named Yettie Road. A sign on Yettie Road announced the short side road which led to the Whispering Wall.

Foster turned into it. It was a short road leading to the car park and Foster decided to stop along it rather than drive into the car park. As far as he could see there was no other car in the car park apart from the Toyota. He would be obvious if he drove in. He would park here for a while and attempt to observe what was happening. Through the telephoto lens of his camera he had an adequate view. He watched and waited.

**

Ventrice was oblivious to the general air of nervousness around him. He walked across to the dam wall. To his left the waters of the reservoir were lapping near the top of the wall; to the right was the sheer fall down the dam face to the valley below.

He knew there were great photographs to be had. He walked back to the car and picked up his heavy camera bag.

"Come on Phillip, let's have a short walk and take some pictures." He turned to his bodyguards and said "there's no-one around. Could you two stay here and keep an eye on things while we have a stroll across the dam?"

Ventrice and Gardner set off across the dam with Ventrice delighted at the thought of the pictures he could compose. The Andersens stood in the car park wondering what to do.

Buckingham's phone broke the silence. He looked at the screen. As expected it was Ben. His voice sounded strained. "Trevor, what's happening?"

"They've gone for a walk across the dam."

"Why aren't you with them?"

"Because Ventrice told us specifically to wait here. What am I supposed to do? Argue with him?"

"No, I guess you had to go along with it."

"What do you want us to do now then?"

"Do you think you can take both of them?"

Buckingham hesitated. "Well I guess. But it's a risk. One false move and we're in the shit."

"All right. Give me some time and I'll think of something."

"Do you think we need to call it off and come up with a new plan?"

"Maybe. Just sit tight for now and we'll see what happens."

Buckingham casually walked over to the dam wall to read the visitors' information sign, located near to the start of the curved wall. The notice pointed out that the wall was such a perfect shape it transmitted even quiet conversations from one end of the wall to the other.

He looked across the dam and listened. He could hear a murmur of voices. He moved closer to the wall and found to his amazement that he could hear a conversation.

It was Ventrice and Gardner who had now walked to the far end of the dam wall and were leaning on the rail talking. He listened for a short while and what he heard alarmed him. He walked quietly away from the wall back into the car park and phoned Ben.

"What's up?" asked Robinson.

"I just overheard those two having a conversation."

"How did you manage that? They're on the far side of the dam."

"Listen, the reason it's called the Whispering Wall is that it's a perfect curve and it transmits even low voices all round the wall."

"All very nice for the tourists I'm sure. But is it relevant?"

"Bloody oath it is. They were talking about us."

"What did they say?"

"Well I couldn't hear the whole thing but I got the gist of it. That guy Gardner was telling Ventrice that he's got some suspicions about us. He said we might not be what we seemed."

"The bastard" said Robinson, "he's trying to nobble the plan. That settles it. I know how to deal with him."

"But if they're suspicious what can we do? They'll be on their guard."

"Don't do anything. I've got a plan. Just walk slowly and casually back towards your car and be ready to get out of here fast."

"How will we know when to move?"

"You'll know all right. Now go." He rang off.

The Andersens walked slowly back towards the car wondering what was happening.

Robinson turned his attention to where Ventrice and Gardner were still leaning on the rail chatting. This was not the right place. He waited. His patience was very soon rewarded when he saw them walk slowly back across the dam. It wasn't what he had hoped for but it would have to do.

In an ideal world he would have taken the Andersens with them but it was not to be. They would have to be dealt with later unfortunately. They would have to be bribed into silence or disposed of. Luckily that was not his problem. He would have achieved the major objective and earned his reward. The Andersens would then be Blaines' problem. He could make the decision.

He waited patiently and watched as the two men walked slowly back across the dam. When they were almost in the middle Ventrice put down his camera bag and pulled out his expensive camera. This was the moment and the location was exactly right. He looked at the screen on his phone and pressed the button.

**

Further down the road Foster was sitting in Debbie's car feeling very sleepy as he watched the not very interesting sight of two men strolling across the dam. He yawned as he saw Ventrice stop and retrieve his camera from its bag. His drowsiness was banished in an instant by the sound of an enormous explosion. He looked up to see a hole at the top of the dam wall where he had only just seen Ventrice and Gardner. Of Ventrice and Gardner there was no sign at all.

It was a tribute to the engineers who designed and built the dam that it appeared to be intact apart from the one smallish hole at the top.

Nevertheless the dam was full and water was pouring across the walkway and down the sheer face of the wall to the valley below.

Foster shuddered. If there was anything left of Ventrice and Gardner it would be part of the growing flood on the valley floor.

Shocked as he was there was enough of the newsman in him to keep taking photographs.

As he did so he was aware of a car in the car park suddenly coming out from an area behind the museum part of the park. Tyres screaming it headed for the white Toyota where it briefly stopped. The driver yelled something to the two men standing near it and took off once more with a screech of tyres.

The car was in a great hurry and would be level with Foster in a few seconds. He crouched down to avoid being seen but pointed his camera at the car and kept taking pictures until it had passed him.

As he put his head up again he saw the Toyota also leaving the car park at breakneck speed. Once more he ducked but kept the camera running until that car had passed.

He sat up and saw that the two cars were heading at speed towards Williamstown. Suddenly it was very quiet. He looked around shocked and realised he was probably the only living soul in the park.

What should he do?

He started the car and drove slowly into the car park. He stopped the car close to the dam and got out. He looked down to the valley floor. He wasn't sure what he would see but at the back of his mind was the vain hope that maybe someone had survived.

But there was no sign of anyone or anything. Nor was there any sound except for the chatter of the birds and the rushing of the water.

He stood there defeated. There was nothing he could do except call for help. He picked up his phone and dialled 999. To his surprise the phone told him there was no such number. What was going on? Then he remembered. Someone had mentioned that the emergency number in Australia wasn't 999. What was it? 111, 100, 000? He had a better idea. He still had Brian Chambers' number in his phone. He tried that and waited hopefully. After a few seconds he heard the familiar voice. "G'day John, how are you?"

"Brian, thank god I've found you. I've got a huge problem."

"Calm down John. Tell me what's the trouble."

Foster forced himself to be calmer than he felt. He told Chambers as quickly as he could what had happened.

"OK John" said Chambers sombrely. "Have you contacted emergency services?"

"No" sobbed Foster, "I couldn't remember the number. I tried 999 but that doesn't work."

"Ok John, stay calm. It's 000, but never mind; I'll sort that out and I'll come over myself. Is there anyone else there?"

"No I'm all on my own. The Andersens have taken off."

"What were the Andersens doing there – if it was them?"

"Well nothing. They were standing near their car and when the explosion happened they jumped in the car and drove off. Oh, after the other guy said something to them."

"What other guy?"

"I couldn't really tell. His car was parked in an area I couldn't easily see. I just saw the car scream over to the Andersens. He shouted something to them and both cars took off."

"I don't suppose you got the rego numbers?"

"No, I was shocked and it all happened so quickly."

"Pity, never mind."

"Wait a minute. I took some photos of both cars so maybe I can get the numbers from them."

"Now you're talking John. Good man. Look, I'll get off now and organise the emergency services. Meanwhile you look at your photos and see what you can find out about these cars. I'll phone you back in a few minutes. Stay put, keep calm and don't touch anything. OK?"

"Yes, I understand."

Chambers spent a frantic few minutes organising fire engines ambulances and forensics. Then he called Foster.

"Hi John, I've organised some help. In just a few minutes you'll be joined by the local fire department, ambulance and police. They should be with you very quickly. Then there'll be Forensics coming up from Adelaide and I'll be over. So I'll see you in an hour or so. How are you coping?"

"I'm OK. I feel a bit sick but I guess that will pass."

"Good, hang on in there. Did you have any joy with the cars?"

"Some. The car the Andersens were driving is a white Toyota sedan. I'm not sure of the model and I can't see the registration number."

"That's OK. It's probably the car they hired so someone at UKIP should be able to give us the number. What about the other car?"

"That's a Nissan hatch, a beige one. Again I couldn't see the number."

"Pity, but I'll put out an alert. You never know."

"I'm sorry Brian, but I've seen the driver before. I watched him in Sydney meet separately with the Andersens and with Phillip Gardner."

"Really? Send me his picture will you and I'll circulate it. Now sit tight. Help will be with you in a few minutes and I'll see you in a while."

"Ok thanks Brian. See you soon."

**

Foster sat in his car and waited. He restlessly tapped his hand on the dash. Very soon he heard the sounds of sirens in the distance. Here come the cavalry, he thought.

The vehicles swept into the car park; a fire engine, ambulance and a police car. Foster got out of his car to talk to them.
"Are you Mr Foster?" asked the burly policeman.
"Yes that's me."
"Good, can you tell me what happened?"
Foster described the events as briefly as he could. The leader of the firemen was looking thoughtfully at the hole in the dam and the water pouring through. He turned to the policeman and said "I don't think there's much we can do about the dam. I'll get onto the Water Board and see what they say."
"OK" said the policeman, "we'll just keep everyone away from the dam until they can erect some barriers. Come with me Mr Foster and I'll get you to write out a full statement."
Foster sat in the police car and scribbled down his statement. The policeman seemed satisfied.
"Thank you sir. Could you please stay for a while? DI Chambers is on his way over and would like a word with you when he arrives."
"Yes I will. I'll go and sit in my car if that's all right with you."
He sat in his car and waited for Chambers, still feeling slightly queasy.
Then he remembered. He had better phone Debbie. He didn't know how and when the story would hit the news but she would worry that he was caught up in it.
She answered almost immediately. "Hi John, how's it going?"
"Hi, things have happened. Are you alone?"
"Yes, I'm still in the hotel room. What's the matter?"
He related the events as succinctly as he could.

"And now I'm just sitting here waiting for Chambers to arrive."

Debbie was shocked. "Poor Francis. And poor Ed. What a way to go. At least you're safe."

"But it wasn't Ed with him?"

"What do you mean? Ed always goes with him."

"Not this time. Ed wasn't there. It was the other guy from UKIP, Phillip Gardner."

"Really! That's odd. I wonder what happened to Ed. And you say it definitely was the Andersens?"

"Yes I'm sure it was them. They beat it pretty quick after the explosion."

"Do you think they were responsible?"

"Well it's tempting to think that but they were just waiting by the car."

"Maybe they planted the bomb?"

"Possibly, but they have no history of knowing anything about explosives."

"What about this guy Gardner?"

"I only met him once but I saw him a lot and he didn't strike me as the type who would be a suicide bomber. My money is on the other guy, the one who spoke to the Andersens and then left quickly."

"But you said he wasn't anywhere near them."

"I know, but I think you can detonate a bomb remotely. Anyhow I guess Chambers and the forensics team will piece together what really happened. Chambers should be here in about half an hour then I'll see what he wants to do. So I could be here a while."

"As long as you're safe. Should I go and break the news to the twins? They'll be devastated."

"No, don't mention any of this to anyone. Let it be handled officially."

"All right, I'll stay here and keep my phone with me. Take care. I love you."
"I love you too and I'll keep you posted. See you later. Bye."

Chapter 36

Michael Robinson drove up Yettie Road back to Williamstown at high speed until it occurred to him that he needed to slow down for a while to allow the Toyota to catch up. His instructions to the Andersens at the dam site had been brief but specific: "Follow me and don't lose me. Stick with me whatever I do."

The two cars hurried to Williamstown where Robinson slowed down to the speed limit. No need to draw unwanted attention.

Robinson carefully looked up each side street as he drove slowly past. He finally found what he wanted and turned into it. The Toyota followed.

The side street was quite long, lined with trees and deserted. Perfect! He drove along it for a short distance and pulled off to the roadside under a tree. Greg Andersen obediently parked the Toyota behind him.

The Andersens got out of their car and approached Robinson who was just climbing out.

"What's happening? Why have we stopped here?" asked Greg Andersen.

"Simple" replied Robinson, "your car is known to the tour team. It won't be long before the police know it too. My car isn't known so get all your gear and I'll take you to the airport. You didn't leave anything behind at the hotel that could identify you?"

"No we gave you our luggage last night as you asked so the rooms are empty. Where is it all by the way?"

"Don't worry; it's in this car. Now empty your car and get in here. I just need to make a phone call and we'll be off."

Robinson walked a few steps up the street and stopped in the shade of a tree to make his phone call. In London it was early evening and Geoffrey Blaines was sitting in the study of his Surrey home when his mobile phone rang.

He noted the caller and picked it up warily. He managed a tense "hello".

"It's Michael."

"Have you got news for me?"

"Yes it's done."

"Plan A or B?"

"Er neither. More a modified Plan B. Circumstances were against us."

"Tell me more."

Robinson related how they had eliminated Ed Hopkins from the outing but that Phillip Gardner had opted to go instead. He pointed out that Gardner had become a problem and was openly hostile to the plan and so would have to be dealt with.

"So what do we need to do?" asked Baines anxiously.

"Nothing. He's been taken care of."

Robinson explained how his explosion had eliminated both Ventrice and Gardner.

"Isn't that a good result?" suggested Blaines.

"Yes it is but it's left us with a problem. The Andersens are still with us. I'm taking them to the airport now."

"But they should have been eliminated as well" hissed Blaines.

"It just wasn't possible. I had one chance only so I took it. They are expecting to fly back to the safe house in England and to be given their reward.

"But they haven't done anything. And there's nowhere near enough money to pay them what we promised them on top of what we are paying you."

"Then you'll have to think up something else. They'll be on their way back later today. And I won't be far behind them."

"OK leave it with me and I'll talk to the MI5 team about what can be done. I need to talk to them quickly anyway and get ASIO mobilised to quash any deep investigation. Get yourself back home and we'll talk again."

"Aren't you going to say 'well done'?"

"Yes of course Michael, but I'm a bit preoccupied with what I have to do now. You've done a good job and we'll celebrate when you're back."

"OK I'll talk to you then. Bye."

"Bye Michael."

Robinson walked slowly back to where the Andersens were waiting by the car.

"Right, let's get you to the airport."

"Who were you calling?" asked Greg Andersen innocently.

"If you must know it's my boss in England."

"You mean Bill?"

"Yes, Bill."

"You told him how things worked out?"

"Yes, but get in the car and we'll talk on the way."

They abandoned the Toyota where it was and headed to the airport, an hour's drive away. Someone would notice the Toyota eventually but by then they would be long gone.

"So you've got your tickets and passports?" asked Robinson.

"Yeah" said Greg.

"And when you get to Heathrow you will be met by one of us who will take you back to the safe house until we sort things out."

"I can't see there's much to sort out" said Greg. "Just give us our money and new ID and we disappear. That was the deal wasn't it?"

"Oh you know; debriefing and final arrangements" replied Robinson vaguely.

Greg Andersen was non-committal and managed only "Hm".

They reached the airport without incident. Robinson dropped them at the terminal and said "that's it guys. You're on your own now. I've got a few things to tidy up and then I'll be on a later flight. I'll talk to you in London. We can celebrate there."

The Andersens took their luggage and walked into the terminal. Robinson was indeed on a later flight and could have gone with the Andersens but he had decided that they were now a liability and he didn't want to be around if they were recognised.

He was safe as long as he was not connected to the Andersens. The fact that that pesky reporter Foster had made some sort of connection had rendered the Andersens a potential risk. But they were now Blaines' problem not his.

He left the airport and found a nearby café where he sat and read a newspaper over a coffee for two hours until he judged it to be safe to return to the airport.

He was booked on a flight that was direct from Adelaide to London via Malaysia.

The Andersens had open tickets to get them to Melbourne by a local airline, from where they had a reservation for an evening flight from Melbourne to London via Hong Kong.

Robinson had purchased the tickets to ensure that the Andersens still believed the plan he had outlined. He had certainly never intended that they should be used, but now there seemed to be no other option. London would have to decide how to pay them off or otherwise eliminate the risk.

**

Meanwhile in London the phones were ringing hot. Blaines had contacted his MI5 colleagues, who in turn had contacted ASIO in Australia and the propaganda machine had been set in motion. The story was released to the international media with the strong implication that it was an act of terrorism, perpetrated by a terrorist, a suicide bomber from Ventrice' own entourage.

ASIO agents in Australia were dispatched to the dam site and the Feathers Hotel to take over the investigation from the local police and to ensure that the correct conclusions were drawn.

**

Before boarding the Adelaide to Melbourne flight the Andersens had changed into casual clothes to make themselves less likely to be recognised. They reached Melbourne without incident and checked in for their Hong Kong flight.

"How long do we get in Hong Kong before we fly on to London?" asked Tony innocently.

"We might not be going to London just yet mate" replied Greg.

Tony as usual was confused. "What do you mean?"

"Mate I smell a rat. Ben was very cagey back there and I thought I managed to catch a few bits of his phone call I wasn't too happy about."

"But the job's done and now we get paid don't we?" said Tony brightly.

"Maybe" admitted Greg. "But I get a sneaky feeling that bomb had our name on it as well, and we were being set up to be the bombers, conveniently blowing ourselves up."

"They wouldn't do that would they?"

Greg smiled. "Tony you wouldn't believe what people can do when there's politics involved. They make our activities look quite tame."

"Are you saying we won't get paid?" asked Tony anxiously.

"If only it were that simple. If they don't pay what are they going to do with us? I think we need to take out some insurance."

"So are we not going to London then?"

"Yeah we are still going to London; or at least nearby, but not by the flight they are expecting us on."

Tony was impressed. Greg always knew what to do. Greg continued.

"At Hong Kong we'll buy ourselves another flight to somewhere else in Europe and then we'll enter England by train or by a different airport. Then I'll call friend Ben and we'll negotiate with them without them knowing where we are."

Tony looked concerned. "But where will we get the money for that?"

"Don't worry. I've still got most of the initial payment they gave us. I made sure I got it out of the account they set up into one of mine. So we're quite rich. We'll be a lot richer still when we've done this deal."

Tony was impressed. "You always think of everything Greg. What would I do without you?"

"Don't I always look after you mate? Come on we're boarding. Next stop Hong Kong eh?"

Chapter 37

Foster sat in his car trying to make sense of what had happened. He was still shocked and queasy. He felt he still had to suspect the Andersens but on the surface they had appeared to play no direct role in the events of the day.
But if they were innocent what were they doing there? And the mystery man had to be involved in some way but how? Foster's mind was racing but he was no closer to any rational explanation of what he had seen. Obviously Ventrice had enemies. All politicians with strong views had enemies but these events didn't fit the picture of a lone avenger with a grudge; they had an aura of organisation about them. But who? And why? His feverish thoughts were interrupted by a tap on the window. He looked up to see the big red friendly face of Brian Chambers.
"Ah Brian, am I glad to see you."
He got out of the car and tried to stand up, but instead almost fell over. An arm came around his shoulder and held him up as a big but gentle voice said "take it easy John. You've had one hell of a shock. Let's sit on this bench over here and you can tell me all about it."
Chambers led Foster to a bench in the shade and helped him sit down. Chamber's face was a picture of concern.
"Are you OK mate?"
"Yeah I'm OK. I just feel a bit sick and wobbly. It's a lot to take in. Why would anyone do that?"
"If I knew the answer to that mate I'd be more than a simple policeman. Now, take your time and try to tell me what you saw, in as much detail as you can."
Foster related to Chambers everything he could remember; Ventrice and Gardner walking to the far end of the dam while the bodyguards remained at the starting

point; the bodyguards walking back to their car; the explosion; the hidden car racing out, pausing only to say something to the bodyguards; the bodyguards rushing out after it.

Chambers listened quietly as Foster tried to remember. Foster suddenly stopped and said "it was horrible. One minute they were there and the next there was nothing." Tears filled his eyes.

Chambers put his arm around him. "It's Ok John. Let it out. No one should have to see anything like that."

Foster sobbed and shook. He would have fallen over had Chambers not been there to support him.

"Thanks Brian, it all happened so quickly. Why did this happen? I didn't like Ventrice all that much but I wouldn't wish that on anybody."

"Frankly mate I don't understand it either. I guess, given the high profile of this, it will be taken away from me and given to someone more senior. And I can't say I'm sorry. In the meantime I think I'll just do what I have to do. What do you make of this other guy Gardner? Could he have been the man who pulled the trigger?"

"I can't see it Brian. He seemed a pretty regular guy. He didn't strike me as being a suicide bomber."

"Whatever type it takes. Fortunately I haven't met too many of them. In fact none. I can see them bringing in the terrorism experts on this one. But the other guys. You seem convinced it was the Andersens. But what the hell were they doing there if they weren't part of the plot?"

Foster shook his head as if trying to clear his mind. "Buggered if I know. I've spent the last half hour trying to work that out and I still have no answers. But I'm convinced the other guy had something to do with it. In fact it could have been him that detonated the bomb."

"I guess we won't know until we've rounded them up and had a chance to question them. We'll see what the forensics team come up with. At least they might be able to tell us how it was done, but then we've still got to figure out who and why."

He paused and smiled. "Anyway, how are you feeling now John? Better?"

"Yeah I think I got spooked being all on my own. Now that you guys are here things seem a bit more normal. I'll be OK."

"Good because I want to go back to The Feathers and have a poke around Ventrice' and Gardner's rooms before other people get to them."

"Haven't you got forensics there already?"

"Yeah they'll be there but I want to have a sniff around myself before they mess things up too much.

"Can I come as well" asked Foster as he remembered something he wanted to do.

"Sure, do you want to come with me?"

"No, I've got Debbie's car here. I'll follow you back."

"Let's go then. The local boys can handle things here and there's not much more we can do."

Chambers had a quick word with the local policeman and returned to his police car. He made his way quickly back to Adelaide with Foster keeping up as best he could.

Chapter 38

John Foster enjoyed an exhilarating drive back to The Feathers. He followed DI Chambers who used his siren and blue lights to cut through the traffic while Foster followed him as closely as he could. After forty five minutes they arrived.

Various police vehicles were already there and the two bedrooms which had been occupied by Ventrice and Gardner had been cordoned off. They made their way to Ventrice' room.

As they approached a police woman beckoned them to the adjoining room. They entered to find the twins sitting on a sofa, red eyed and tearful, with Debbie sitting alongside consoling them. In another chair sat Ed Hopkins, already pale and drawn from his food poisoning, trying to come to terms with what had happened.

"Hi Debbie" said Chambers in as quiet a voice as he could muster. "Could you introduce me?"

"Hi Brian, these ladies, Alice and Grace, are Francis' assistants and Ed Hopkins here is Francis' right hand man. This is DI Chambers from Mannum Police."

Everyone nodded soberly not really knowing what to say. Eventually Hopkins looked up and said in a quiet voice, "poor Phillip; it's all my fault."

"Why do you say that Ed?" asked Chambers.

"It's obvious isn't it? Whoever planned this wanted Francis on his own. They made sure I wouldn't go with him. What they couldn't have known was that Phillip would volunteer to take my place."

"What did you mean by 'they made sure I couldn't go with him'?"

Hopkins sighed. "I was supposed to go, not Phillip. After the reception last night I was taken ill and have been vomiting and shitting ever since. I couldn't make it this morning."

"Couldn't it have been co-incidence? These things happen you know."

"Possibly, but it seems no-one else had a problem with the food. Just me. And then I remembered; a waiter came to me with a drink, the only drink on the tray. I thought at the time it tasted a little odd but I was talking to people and just drank it. I think it was laced with something."

"It's possible" admitted Chambers. "Do you mind if we take a blood sample to see if we can identify anything?"

"Of course not; do what you have to do. What a mess. Francis was a great man, one of the best."

"Yes sir; what I'd like to do is to line up all the waiters who were on duty last night and see if you can pick him out."

"Yes that's fine. I think I can remember him."

Chambers delegated one of the constables present to seek out the manager and arrange for an identity parade. He turned to the twins.

"Ladies, I am truly sorry for your loss, however I must insist that you remain here for a while. We will undoubtedly have more questions. If we can assist you in any way in the meantime please ask the policewoman here."

"I'll look after them Brian" added Debbie.

Ed Hopkins stood up. "Does that apply to me also Detective Inspector? As you can imagine I have lots of things to do."

"No I guess not" replied Chambers. "But don't leave the hotel in case we need you."

"I won't, and thank you". Hopkins left the room still looking as if he should be in bed.

Chambers and Foster left the mourners and entered Ventrice' room. Apart from sealing off the room no significant work had yet started. The main forensics team had been despatched to the dam wall to see what they could discover."

"Nothing much unexpected here" remarked Chambers. "The room is pretty tidy."

Foster, who had entered the room behind him, looked about. "Brian, his laptop is over there. How about we take a look?"

"I don't know much about computers" admitted Chambers, "but aren't they usually password protected so you can't get in?"

"Usually, but maybe one of his girls knows it. They are his assistants after all."

Chambers smiled. "Very nice assistants too. Go and talk to them while I have a look around."

Foster went back to the adjoining room and asked the twins for the password. They looked at each other with shock on their faces. Grace said "but it contains Mr Ventrice' private files. I'm not sure we should."

"Look Grace" said Foster patiently, "if you don't tell us the computer will be handed over to forensics who will know how to get round the password. They will assume there is incriminating evidence on it and will examine every file minutely. Is that what you want?"

"Well no" said Grace nervously. "But can I have a word in private with Debbie before I give it to you?"

"That's a strange request but go ahead" replied Foster cautiously.

Grace led Debbie into the bathroom and closed the door. After a few minutes the door opened and the women emerged.

Debbie walked up to Foster and said "John, Grace will give you the password but I want to be there when you look at the files. OK?"

"That's fine" said Foster, already thinking he knew what this was about. "I'll bring the laptop in here and you can see what's on it."

He went back to Ventrice' room, picked up the laptop and returned to the twin's room. He opened the lid and switched it on. Grace had already written the password on a piece of paper. Foster looked at the Documents folder. It consisted of three main sections: Ventrice' business affairs, UKIP related matters and photographs. He glanced through the titles of the files struck him as particularly interesting or relevant.

I guess the police will go over the documents in some detail, he thought. No need to do a thorough search. Besides he didn't have the time. Instead he turned to the photographs.

He examined the structure of the folder. As he expected of Ventrice everything was neatly organised into years and locations. How many pictures of vineyards do you really need, he wondered.

There was one other folder obliquely titled 'Specials'. He clicked on it. Immediately he was informed that this folder was password protected. Foster knew he was on to something. He looked up.

"Grace, what's the password for this folder please?"

Grace glanced at the screen and turned very pale. "I'm not sure" she mumbled.

"Come on Grace" said Foster, "remember what I said before about forensics. I think I know what pictures are in here and I would like to remove some of them."

"I don't know what you mean" said Grace.

"I think you do Grace. I think Debbie would be interested to see them as well. Isn't Debbie a friend of yours?"

"Come on Grace" urged Debbie.

"All right" said Grace quietly. She gave them the password with tears streaming down her face.

Foster examined the folder structure. Ventrice had been thorough and organised as usual. Some of the folders had women's names in the title. He opened one at random tagged 'Provence – Yvette'.

It contained a large selection of stills and movie clips which appeared to have been taken in a Mediterranean villa with a walled courtyard and a pool. Many of the shots showed a naked lady in various poses, presumably Yvette, sometimes alone, sometimes with one or both of the twins. It appeared that Ventrice enjoyed taking photos of girl on girl action.

He selected one of the movie clips. It was, as he expected, a movie of the three women exploring each other, presumably taken by Ventrice. Towards the end the camera angle changed and Ventrice himself was part of the action. It seemed to Foster that this sequence was taken by a fixed rather than a hand held camera.

He closed the folder and began to look at the more recent ones. He was not surprised to find one tagged 'Sydney – Debbie'.

He opened it and looked first at the stills. It was as Debbie had described: poses in her red dress followed by topless poses at the "beach bar". There were many more. Foster steeled himself and pressed on. Next a sequence of the three girls totally naked at the bar, exactly as Debbie thought she had dreamed.

"I think you need to look at these Debbie" muttered Foster.

They both watched as the relatively innocent nude shots moved on. At one point Alice separated herself from the others and walked towards the camera, hips swaying provocatively. Debbie knew exactly what was happening at that point. She could recall vividly what she had hoped was a dream.

My god, she wondered, what else is there? Then she remembered with a shudder the point at which Ventrice had put down his camera, but at least that was the end of the still photos.

Debbie looked up from the screen to Foster. "So it was real" she said.

Foster nodded. "Are you OK?"

"Yes I'm all right. At least now I know the truth – don't I Grace?"

Grace was sitting to one side with her head in her hands. She didn't reply.

"There's more" said Foster. There's a movie clip. Do you want to see it?"

Debbie nodded. "I need to know what happened, however bad it is, and then I can put it behind me. Go on, play it."

The movie appeared to have been taken with a fixed mounted camera. It started at the point where the twins had removed their panties and were persuading Debbie to do the same.

"There must have been a hidden camera" murmured Debbie. "I don't remember seeing one."

The movie recorded every detail as Debbie had described it right up to Alice tugging at Ventrice' trousers. That's when I passed out, she thought. Was there any more? There was. There was a short sequence of Alice and Ventrice enjoying each other, after which it ended.

"Thank goodness that's ended "said Debbie with a sigh. "Are there any others?"

"No" replied Foster. It's the only movie clip in this folder and I can't see any other folders that look relevant.

"Good" said Debbie. "Grace, I want the truth from you. Don't mess me about. Is that all there was or is there more?"
Grace looked up and through her tears said quietly "That's all there is Debbie, I swear."
"But did Francis do anything to me?"
"No he never touched you. That wasn't his style."
Debbie raised her voice "What do you mean 'wasn't his style'? Just what was his style?"
"Don't be angry Debbie. He certainly wanted you, as he had wanted lots of other women, but he wanted you to come to him of your own free will. Those photos were just a warm up. He would have charmed you into bed eventually."
"Would he now? I'm really sorry he's dead but it looks as if I've had a lucky escape."
Grace had recovered her composure. "Don't look at it like that Debbie. I think all the women that Francis was involved with will look back on the experience with fond memories. He was a very generous man, as well as a lot of fun."
"But how could you and Alice put up with all this?"
"It was fine, really. Francis was very good to us and our job was interesting and exciting. We went along with it and enjoyed it. I'm sorry if you think we exploited you."
"No that's OK. I'll put it behind me. What will you do now Grace?"
"I don't know really. It's too soon to think about it. Francis always said he would look after us in his will so we'll have to see."
Foster interrupted the conversation. "I think we should delete that folder of you Debbie before forensics come in and take the machine to pieces."

"But isn't that tampering with evidence? And what would Chambers say?"

"Chambers is still shuffling about in the other room. But not for long. It's now or never. You don't really want this stuff examined do you?"

"No I don't. OK do it." She looked at Grace. "Grace not a word to anyone about this."

"I won't, I promise" said Grace.

Foster deleted the folder and then deleted it from the recycle bin. He knew that it might be possible to resurrect files that had been deleted but he hoped they would see no reason to do that. He was only just in time as Chambers re-appeared.

"I've had a good look round and I can't see anything noteworthy in there. I'll let forensics loose on it. Have you found anything interesting on the computer?"

Foster recovered quickly. "Not much that I can understand. There are business documents and UKIP stuff, mostly pretty boring. The highlights are the pictures of Ventrice' past girlfriends, some of them quite steamy."

Chambers smiled."So he had an eye for the ladies eh?"

"You could say that. But I couldn't see any clues that would help you solve your case. Maybe forensics can do a better job."

"Yeah I'll get them to take a look. And maybe get some political analysts on the job; see what they come up with. I think I'll take a look at Phillip Gardner's room. Do you want to come with me?"

"Sure" replied Foster and they went off to find Gardner's room.

The room was on another floor but was easy to identify by the policeman on guard outside it, making sure that no-one entered.

"Constable have you got the key?" asked Chambers.

"Yes sir" he replied and opened the door for them.

Apart from an unmade bed the room was tidy. Chambers opened the wardrobes and rummaged through what few contents there were while Foster walked over to a small table on which a few documents were strewn about. Among them was a diary.

Well, thought Foster, a man who still keeps an old fashioned paper diary. He picked it up and flicked through. He could see it was used mostly for keeping track of appointments with almost no personal narrative. He flicked to the pages for the tour and noticed a number of appointments for someone described only as 'MR'. The latest was for only two days ago, on Sunday when he would have been in Sydney. Foster looked at the time and realised with a sense of triumph that this was an appointment he had witnessed; the meeting with the mystery man. So he knew now the mystery man's initials were probably MR.

"Yes" he exclaimed.

Chambers looked round and said "have you found something John?"

"Well a clue at least" said Foster. "I've just worked out from this diary that the mystery man's initials are 'MR'."

"Good one, but it's only a start. There must be a lot of MRs in the world."

"Yeah I know. I'm just looking to see if there's any further mention of him. Bingo, look at this."

Chambers looked as Foster pointed to a diary entry on Sunday May 15. 'Odd message from John Foster. Need to talk to Michael'.

"Well you get a mention John. What's it all about?"

"I caught him at the evening drinks and just said to him to watch his security men. They might not be what they seem. So then he needs to talk to Michael. The next day he has a meeting with MR, the mystery man. Doesn't that mean the mystery man, who also meets with the Andersens, is called Michael R something?"

"It's a reasonable theory" admitted Chambers. "Have a flick through and see if there are any more clues."

"It's a pity we haven't got his mobile phone. I'll bet the full name is in there."

"True" said Chambers, "but I don't think there will be much left of it after that explosion. Keep looking though the diary; there may be more stuff. And don't forget we can interview the UKIP staff. One of them may know who Michael R is."

Just then a voice came from the doorway. "Would you stop right now please?"

Chambers looked around to see a tall, hard looking younger man standing in the doorway. "Who the hell are you" said Chambers.

"I might ask you the same question."

"Well if you can't work it out from my uniform I'm DI Chambers of Mannum Police and I'm conducting an investigation."

"Not any more you're not sport. It's mine now."

"On who's say so" asked Chambers as politely as he could be.

"On the Government's say so DI Chambers. My name is Andrew Koomer. I'm with ASIO. Here's my ID card and authorisation." He held out two documents.

Chambers scanned the documents and looked up.

"Well I guess it's yours all right. I can't say I wasn't expecting this but why are ASIO interested?"

"A foreign politician of high rank is murdered by international terrorists on our soil. Of course we're interested."

"How do you know it's international terrorists?" asked Chambers.

"Well it seems pretty obvious to us. We need to determine who and why."

"We may have a different theory."

"Who's we?"

"John here and myself. This is John Foster. He's a reporter and was at the dam scene to witness the explosion. In fact he is probably the only witness there is."

"Well Mr Foster, we will certainly want to interview you. In the meantime both of you are under orders to talk to no one about this case and to cease any investigations you may be contemplating. Do I make myself clear?"

"Crystal" said Chambers, "but it seems a little high handed to ignore the opinions of people who are close to this."

"You can express any opinions you have DI Chambers, but only to me. How I treat them is my business. Now I want you to hand over any evidence you have collected to date. Have you taken anything out of these rooms?"

"No we haven't. We've just sealed them off and we were having a preliminary look round before the forensics team arrives. At the moment they are at the dam site."

"We've already sent our agents to the dam. And you can call off your forensics. We have our own team. Now if there's nothing else could you please vacate these premises and go back to your normal duties."

"I will be making a report of what we've done so far and what our interim thoughts are" said Chambers formally.

"That's fine" replied Koomer, "and please send me a copy. Here's my card. You can email it to me. But I repeat you are to do no further work on this case. I hope that's very clear. You too Mr Foster. No wild speculations for your readers. Now I have work to do."

Foster and Chambers left the room and walked back down the corridor.

"Supercilious sod" exclaimed Chambers. "I guessed it would be taken from me and given to someone more senior. But bloody ASIO! And did he have to be so snotty about it?"

"I guess it's very high profile" said Foster. "And look on the bright side. It's not your problem anymore."

"No I guess not. But the Andersens are and I would have liked to solve that little mystery."

"Speaking of which, I noticed you didn't mention that we have photos of the two getaway cars as well as the mystery man, Michael R and the Andersens. What do you intend to do with them?"

Chambers smiled for the first time since they had met Koomer. "Oh I might just string Koomer along for a bit until I hand those over. Can't make it too easy for the little bugger can we? In the meantime I might do a little digging of my own."

"I like your spirit Brian" said Foster, "But you've just been warned off big time."

"I'm merely following up some leads on my Anderson case" said Chambers innocently. "No law against that is there?"

The two men laughed.

"What's next then?" asked Foster.

"We'll wait and see if any of the vehicles are sighted but otherwise we'll lie low. Personally I don't hold out much hope. There are a lot of white Toyotas and Beige Nissan hatches out there, but you never know. You and I need to compose a full report of what you've seen and what our theories are. I'll send that to my boss. He can decide what to do about ASIO. It's above my pay grade."

"When do you want to do that?"

"How about right now while it's still fresh?"

"Fine. Let's go and see if we can find a room somewhere. We can use your laptop. It saves going back to Mannum."

"OK" agreed Foster. You go down to reception and see what you can sort out and I'll let Debbie know what we are doing."

Chambers walked away towards Reception while Foster made his way back to the twin's room. Debbie was still there with the twins, who were very tearful. He explained what they were doing and Debbie volunteered to stay with them a while longer and offer what comfort she could. As Foster walked away he heard a voice call "Mr Foster, a moment please."

He turned around to face Andrew Koomer. "Oh it's you" he said without enthusiasm.

"Don't sound so delighted" quipped Koomer. "As you're still here we might just have that little chat we talked about. Ventrice' room is free. Let's go there."

Foster followed him into Ventrice' room.

"Sit down John" said Koomer, "and tell me all about it."

"Before I do I must text DI Chambers. I was supposed to be helping him with his report. He'll wonder where I am."

Koomer's face was impassive. "If you must."

Foster sent Chambers a quick text 'caught by Koomer. See you when I'm free'.

Chambers read the text, smiled and found himself a quiet spot in Reception to collect his thoughts and scribble a few notes. He sent Foster a curt reply. 'don't let the bastard grind you down'.

Foster smiled as he read it while Koomer's face remained impassive.

"Are you ready John?"

"Yes, what do you want to know?"

"Just tell me in your own words what you saw."

Foster related how he was parked up the road but through his camera lens he could see Ventrice and Gardner walk to the other side of the dam while two other men stood by the car.

"And these other two men were?"

"They were Ventrice' Australian bodyguards. But I'm not sure they were who they claim to be. I think I've seen them somewhere before."

"Let's just leave the realms of speculation and imagination for the moment shall we? The other men were Ventrice bodyguards. Right?"

"Right."

"Go on."

"There was a sudden explosion and Ventrice and Gardner were gone. There was just a hole in the dam where they had been."

"Did you see any sign of anyone causing the explosion?"

"No, none at all, but I've got a theory."

"Let's leave your theories for a minute. You didn't actually see how the explosion was caused?"

"No."

"So it could have been the man with Ventrice could it not?"

"Well I guess but….."

"No buts. It could have been this man, er, Gardner?"

"I suppose so, but I didn't pick him as a suicide bomber."

"So you're an expert in these matters John?"

"Well no, of course not, but I met him once or twice."

"You met him once or twice" repeated Koomer slowly. "And on that basis you decide he's not a suicide bomber?"

"But there was someone else there."

Koomer sighed. "Go on, tell me."

"Just after the explosion another car came out of the far corner of the car park at speed. He stopped outside the bodyguards' car, yelled something and took off again. Then the bodyguards took off after him."

"You hadn't noticed this car before?"

"No he must have been hidden by all those bits of old machinery they've got there."

"Did you hear what he said?"

"No, but I think he could have detonated the bomb and then warned the others to get out."

Koomer leaned back in his chair and smiled. "So it's a conspiracy between these three men is it? I have to say you have a vivid imagination. Isn't it just possible that he was an innocent tourist and was panicked by the explosion, as were the others?"

"But I think I've seen him somewhere before. He....."

"You seem to have seen everyone before John. You have quite an imagination. Let me ask you a question. What were you doing there and why were you the only reporter?"

"I was trailing Ventrice hoping to get a story. That's what I do for a living."

"But how did you know he was going to be at the dam? It was supposed to be a secret."

"I had a tip off from a person in Ventrice' party."

"Have you any more to tell me?"

"No not really, that's what happened."

Koomer was sombre. "So John, you worm your way into a secret meeting and then you start making up all manner of conspiracy theories. I think I've heard enough, but I will warn you again. Not one word of your wild theories is to be published or communicated to anyone else. If you do I shall arrest you under the terrorism act and you will be in lots of trouble. Am I clear?"

"Yes that's clear. But I don't think DI Chambers shares your view of this."

"You just leave DI Chambers to me. Now I think we're done. I hope for your sake we don't have to meet again. Now go before I change my mind and arrest you."

Foster knew when he was beaten. He stood up and left the room and went back to reception to find Chambers in a chair waiting for him.

"You look as if you've been sucking on a lemon John."

"Yeah, it's that bastard Koomer."

"He's a case isn't he? Tell me all about it."

Foster told him the gist of the interview and added "he wasn't interested in anything I had to say. It's as if he'd made his mind up that Gardner was a suicide bomber and that's all there is to it. The other people were just innocent bystanders who panicked."

"Yeah, very convenient isn't it?"

"What do you mean?"

"Maybe the others are being protected somehow, or am I just getting caught up in your theories? Anyway let's get this report done and sent to my boss – and we'll put all our thoughts in it. He can work out what to do. I've got a room organised just here. Let's get on with it."

As Chambers was getting up there was a shout from the corridor. "DI Chambers."

Chambers looked around to see Ed Hopkins hurrying towards them.

"I'm glad I caught you before you left. There's been a development."

"What's that?" asked Chambers.

"You know that identity parade you were organising to find the waiter who spiked my drink? No need for it. I've seen him again. He's on duty now in the Georgian Room. I was passing by and I saw him."

"Let's have a word then" said Chambers. "Lead me to him."

Hopkins led them back to the Georgian room and pointed to a waiter who was setting up glasses. He was a small, slight young man who appeared to be barely out of his teens judging by his pale, spotty face.

Chambers walked over to him and said quietly "excuse me, can I have a word sir?"

The young man looked startled but recovered quickly. "What about?"

"You were on duty at the reception last night I believe."

"What if I was? I haven't done anything."

"No one has said you have. We just need some help in piecing together the events of last night. Could you spare us a few minutes?"

"Well all right, as long as you're quick. I'm pretty busy."

"It won't take long. Just a few questions. I've got an interview room organised if you'll just come this way."

The young man looked startled again but obediently followed Chambers to the room he had commandeered.

"Sit down and relax" began Chambers. "This won't take long. First what's your name son?"

"Darren."

"Darren what?"

"Darren Pilkington."

"That's better Darren. And you are employed here at The Feathers as a waiter?"

"Yeah, I've been here a few months."

"And you were on duty last night in this room?"

"Yes, I was handing out drinks."

"And you served this gentleman a drink" said Chambers pointing to Ed Hopkins.

"Maybe; I can't remember everyone I served drinks to."

"Well he says you did, and it tasted a bit odd. And soon after he was violently ill."

Darren was by now looking decidedly nervous but he was defiant.

"What's that got to do with me? I handed out drinks to lots of people and they didn't get sick did they? It's hardly my fault if the guy is ill is it?"

"That depends on whether you slipped something into his drink."

"Why would I want to do that?"

"That's what we want to know."

"I don't even know this guy. Can I go now?"

He made to stand up. Chambers also stood up and towered over him. He raised his voice and yelled. "Sit down Darren. You know a lot more than you're telling us. Now I've had enough lip from you. Two men have died and you may have something to do with it. I could arrest you now under the terrorism act and throw you to the wolves. So one more time. Was Mr Hopkins' drink tampered with?"

Darren turned white, looked down to the floor and whispered "yes, but it wasn't me."

"What do you mean it wasn't you?"

"It was this other guy."

"What other guy?"

"I don't know his name. He came up to me when I was delivering some drinks and asked me if I'd like to earn a quick hundred bucks."

"Go on."

"I said what for? He pointed to this guy, Mr Hopkins here, and said he was a good friend of his and wanted to play a practical joke on him."

"What kind of practical joke?"

"That's what I asked. He said he just wanted to put some stuff in his drink that would make him giggly and silly for a while."

"And you went along with it?"

"Well it seemed a pretty harmless prank."

"You stupid boy. Didn't you think about the consequences?"

"I guess not" said Darren miserably.

"OK, what did this man look like?"

"Tall, a bit posh looking, dark hair, looked as if he could handle himself. Oh and he had a pommie accent."

"Did he indeed? John, how would you describe your mystery man?"

Foster had been sitting quietly in a corner of the room as Chambers conducted the interview. "It sounds a bit like him doesn't it?"

A confused Darren sat quietly as Chambers pulled his phone from his pocket. He flipped through the recent photographs until he came to the pictures of the mystery man that Foster had taken in Sydney.

"Now Darren" he said in a quieter voice. "I want you to look at this photo and tell me if this is the man you spoke to."

He passed the phone to Darren who examined it carefully.

"Yeah that's him" he said quietly. "Who is he?"

"I wish we knew" admitted Chambers. "Now you are absolutely sure. The penalties for giving false evidence in a case like this are very severe."

"No I swear that's him. What are you going to do with me?" he asked nervously.

Chambers gave him a hard look. "Darren you've been bloody stupid but I don't think there was any criminal intent. What you have told us may be useful so for now

I'm not going to charge you with anything. But don't go away. I may want to talk to you again. Go on, you can go."

A very relieved Darren stammered "yes sir" and left the room as quickly as he could.

"So it was deliberate" said Hopkins.

"Looks like it" agreed Chambers. "Of course it may just have saved your life."

"True, but it didn't do much good for Phillip. Who is this person?"

"That we don't know. Do you recognise him?"

Hopkins took the phone from Chambers and looked at the picture. He shook his head. "No I don't know him at all. How come you're so interested in him?"

"He's been observed having meetings with the two bodyguards and also separately with Phillip Gardner. We wondered why, especially as we have our suspicions about the bodyguards. Anyhow we are all done. The case has been handed over to ASIO and we've been told not to do any more. They seem to want to believe that Gardner was a suicide bomber."

"That's ridiculous" said Hopkins. I've known Phillip for a few years now and I can't think of anyone less likely to be a suicide bomber."

"I agree with you Ed but my hands are tied. I'm going to report everything I know to my boss and then it's his problem what he does with it. What are you going to do now?"

"I don't know. I guess we'll wrap things up here and go home. I suppose UKIP will want to look for a new leader, although it's going to be hard to find someone as good as Francis. It will be a big blow to them."

"Will it?" said Chambers thoughtfully. "So this is actually a very good result for UKIP's opponents."

"What are you getting at Brian?"

"Oh just letting my imagination roam a little. I'm starting to get a hint of a motive."

"You couldn't possibly think……. Could you?"

"No it's probably just wild speculation. Anyway I've got to get my report to my boss so if you'll excuse me. I'll keep you posted but as I said it's out of my hands now."

"OK thanks Brian. I've got plenty to do. I'll see you."

Chapter 39

While Foster and Chambers continued to work on their report Andrew Koomer was doing some reporting of his own.

He phoned his superior in ASIO to report that he had taken over the case from the local police and secured all locations. The ASIO team were assembling the evidence and suggesting their conclusions.

"Good" said the superior "and we know what those conclusions have to be. Well done Andrew."

"Thank you" said Koomer "but" and he paused slightly. "We have a problem."

"I don't like problems. Tell me all about it."

Koomer explained the discussions he had had with Foster and suggested he was a loose cannon who somehow needed to be silenced.

The superior listened carefully and finally said. "So he's clutching at a few strands but what does he actually know?"

"I don't think he knows much at all but he's got a lot of suspicions. If he keeps digging maybe he will unearth something embarrassing."

"OK Andrew, and thanks for the warning. Obviously we have to do something to curtail Foster's activities. Leave it with me and keep up the good work you are doing. I'll talk to you later."

While Koomer went back to his task of managing the local ASIO team his superior conferred with other senior officials in ASIO.

The remedies suggested varied from "do nothing; he'll not discover anything" to "Maybe we should arrange an accident" to "why don't we just deport him back to the UK?"

Having listened to all the ideas the most senior officer made his decision. "I'm not keen on the accident option. It's too dramatic in the current circumstances, but I don't think we can sit back and do nothing. Deporting him is not a bad option but it could be seen as a trifle heavy handed and suspicious, but it has given me an idea. I'll have a word with our colleagues at MI5 in London."

Luckily the timing was right. By then it was early morning in England. Various MI5 staff were awakened by phone calls at what was for them a very early hour. The plan was agreed and a senior MI5 official made a discreet phone call to the chief editor of The Sun newspaper.

**

Back in Australia it was evening and Foster and Debbie were back in Debbie's flat exhausted by the traumatic events of the day. Debbie had finally prised herself away from consoling the twins after Ed Hopkins had promised to look after them.

Too tired to cook or go out for dinner they had eaten what meagre food was in the flat and planned to have an early night. Maybe things would look different in the morning.

They sat talking yet again about the events of the day and speculated on what had really happened but were no nearer to an understanding. Their discussion was interrupted by the musical ringtone of Foster's phone.

He noted the caller and was not totally surprised to see it was his editor in London, Mervin O'Grady.

"Hi Mervin" said Foster trying to sound less exhausted than he was. "What's new?"

"What do you mean what's new? I've just heard what happened."

"So the story has broken over there has it? Here we are being tightly controlled as to what we can say."

"Not exactly broken. I had a call from MI5. They too are trying to piece together what happened."

"Good luck to them" said Foster. "I was caught up in the middle of it and I can't figure out what happened."

"That's why I rang. They want to talk to you as you are one of the few witnesses. Just how you managed that you'll have to tell me sometime."

"OK, will they phone me or shall I set up a Skype link?"

"Not exactly John. They want you in person in London. They think you can be useful to them."

"Well I hope they take more notice of me than ASIO did. They didn't believe a word I said and told me to stop spreading silly rumours."

He paused suddenly aware of the enormity of going back to London.

"Er, when do they want me in London?" he asked cautiously.

"Yesterday. I want you to get on the first available flight and come back straight through."

Foster thought quickly. "But what about the work I'm doing on the tour here?"

"Come on John, the tour is stuffed. You know that. Any bits of mopping up can be handled by one of the local guys from The Australian so get going and I'll see you in a day or two. OK?"

"Fine Mervin, see you" said Foster and put the phone down.

Debbie could tell from Foster's expression that something was wrong. "Tell me John, what's going on?"

Foster looked at her and was on the verge of tears. "I've been recalled to London and I have to leave immediately."

"What? Why?"

Foster related the details of his conversation with Mervin.

Debbie frowned. "Don't you think it's all a bit odd?"

"I don't follow you."

"Well ASIO treat you as if you're a bumbling idiot with conspiracy theories while MI5 think you're a valuable witness. Don't you think that's odd?"

"I hadn't thought about it like that. Maybe they know something that ASIO don't. Or maybe that guy Koomer is just a silly ass."

"Maybe, but I'm suspicious. I'll tell you what though. You're not going to get away from me that easy. I'm coming with you."

"You're kidding. How could you manage that?"

"Well I've got a bit put by that will buy me a flight and I suspect some nice man would offer me free accommodation wouldn't he?"

"I suppose he would but what about your job?"

"Don't forget Peter's already agreed for me to be on leave for the duration of the tour. That gives me two weeks yet. Besides it's time I saw something of England; I've never been there."

She looked at him coyly. "Don't you want me to come? Do you think I would spoil your nice bachelor life there?"

Foster smiled. "I wish. I just can't believe you would actually come. I can't think of anything better."

"That's settled then. Come on let's get to bed. We've got to find a flight tomorrow."

**

The following day was a busy one for Foster and Debbie. Foster already had an open return ticket from London to Adelaide which had been supplied when he first came to Australia to follow up on the disappearance of Alan Warner. How long ago that now seemed, even though it was only a few weeks.

They talked to the airline and managed to get both of them on a flight leaving Adelaide that evening. With the airline's help they applied for a fast track visa for Debbie to enter the UK as a tourist and by mid afternoon they were back at the flat organising their packing.

Foster had one last task he had to do before he could return to Britain. He picked up his phone and dialled Brian Chambers. He now regarded Chambers as much more than a colleague. They had been through so much together he was now more of a personal friend.

Chambers was sitting at his desk deep in thought when Foster rang. He sighed, picked up his phone and said in a tired voice "Hi John, what can I do for you?"

"You don't sound very happy Brian. What's the matter?"

"Oh I've just had some news I'm not very happy about. But never mind. How can I help?"

"It's not that so much" said Foster, "it's more of a goodbye phone call."

He told Chambers how he had been summoned back to London to be interviewed by MI5 and that he was leaving that evening.

When Foster had finished his narrative Chambers was quiet for a moment then said "That's a bit strange."

"Well I always had to go sometime" said Foster. "And there's nothing much I can do here now."

"No that's not what I meant. The whole thing is starting to feel a bit strange."

"Sorry I don't follow you."

Chambers took a deep breath. "Let me tell you what's happened to me. I put my report in yesterday and spelled out the suspicions that you and I have about the bodyguards and the mystery man."

"What and they want you to investigate further?"

"No, quite the opposite. I've been ordered to drop it and hand over all the files I've got."

"Did they give any reasons?"

"Yeah, they said the case was now being handled by ASIO and ASIO were convinced that Phillip Gardner was a suicide bomber and that's all there is to it."

"That's ridiculous. We both know that. What about the bodyguards?"

"Just wild speculation on my part they reckon. They probably just ran away in a panic and will turn up eventually."

"What about the mystery man then?"

"I got much the same response that you got from Koomer. They think it was probably an innocent tourist who just panicked and ran. Anyway I've been ordered off and told not to talk to anyone about it anymore. They say this is now a matter of national security and my wild speculations aren't helping."

"What will you do Brian?"

"There's not much I can do is there? I'll continue to look for Tony Andersen but I don't hold out much hope now. I think there's some sort of cover up going on but I can't work out who or why."

"It certainly looks that way. I'll be interested to see what treatment I get in England."

"When did you say you were going?"

"I've got a flight this evening."

"That's quick. OK John, good luck with it all. Stay in touch and I'll keep you posted if I find out anything."

"I sure will. It's been great knowing you Brian. I hope to see you again one of these days. Bye for now."

"See you John" said Chambers in a quivering voice as he put the phone down. He sat quietly while his eyes roamed around the room as if searching for something that would give him a clue as to what was happening and why. With Foster gone he felt alone against a hostile world he didn't understand.

For some time he sat there brooding, not sure what to do next, until there was a knock on his door. Roland came in and said "is it OK if I go now? My shift is finished."

Chambers looked up and made his decision. "Yeah no problem mate. I'll sort things out here then I'm heading home as well. Tomorrow is a whole new day."

Chapter 40

The arrivals hall at Paris' Charles De Gaulle airport was its usual hectic self. Passengers were streaming in from all parts of the globe; some looking out for friends and relatives; some for chauffeurs and taxi drivers; others bewildered and anxious to know where to go next.

Two men sat at a table in a small café watching the countless comings and goings. They had arrived early in the morning from Hong Kong and were treating themselves to an early lunch.

One of the men turned to the other and said "Didn't I say I'd get you safely to Paris?"

Tony Andersen was concentrating on cutting another slice of his steak. He paused momentarily.

"Yeah you did Greg. And they sure know how to cook a steak and chips here don't they?"

"They call it steak-frites here but never mind. Did you ever see so many gorgeous girls in one place?"

Tony pondered. "Yeah they look very classy. A bit scary if you ask me."

"Don't be scared mate. I'm told they like big Australians. And pretty soon we'll be big rich Australians. You'll be able to take your pick."

As usual Tony was easily confused. "But I thought you said we were going to live in Spain in a big house with a swimming pool."

"Maybe we will. But France has big houses with swimming pools as well. It's up to us where we go."

Greg let Tony carry on eating his steak as he idly watched the passersby and reviewed his plan.

They had arrived in Hong Kong early in the morning on schedule but instead of waiting for the evening flight to London he had used some of their funds to buy another ticket, this time with Air France, scheduled to leave Hong Kong later in the day bound for Paris.

His plan was simple but he believed it was foolproof, certainly for long enough to conclude their negotiations, collect their payoff and disappear.

He supposed that by now Ben's associates, whoever they were, would have realised they had not been on the Hong Kong flight to Heathrow.

He still did not know for sure who Ben's employers were but the treatment he had received from them, together with the impressive safe houses in London and Brisbane added to his belief that they were one of the security services. The whole operation seemed too sophisticated to be the work of an individual or small group.

If he were right it wouldn't be too long before they would be able to track them down to the Paris flight. But they were not to know if he and Tony had stayed in Paris or moved on. He had taken the precaution of keeping their mobile phones switched off to avoid leaving any clue as to where they were.

Otherwise he wasn't too concerned. His plan was to confuse them and make his way to England without them knowing exactly where he was.

With lunch over it was time to start the next phase of the plan. They still had a long and tiring day ahead of them and they were already weary from two nights of flying.

They made their way across to one of the public access internet connections where Greg made a booking for them on Eurostar to travel to St Pancras, London, by fast train later that day. He used the names and passport numbers that had been given to them by Ben.

He looked at Tony and grinned. "I'd love to see their faces when we don't show up on the London flight."

Chapter 41

Early on Thursday morning a persistent ringing of the bedside phone roused Geoffrey Blaines from his slumbers. What could anyone want at this unearthly hour?

He heaved himself into a reclining position and managed to mumble "hello".

His temper was not much improved when the caller identified himself as Harry, one of the team from the safe house.

"What do you want at this time?" he grumbled.

"I'm sorry sir. I have some urgent news for you. And it's not good."

"Well spit it out then."

"It's the Andersens" said Harry hesitantly. "They weren't on the flight."

"Are you sure?"

"Definitely sir. When they didn't show we talked to the airline. They confirmed that those passengers never turned up. So we can't take them to the safe house if we can't find them. What do you want us to do?"

Blaines thought quickly. He instructed Harry to stay at Heathrow and monitor all flights coming in from Hong Kong regardless of which airline it was.

"Have you spoken to Michael Robinson?" he added.

"No we can't. His flight isn't due in for a while yet."

"Well wait for him and when you see him tell him what's happened and get him to phone me. And let me know if there are any developments. Got that?"

"Yes Sir, anything else?"

"No just get on with it" barked Blaines as he slammed the phone down.

Harry slipped his phone back into his pocket and grinned at his colleague. "Well he's not a happy man. It looks like we'll be here for quite a while. Let's grab a coffee."

**

Blaines knew he had a potential crisis on his hands. It was just possible that the Andersens had somehow missed their flight and would be on a later one. It was also possible that they were suspicious and had gone into hiding somewhere. But where?

He took the most obvious action open to him and telephoned his MI5 contact. Sir Marcus Tomelly was also another who detested early morning phone calls. However he listened patiently while Blaines explained his predicament.

The years that Tomelly had worked in the special services had taught him when to act and when to wait. On this occasion it was necessary to do both.

He told Blaines to do nothing in the short term except to get hold of Michael Robinson as soon as he was back in the country. While they waited he would initiate a search of all flights out of Hong Kong to see if the Andersens had taken any of them.

Blaines accepted Tomelly's judgement prepared himself for a day of waiting and worrying.

**

Later that morning a bleary eyed Michael Robinson walked into the arrivals hall of Heathrow's Terminal 3. He was exhausted by the long flight from Adelaide and looked forward to a sleep in a bed that wasn't moving. He was scanning the signs to find out where to catch the Heathrow Express back to London when he was shocked to hear a familiar voice.

"Good morning Michael. And welcome home." He looked around.

"Harry, what are you doing here?"

"Let's get a coffee and I'll tell you."

He guided Robinson to the nearby Costa Coffee outlet.

"Better make it a strong one" said Robinson. "I'm very tired. It might just keep me awake for a while."

Harry ordered two strong black coffees and found a table in a quiet corner where they wouldn't be overheard. As soon as Robinson was seated Harry broke the news to him, that the Andersens hadn't shown on their expected flight and so far there had been no sighting of them. He added that he and his colleague were hanging around in case they came in on a different flight.

This was the last news Robinson wanted. All he really craved was a long sleep. He tried to think through the implications.

"Does anyone else know?"

"Yeah, Blaines knows and he's not very happy."

"I'll bet he isn't. What did he say?"

"He's got us hanging around here all day in case they come in on another flight and he wants you to join him in his Westminster office."

All Robinson wanted was to sleep but he knew what he had to do.

"OK I'll get up there. But first I need another coffee. It's going to be a long day."

**

When Robinson finally arrived at Blaines' office via the Heathrow Express and a taxi he discovered, to his great surprise, that Blaines was surprisingly cheerful.

"Michael, good to see you. How was the flight?"

"Long, boring and tiring; otherwise OK. What's the latest?"

"Good news. We know where they are. We called in a few favours in Hong Kong and they have delivered for us. The Andersens arrived in Paris this morning."

"Paris! Why Paris?"

"Well I don't think it's to look at the Eifel Tower! I think they will attempt to get into England by train."

"So what can we do?"

"We've already done it. We are monitoring all bookings on Eurostar. It's only a matter of time. While we wait you can tell me the details of what happened out there."

Robinson narrated to Blaines the full story of the events of Tuesday, right up to the time when he dropped them at Adelaide Airport.

Blaines listened intently, occasionally firing questions at a very sleepy Robinson in an attempt to keep him awake.

Finally Blaines had heard enough.

"Thank you Michael. I can see why you did what you did. So our plan B very nearly worked. In fact it did work except that we are left with the Andersens to deal with. Not a perfect result but pretty good."

"So what do we do now?"

"We wait and see what they do next. I think…………"

Blaines' comment was cut short by the sound of his phone ringing. He picked up the phone, greeted the caller and listened. He smiled and put down the phone.

"Good news Michael. They are booked on Eurostar later today. We know which train they're on. They've outsmarted themselves this time. There'll be a reception committee waiting for them at St Pancras. Once we have them locked up we can decide what to do with them."

Robinson was relieved. "Does that mean I can get some sleep?"

"Of course. You get yourself home and have a good rest. You know you've done your country a great service, even though no-one will know about it. I'll talk to you in the morning."

Robinson made his way home, weary but triumphant. He had delivered and would now get his reward. Blaine's security men would pick up the Andersens from St Pancras Eurostar Terminal and the job was done. There was nothing else to go wrong. Or was there?

****

If you enjoyed this story, look out for the third and final book in the series, "Too Many Plotters", published on Amazon.

Too Many Plotters

This story continues from where Too Many Assassins ended.

The Andersen brothers have made their way back to England to claim their reward. At the same time they have become suspicious of Michael Robinson's true intentions and a game of cat and mouse ensues between the True Believers and The Andersens.

John Foster has been summoned back to England to face a questioning by MI5. After his treatment by ASIO in Australia he is suspicious of the motives of the security services.

Alan Warner is back in England and working for Peter Carney, currently unaware that the man he most wants to talk to, Tony Andersen, is also in England.

Ed Hopkins has also returned to England. He does not accept the official view of the assassination of Francis Ventrice and Phillip Gardner and is determined to investigate further.

Suspicions about the death of Ventrice are also surfacing among some members of the True Believers who were not aware of the plot.

When Foster learns from his Australian contacts that the Andersens appear to have left Australia and gone to England he teams up with Warner and Hopkins in an attempt to penetrate the fog of propaganda coming from official sources and find out what really happened in Adelaide, as the Andersens move closer to their reward.

Made in the USA
Charleston, SC
21 April 2015